ZANE PRESENTS

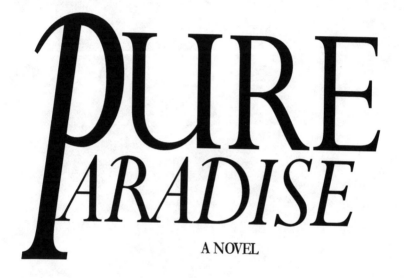

PURE
PARADISE

A NOVEL

Dear Reader:

Allison Hobbs is on fire, on a roll, on top of her game, and everything else in between. I envision Allison writing more than fifty novels before long because she is that talented. Every book is a page turner; a masterpiece; a journey into the erotic and vivid imagination of one of the most prolific writers to ever grace readers with her words. In *Pure Paradise*, she continues on her quest to fan the flames of the freakiness that exists in all people; even if they are not prepared to embrace it.

Milan Walden, a young African-American woman, is the owner of Pure Paradise, a cutting-edge day salon. Pure Paradise presents an array of salon services to its affluent clientele. Additionally, the salon offers a salacious menu that consists of an assemblage of naughty notions, designed to whet and satisfy the sexual appetites of the most discriminating palates.

While Pure Paradise is raking in the dough, Milan indulges her own kinky desires by building a personal stable of pleasure providers— a chattel of willing men and women who crave to indulge Milan's voracious and varied carnal desires.

Enough said. I have no intention of giving the details of the book away. You have to savor that delight yourself within the following pages. If you have not read Allison's other books, you have missed out on a lot. Fans of my work will surely appreciate Allison Hobbs. I often state that she is the only woman on the planet freakier than me, and it's the truth.

Her titles include *Pandora's Box*, *Insatiable*, *The Climax*, *Big Juicy Lips*, *The Enchantress*, *One Taste*, *Disciplined*, *A Bona Fide Gold Digger*, *Double Dippin'* and *Dangerously in Love*.

Thank you for supporting Ms. Hobbs' efforts and thank you for supporting one of the dozens of authors published under my imprint, Strebor Books. I try my best to bring you cutting-edge works of literature that will keep your attention and make you think long after you turn the last page.

Now sit back in your favorite chair or, better yet, chill in the bed, and be prepared to be tantalized by yet another great read.

Peace and Many Blessings,

Zane

Zane
Publisher
Strebor Books International
www.simonsays.com/streborbooks

ZANE PRESENTS

PURE
PARADISE

A NOVEL

ALLISON HOBBS

STREBOR BOOKS

NEW YORK   LONDON   TORONTO   SYDNEY

Strebor Books
P.O. Box 6505
Largo, MD 20792
http://www.streborbooks.com

© 2009 by Allison Hobbs

ISBN 978-1-59309-224-5
LCCN 2009924326

First Strebor Books trade paperback edition July 2009

Cover design: www.mariondesigns.com
Cover photograph: © Keith Saunders/Marion Designs

10   9   8   7   6   5   4   3   2   1

Manufactured in the United States of America

For information regarding special discounts for bulk purchases, please contact Simon & Schuster Special Sales at 1-866-506-1949 or business@simonandschuster.com

The Simon & Schuster Speakers Bureau can bring authors to your live event. For more information or to book an event, contact the Simon & Schuster Speakers Bureau at 1-866-248-3049 or visit our website at www.simonspeakers.com.

FOR DANTE FEENIX
Not just a handsome face,
but one of the nicest people in the world.
Thank you for all you've done on my behalf.

CHAPTER 1

"What do you think? Do I look like a dominatrix?" Sumi asked Milan. Wearing thigh-high latex boots, a short black rubber dress with a zip-up front, and matching arm-length gloves, she held a black whip and struck a threatening pose. Sumi was an exceptional beauty, an exotic mix of Korean and Italian heritage. Her large doe-shaped eyes sparkled with sensuality. She twisted her pretty face into an exaggerated angry mask and cracked the whip.

Looking dangerously sexy, she wielded the whip like she was eager to thrash the crap out of a man and have him cowering and begging for mercy. Unwilling to admit that Sumi had captured the authentic look of a dominatrix, Milan gave her only a cursory glance. "You look cute," Milan said with amusement in her tone.

"Cute?" Sumi questioned.

"It's not Halloween, so what's the deal? Did you get an invitation to a masquerade ball?" The thickly layered sarcasm was intended to let Sumi know that Milan refused to take her seriously.

Sumi's red-painted lips turned down in disappointment. "Are you for real?" She glanced in the mirror and struck a pose. "I look hot." Her words did not ring with conviction. "Don't you think I look hot?"

Milan sneered. "I doubt that anyone would take you seriously enough to pay for your services. You look gorgeous. That dress is really sexy, but you're not a convincing dominatrix."

Sumi placed both hands on her hips, indignant.

"You are not a qualified dominatrix." Milan went on, "so stop trying to add that to your job description. You're my personal assistant and I want you to find a qualified person to do the job."

"But you promised *me* the job—"

"That was pillow talk. I'm not responsible for the things I say when we're in bed. Now, bring your sexy self over here and let me unzip that hooker dress."

Sumi arched a brow. "Oh, now you're calling me a ho?" There was more than a hint of defiance in her tone.

"If the shoe fits." Ready to break the tension, Milan flung her a teasing smile. "Aw, don't worry, Sumi. You're not any ol' ho—you're my personal ho. Is that better?" Milan winked at her tauntingly.

Possessing a severe temper, Sumi stomped over to the bed where Milan lounged naked atop the satin sheets, waiting for her girl toy to join her. "I'm not your ho! I'm your lover. We're in a relationship!"

Milan wanted to burst out laughing but Sumi was reaching her boiling point. And she was proficient in martial arts, so Milan switched to a placating tone. "Don't I pay you a hefty salary?" she reminded her assistant. Sumi had not been a very good secretary—her typing skills were awful. Back when Milan merely managed Pure Paradise, Sumi was hired mainly as eye candy, a good advertisement. She was the look of perfection, sitting at her desk in an open area where potential clients could see her. Her exceptional beauty promised similar results to those willing to pay Pure Paradise's steep prices.

When Milan became the owner, she'd elevated Sumi to the position of her personal assistant and Sumi had blossomed. She performed her numerous duties without complaint and with unfailing devotion. Now, she wanted to do more and Milan didn't like it.

"Sure, you pay me a good salary, but I work very hard, so don't insinuate that you're giving me a handout." Sumi was hurt, and her voice took on a higher pitch. "Every week I put in sixty hours or more and I never request overtime."

Milan sucked her teeth. Screw Sumi and her freakin' martial arts. She was taking her tirade much too far. "If you dared to ask for overtime, I'd fire you on the spot. I elevated you from a lowly secretary to your current prestigious position. You're earning four times the amount you made before I took over Pure Paradise."

Sumi shot a glance at the whip she still held, which made Milan feel a bit uneasy. "You practically run Pure Paradise! I allow you to strut around barking orders at the staff as if you were the actual owner of my establishment. What else could you possibly hope for?" She'd intended for her words to make Sumi melt but now Sumi was huffing and puffing, angrier than ever.

"I want respect. I'm doing the job of three people and I do it for you. I do it because I love you, Milan."

What's love got to do with it! Milan felt like belting out that old Tina Turner song but she couldn't sing and Sumi didn't have a sense of humor. It was sad but true; Sumi was confusing good sex with love. Though the moment was awkward, Milan wanted some of Sumi's fabulous sex right now, so she forced her mouth to curl into what she thought would imitate a loving smile. "Unzip that dress, sexy, and bring your cute ass over here."

Disappointment dimmed the playful sparkle that had shone in Sumi's eyes when she first demonstrated her ability to crack a whip. "I'm not unzipping shit," Sumi said with saucy impudence. "Why do you get such malicious pleasure from treating me like a plaything? I'm not your toy."

Yes, you are! You're my prized sex toy, my precious Sumi-toy! Milan was tempted to say, but she didn't dare utter her inner thoughts while Sumi had hold of that damned whip.

Using amazing cunt tricks, Sumi had catered to Milan's freakish desires, and had become a human replacement for Milan's entire collection of battery-operated pleasure providers. She didn't need them anymore. Sumi could get Milan off faster and with stronger eruptions than even her expensive, gold-plated fuck-buddy. And Sumi didn't have to rely on a synthetic strap-on phallus to make Milan cum. She could do things with her cute little cunt that drove Milan to the brink of madness.

But the pretty little thing was so sensitive, Milan knew better than to piss her off by telling her to her face that she was nothing more than a sex toy. Sumi's temper, along with her Asian pride, made her unpredictable. She was apt to fly off the handle and karate chop all Milan's exquisite bedroom furniture. Knowing Sumi the way she did, it wouldn't surprise her if the girl quit on the spot if Milan insulted her by calling her a "Sumi-toy." Milan frowned as she was struck by the realization that it would be very difficult to replace her sexy Sumi.

With a placating smile, she gently grasped Sumi's wrist and

pulled her closer to the bed. "I'm sorry." Milan tugged her wrist until Sumi dropped the whip and started unzipping, displaying pert breasts and a curvy petite body.

Sumi's mons pubis, covered by a layer of jet black silky hair, was an alluring sight, causing Milan to unconsciously lick her lips.

Sumi bent and peeled down the top of her right boot. "Keep them on," Milan insisted. She didn't feel like waiting for her assistant to struggle out of the skin-tight boots. Besides, Sumi looked hot with the boots on.

Propping herself up on an elbow, Milan tugged Sumi forward until Sumi's crotch was flush with her face. Playfully, Milan blew out a stream of cooling breath, blowing Sumi's silken pubic hairs, making them flutter and lift until they parted and an olive-colored nub poked through.

Mmm. Milan's mouth and her pussy started watering at the same time.

Flicking her tongue against Sumi's little clit, she slowly broke her assistant's resolve. She sucked softly, relishing the taste and texture as much as Sumi enjoyed getting her clit sucked. Milan sank her tongue into Sumi's pot of tangy spice, which had a zesty bite that left a pleasant ginger-honey aftertaste. She ate Sumi's pussy until Sumi was sufficiently stimulated.

It was her turn now. Milan lay flat on her back. Sumi climbed on top of her, fitting her petite body against Milan's and running her hands along Milan's lean mocha-colored limbs.

Milan grasped the sides of Sumi's face and pulled her mouth to hers. Sumi closed her eyes blissfully as Milan slid her tongue between her lips, sharing the ginger-honey flavor.

Moaning, Sumi responded to Milan's pussy-flavored kiss with slow gyrations and soft pelvic thrusts. With each thrust, Milan's legs spread a little wider, giving Sumi more access to her opened treasure chest.

"Fuck me," Milan murmured.

Lifting up, Sumi gazed at her lovingly as she stroked the bushy hair that covered Milan's mons. She parted Milan's pussy lips and toggled her clit until it moistened, became engorged, and darkened to a deeper hue. Sumi was gearing up for the good part.

Milan inhaled deeply as she readied herself. Sumi's pussy tricks gave a stiff dick some hellified competition.

She straddled Milan, her silky snatch brushing against Milan's bushy forest. Sumi aligned her parted pussy with Milan's sensitive clit, and then sank down, clamping her tight pussy muscles around Milan's swelling pleasure bud.

Each pussy bite from Sumi was thrillingly electrical. Sumi would soon take her over the edge. Milan had had her share of sexual experiences with other women, but the pussy she'd been acquainted with couldn't compare to Sumi's. Milan had no idea how Sumi had trained her pussy to snap the way it did. Maybe it was all that exercising and martial arts training that made Sumi's cunt so unusually agile, like a pair of lips, only tighter and with more grip.

With blissful expectation, Milan took in a deep breath. Using rapid vaginal clenching, Sumi's strong cunt muscles seized Milan's taut clit, tightening and then releasing, taking a series of nibbling pussy bites that stimulated Milan's hot spot better than a mechanical device.

Milan shuddered and bit down on her bottom lip, bracing herself for the inevitable torrent of hot sexual release.

"Wait! Please, Sumi! Don't make me cum yet!" Temporarily

out of her mind with sexual tension, Milan was not too proud to beg.

Once the pleading began, the tables turned in Sumi's favor. On top, her expression confident, Sumi lowered her head. "Kiss me, bitch."

Helplessly, Milan sought Sumi's lips; all the while frantically twisting her hips, silently pleading for more tantalizing pussy bites.

"You need my cunt, don't you, bitch?" Sumi demanded angrily, nostrils flaring.

"Yes!" Milan gave a cry of agonized joy. Her hand touched the small of Sumi's back, pressing her small breasts against her own. Their peaked nipples rubbed together, creating more excitement and friction. Sumi fastened her walls even tighter around Milan's protrusive sex organ, making it throb, making Milan gasp with pleasure.

"Slow down, I don't want to cum. Not yet," Milan said, her voice hoarse with passion. But her body movements spoke otherwise. Undulating, she lifted up and then ground her distended female organ even deeper into Sumi's extraordinary pussy.

Dispensing vicious cunt snaps, Sumi pulled and twisted Milan's pearl of passion, giving her pleasure so unbearable, Milan had to bite down on her bottom lip to keep from screaming.

Sumi palmed Milan's taut buttocks, pulling her closer, intensifying the pussy friction as she fucked Milan senseless. "I don't like sharing you and I shouldn't have to. Nobody can fuck you like I do. That pussy is mine. All mine!"

Having Milan at a sexual disadvantage, Sumi put her in an awkward position. "You know how much I love you, Milan. Why can't you love me back?" Her expression was a blend of lust, love, and sorrow. Lust, the dominant emotion, was spectacularly expressed as she clenched and grinded against Milan's feminine region. With her swiftly rotating hips, her snapping pussy pulling on Milan's engorged clit, Sumi demanded, "Do you love me?"

Milan was out of her mind with passion and willing to say anything to keep Sumi giving up the cunt. "Yes, I love you. You know I do," she whispered. Milan felt confused by her own words, unable to distinguish fact from fiction. She actually felt something close to love as an orgasm pulsed through her. But survival had also kicked in. If she didn't return Sumi's declaration of love, the little hothead was apt to hop off her pussy, throw on her clothes, and storm out into the night, leaving Milan hanging in an awful state of sexual duress.

Holding Sumi and pressing her down, assisting her in using her hot-red snapper to get a tighter grip on her own peaked flesh, Milan could feel a fiery sensation, simmering at first, and then burning wildly through her lower region. She squeezed Sumi's delicate shoulders, quivering and moaning as she convulsed and then exploded.

Keeping up her rhythm, Sumi kept winding her awesome little body until she joined Milan in soul-shuddering ecstasy.

Finally catching her breath, Milan smiled sardonically and stroked Sumi's silky hair. "You're getting out of hand, Sumi," Milan whispered, her voice raspy with residual lust. She pulled Sumi's silky hair hard enough to inflict pain and to remind her who had the real control in their relationship.

"Ow! Stop, I hate that rough stuff." Sumi rolled her eyes and then began to sulk, begrudgingly relinquishing the power to Milan.

Back in full control of her sanity, Milan gave Sumi's hair another yank.

"Ow!" Sumi screamed and moved away from Milan's reach. "I'm going home," she spat.

"Go! I got what I wanted," Milan fired back.

"You're such a bitch. I hate you." She leapt from the bed and grabbed the dominatrix dress. "I thought you loved me."

Milan laughed tauntingly while Sumi angrily pulled on the dress and yanked the zipper up. With her head tilted in thought, Milan watched Sumi. She seriously had to figure out a way to get more control of her hot-tempered assistant. Clearly, the surly little sexpot needed a few lessons in obedience training. Milan had tried and tried to break Sumi's will, but she had only a loose grasp on the spitfire. Thank good- ness she usually had sense enough to placate the pussy-snapping hussy until she gave Milan the blood-rushing climaxes she craved.

Sumi stormed out of Milan's bedroom and stomped down the long corridor. Milan jumped out of bed and ran behind Sumi. "Sumi," she yelled. Sumi turned around, her expression hopeful.

"You forgot something!" Milan tossed the black whip at her and slammed her bedroom door.

CHAPTER 2

P ure Paradise Day Spa with its enchanting ambience—handpicked flowers, potted foliage, tinkling music, flickering candlelight, and intoxicatingly fragrant scents that wafted throughout the establishment—appeared to live up to its name. Swathed in comfy robes and slippers, the clientele looked pampered and relaxed. They milled about, sipping mimosas or herbal tea as they waited to be indulged with a Chocolate-Bliss facial, a sea kelp body massage, hot stone therapy, hydrotherapy, waxing, manicures, pedicures, or any of the numerous services offered.

On a lower level, private fantasy theme rooms equipped with costumes and props were provided for couples. A fantasy session was ridiculously costly, but affluent patrons didn't mind spending big bucks to indulge their freaky imaginations.

In a separate room on the lower floor, Milan Walden, owner of Pure Paradise, greeted prospective clients, a husband and wife, with a very tight smile. Compared to her lavish office suite upstairs, the consultation room was rather smallish. She felt boxed in and out of her element in the modestly furnished office. Actually, Sumi should have been interviewing this couple, but Sumi was visiting a local dungeon, observing Mistress

Veronique, a premier dominatrix, at work. If the woman was as cruel and intimidating as reputed, Sumi was to offer her a contract to work as a consultant at Pure Paradise.

Milan sighed. She needed two assistants. No, strike that. The way her business was booming, she needed three or four assistants. Sumi was not going to like sharing the power, but she'd have to deal with it. The poor dear was being stretched to capacity as it was, and business was suffering. Milan corrected her thought. No, business wasn't suffering...Milan was. She absolutely despised having to interact with clients.

Yet matters of a sexual nature were too delicate to be handled by any staff member other than Sumi. Admittedly, her assistant was good at her job—so good, she thought she was capable of taking on the additional job title of "in-house" dominatrix. What a laugh. Sumi didn't have any real power. Milan allowed her assistant to execute her precise orders: reprimanding, hiring, and firing on Milan's behalf. But the girl didn't have a dominant bone in her cute little body. What a pity.

Lately, Sumi had started behaving like a diva. Milan didn't like her assistant's new attitude, so today she'd sent Sumi on a mission that would give her a badly needed reality check. After observing an authentic dominatrix at work, with her foot pressed down on a naughty slave's neck, Sumi would come to her senses and realize she was too delicate to really crack a whip. Sumi needed to get rid of that latex dress, the boots, and the whip and devote all her attention and concentration on angling her snapping pussy around Milan's ripened clit.

She was suddenly struck with a brilliant idea, a scheme that would put Sumi in her place. Milan shook her head, marveling at her own sheer genius. She gazed at the paperwork and then returned her attention to the oddly paired couple who sat on the other side of the rather ordinary desk. The plain oak desk made her yearn for her custom-designed power desk. Her desk screamed success! Made of six different types of exotic wood, it cost seventy-two thousand dollars—as much as some people spent on a luxury car. It was a spectacular piece of furniture and was most fitting for an extraordinary woman such as herself.

Milan glanced at her surroundings and wrinkled her nose. As soon as she got rid of this bothersome pair, she'd make a mad dash to her elegant office suite.

The wife, an attractive, slim blonde, had a snooty air about her and she had irked Milan on sight. She looked to be in her late twenties, professionally attired in pearls and a nicely cut business suit. The husband, on the other hand, swarthy with a big belly, was considerably older than his wife. Additionally, he had the unpolished look of a laborer and wore a T-shirt bearing the logo of a roofing company. The man was totally icky!

"Well, it looks like everything is in order," Milan said, looking down at the paperwork on the desk. "You've passed our requirements with flying colors." She didn't smile and maintained a business-like demeanor, sitting erect with her lips pursed, her eyes intense, her expression serious. She found the ill-matched couple nauseating and couldn't muster any more than the same tight smile. "So...which fantasy interests you?"

"I own a roofing company. There's good money in roofing, but I have to put in a lot of ridiculously long hours—"

Do I look like I give a shit? "And your point is?" Agitated, Milan glanced down at the application again. "Mr. Tamburro," she said with a sigh.

"I'm getting to the point," the husband said brusquely.

Milan searched the wife's face, hoping for some type of intervention, but the wife squirmed and refused to meet Milan's agitated gaze.

"I put my wife through six years of college," the husband went on. "She has a master's degree in business. I don't claim to be a scholar, but I make a lot more money than she'll ever dream of earning." Mr. Tamburro looked at his attractive wife with contempt. The wife gave Milan a "See what I have to put up with" look, which Milan chose to ignore.

Mr. Tamburro would be footing the bill for the couples' fantasy so Milan decided to reserve her attention for him.

"You've looked over the brochures," Milan said with a sigh. Her patience was dwindling quickly. "Have you made a selection?"

A crimson shade of rage suddenly tinged Mr. Tamburro's olive complexion. Clutching the glossy brochures, he blurted, "My bitch of a wife cheated on me! Not once…but twice…and with her coworkers." He glared at his wife. "Seems she's developed the hots for the suit-and-tie type. I'm not good enough for her anymore."

"That's not true," Mrs. Tamburro whined.

Milan waved her hand, cutting off the adulterous wife and returning her attention to the bill-footing husband. "Is that what you'd like—a fantasy that involves wearing a suit and tie?" Keeping the annoyance out of her tone was difficult. She'd given the couple a brochure with every fantasy Pure Paradise offered. She hadn't anticipated taxing her brain to come up with an impromptu suit-and-tie fantasy session for the kooky couple.

"Hell no! I want her to get a sound spanking for cheating on me." He rolled his eyes at his wife. The wife tried to maintain an impassive expression but couldn't. Cringing with embarrassment, she dropped her gaze. Her cheeks took on a pink tint.

"Oh!" Milan perked up. "Well, you'll be delighted to know we have a special room for corporal punishment. It's equipped with an array of thrashing devices from paddles and hair brushes to whips and canes. I'll need you both to sign a consent form." She pushed the form across the desk.

"Not so fast. There's a slight hitch." Mr. Tamburro's angry expression changed to embarrassment. "I can't do the spanking." He cast a warm gaze toward his wife. "I love my wife. Besides, I wasn't raised to mistreat or put my hands on a woman. I behave like a gentleman, even when my wife takes it upon herself to carouse around like a stinking whore."

Milan sighed in exasperation. "Okay, if you're not in the mood for a paddling session, which fantasy interests you?" She spoke through gritted teeth. Pure Paradise offered a vast array of sex services but she'd be damned if she'd waste her breath with a high-spirited sales pitch. She would have never allowed the couple in the consultation room had she known they had yet to select a service.

It was obvious that the communication at Pure Paradise was badly flawed. But not for long. Milan would start interviewing new assistants immediately. She'd hire as many as she thought necessary to ensure Pure Paradise operated smoothly. Sumi would have to get over herself and deal with some competition.

Milan stood. "Why don't you two go home and look over the brochures again. When you've made a decision, call Sumi Cranston, my assistant." She forced a smile and cut a dismissive glance toward the door.

"I've made up my mind and I'm prepared to pay in advance," Mr. Tamburro said, leaning forward as he pulled his wallet out of a back pocket. He whipped out a credit card.

Milan ignored his offer of payment. She remained standing,

hinting that the interview was over. "Mr. Tamburro. I'm a busy woman. You and Mrs. Tamburro should go home and discuss the service that suits your needs."

"I already told you. My wife needs a good spanking." He looked at his wife for confirmation. Wearing an expression that looked as pained as if she were being flogged at that very moment, the wife gave a curt nod.

"Like I said, I'm too much of a gentleman to hit my wife, but I'm willing to pay top dollar to get the job done."

The wife gasped. Suddenly interested, Milan jerked her head toward the husband. "You want someone else to do your dirty work?"

Looking embarrassed, he nodded.

"I'll have to bring in a trained master and that will double the cost."

"Not a problem," Mr. Tamburro said.

"Honey," the wife whined, her eyes wide. "I think we should discuss this matter privately."

"My mind is made up," he barked at his wife. "Either you get your tail whipped or go get yourself a lawyer."

It was an unusual request. Most couples used the themed rooms that were listed in the brochure. They enjoyed experimenting with the equipment to indulge their perverted fantasies. She could have turned down Mr. Tamburro's request, but Milan was eager for the challenge.

She cleared her throat. "Mr. Tamburro," she said softly, "we offer several choices…" The husband nodded for Milan to continue. "There's verbal humiliation with a light thrashing— a sort of erotic spanking, which is what I recommend—"

"What else do you offer?" He eyed Milan intently.

"Well…" Milan took an excited breath as she struggled to

contain her own sexual arousal. The topic was quite stimulating and had her juices flowing. "We also offer a more harsh punishment. Your cheating spouse would be bare-assed and given a severe spanking."

Mr. Tamburro's face lit with interest.

"You should be aware that a severe spanking will leave residual welts and bruising," Milan said casually, though her mind was racing to come up with a more sadistic form of punishment. And there was a problem.

She didn't have a trained master. All her employees were certified in massaging, aromatherapy, polishing toenails, and all sorts of therapies that didn't meet Mr. Tamburro's requirements. Hopefully, Sumi would get Mistress Veronique to sign the contract. If the woman was a true dominatrix, she would be willing to dispense punishment to women as well as men.

The husband sat on the edge of the chair, rubbing his chin excitedly. "I want her to get a harsh spanking," he said, nodding and looking vindicated. "The full treatment! Whatever it costs, I'm willing to pay."

The wife jerked back, gawking at her husband. Her words came out in a sputter. "I'm not, uh, sure about this. We really have to talk."

Milan ignored her. "Would you like to sit in on the session, Mr. Tamburro?" A devilish smile played on Milan's lips.

"I sure would!" he exclaimed as he gleefully rubbed his hands together. The wife groaned. A sudden shadow fell over the husband's face. "No. I couldn't sit back and watch while some sadistic fella beat the crap out of my wife."

The wife brightened perceptibly.

Milan shrugged. "I was actually going to have a woman spank your wife. A skilled dominatrix."

"A woman!" Mr. Tamburro reared back and snorted in disapproval. "What kind of pain could a woman inflict? If I'm going to spend top dollar for punishment, I want my money's worth. I want a man to beat her. A big black buck!" he added and glared at his wife.

Where the hell would she find a big black buck who was a trained master? Gerard, her former trainer, came to mind, and she instantly tried to dismiss him from her thoughts but couldn't.

At Milan's insistence, Gerard's benefactor, the evil Mistress Ming, had been financially crushed. Ming's illegal "training center," along with her wealthy husband's chain of fitness centers, had been gobbled up by one of Maxwell Torrance's corporations. Maxwell Torrance, billionaire and tycoon, was Milan's personal sex slave.

Maxwell had put Ming out of business, sent her packing. Milan felt a shiver of delight, imagining the arrogant hussy back in China, living in poverty. Stripped of her jewels and couture wardrobe, and all her money, Ming was hopefully working her fingers to the bone in some rice field. Though Milan had no idea what had become of Ming, imagining the evil wench sweating as she toiled for a few coins was a delicious fantasy.

Gerard? He was most likely still in the States. Oddly, her heart didn't race. She was over Gerard. Her heart was set on someone else—and once again, the man she'd set her sights on was playing hard to get. Milan sighed. She sure knew how to pick them.

Returning her thoughts to the present dilemma, she smiled at the couple. "Mr. and Mrs. Tamburro, as you know, Pure Paradise has designed numerous couples' fantasies, but we're flexible and are fully capable of tailoring a program that meets your needs. Don't worry, Mr. Tamburro, you don't have to go in the room with your wife. You don't even have to accompany your wife here. I understand your unwillingness to view her chastisement firsthand, but might I suggest that you accept the complimentary DVD of her punishment session? I highly recommend that you and your wife view the DVD together, and often. Reliving the pain and humiliation repeatedly should discourage your cheating wife from engaging in future adulterous affairs." Milan amazed herself with her brilliant creativity. Feeling proud of the sales pitch that she made up as she went along, Milan beamed at the married couple.

The wife cringed with horror.

"Oh, boy. That sounds like a winner," Mr. Tamburro gushed, jubilant. "I'll get a lot of pleasure watching the DVD with her." He scratched his head. "How many times should we watch it?"

"Every night before sex," Milan responded quickly.

"We don't have sex every night," Mrs. Tamburro stated, balking at the idea.

"It's not too late to start. This woman here…" He pointed to Milan. "She's a sex therapist and she knows what she's talking about."

Sex therapist! Sounds good to me. "You absolutely need to have intercourse with your wife on a daily basis, but without tenderness," she cautioned, taking her new title seriously.

"You hear that, hon? I don't want to hear anything about headaches or any talk about your menstrual cycle. No excuses. I want my daily ration of sex without a word of complaint."

"Oh, fabulous," the wife said sarcastically.

To Milan's satisfaction, the deal was about to be sealed. She bestowed Mr. Tamburro with her most winning smile. "Sign right here." She pointed to the lines marked with an X and sat down as the husband perused the form. He affixed his signature and then handed the pen to his wife.

Picturing the prissy Mrs. Tamburro getting her ass spanked made Milan terribly horny. The unmistakable twitching between her legs was getting stronger and more demanding by the second. She needed to get rid of the Tamburros and take care of her personal situation. "We can accommodate you next Wednesday at two."

The wife consulted her BlackBerry and frowned. "I have an important meeting on that date. Do you have another open-ing—can you fit me in after five?" Her trembling tone pleaded for a different time slot.

"There you go...putting that friggin' job before our mar-riage." Mr. Tamburro gave his wife a stern look. "Listen up, Mrs. Cheater, I want you to cancel that meeting and get your buns over here at two o'clock on the dot. If you can't make it, well, I guess I'll see you in divorce court. I'm serious. Our prenup protects my money. You won't get one single dollar. Let's see how far you get with your measly salary." He sneered at his wife and then looked at Milan. "Her job is nothing but show," he said to Milan. "With all those degrees I paid for, she still doesn't earn the kind of money she enjoys spending." He poked himself in the chest. "I'm a wealthy man, but I don't have to wear fancy clothes to broadcast how much I'm worth."

At the mention of the prenuptial agreement, Milan felt an uncharacteristic stab of sympathy for the wife. Over a year ago, she had experienced the humiliation of being forced to sign an outrageous prenup and could relate to Mrs. Tamburro's dilemma. But that was all behind Milan. She'd come out on top. Now large and in charge, Milan defied anyone to try to tell her what to do. She owned a thriving business and, as shocking as it seemed, she had billionaire business tycoon Maxwell Torrance by the balls. Literally. She owned the man. She made him wear an engraved collar of ownership as proof.

Nothing had been handed to her. Unlike Mrs. Tamburro, Milan had overcome many obstacles to get to her station in life. Withdrawing her sympathy, she turned cold eyes toward the wife. "Do you agree to the two o'clock appointment?"

Tears clouded Mrs. Tamburro's eyes. She turned to her husband. "I don't think this is necessary. I've learned my lesson. Please, sweetheart."

"It's your choice…take the whipping or we're getting a divorce." Mr. Tamburro was adamant.

Resignedly, Mrs. Tamburro nodded. The husband gave Milan a conspiratorial wink and then tried to hand Milan his credit card. Milan recoiled as if handling the payment process would tarnish her. "Pay at the front desk, please," she said with a grimace.

The moment the couple left the consultation room, Milan picked up the phone and called security.

"Royce, there's an emergency in the basement consultation room. Get down here, fast!"

CHAPTER 3

Responding to Milan's urgent tone, Royce, the security guard, rushed to the consultation room. His hand was on his gun; clinking and clanging metal cuffs dangled at his side. His head turned back and forth swiftly, making the loose skin of his jowls swing in the air. With his badge, big and gleaming, and with the excessive layers of wrinkled facial skin, he reminded Milan of the old cartoon character Deputy Dawg.

Royce's eyes, anxious and wide, swept the room searching for the source of Milan's distress. Finding nothing out of order, he cocked his head quizzically. "What's wrong, Ms. Walden?" Breathless from running down several flights of stairs, Royce wiped perspiration from his forehead.

"Nothing's wrong!" she spat, annoyed by the inquiry. "I'm experiencing a personal crisis."

Milan leaned back in the chair. Brushing her fingertips against the silk top that concealed her small breasts, she drew the security guard's attention to her protruding nipples. Clipping the twin pearls between her fingers, she displayed her state of arousal.

Hit with sudden enlightenment, Royce exclaimed, "Oh!"

Milan rose and stuck out her hand. "Give me your cuffs,

Deputy Dawg," she taunted. Royce's face dropped. Visibly impacted by the cruel nickname his boss had given him, Royce was humiliated and his shame and sorrow caused his face to sag even worse. Resignedly, he unhooked the handcuffs from his belt loop and handed them to Milan.

"Hands behind your back," she ordered, wearing a wicked smile. Then she sauntered to the other side of the desk and cuffed the beleaguered security guard. "I want to try something different today. Let's see how well you perform without the use of your hands."

More perspiration dotted Royce's forehead. He looked miserable as he tried to keep his balance. Slowly and quite shakily, he lowered himself to the floor.

Milan inched up her tight skirt and snaked her hand between her legs. Her pussy, aroused from the conversation with the Tamburros, was hot and overly moist. She pulled her thong to the side and ran the length of her palm up and down her slippery entrance. Sighing with pleasure, she withdrew her hand and presented Royce with her cupped palm, which she proceeded to fit over his mouth. "Have you been a good boy today?"

As he was supposed to do, Royce slackened his jaw and nodded on cue.

"Excellent." She rubbed her palm against his lips. "Here's a little pussy treat for you."

She closed her eyes as Royce darted out his extremely long and wide tongue. Quick tongue flicks sent naughty tingles up her spine. Slowly and sensually, Royce lathed her cupped palm until it unfurled in surrender. Royce was not easy on the eyes and had zero sex appeal. He'd worked two or more jobs most of his adult life. Money worries, limited exercise, and too much fast food had Royce looking ten years older than his actual thirty-nine years.

An abundance of taste buds covered the surface of his tongue. It was a birth defect, but for Milan's purposes his deformity was a blessing. His roughened tongue felt like moist sandpaper as it brushed against Milan's smooth palm. The sensation was ticklish and oddly tantalizing—both gross and stimulating at the same time. As he swiped her flesh with his harsh and bumpy tongue, her nipples tightened to the point of feeling like unbearably hard pebbles. Murmuring softly, she lifted her bra and fondled her small breasts. Her soft sighs were accompanied by Royce's loud lapping. Her pussy contracted as hot passion trickled out.

"Eat it!" Milan smashed her open palm against his mouth, grinding it harshly, commanding him to increase the tempo and intensity of his tongue strokes. Royce licked harder and faster, panting and groaning in a manner so vile and yet seductive, Milan could feel more cream oozing out of her pussy. Royce knew exactly how to appeal to her freakier side.

Royce licked her opened hand until it gleamed and then narrowed his long tongue into a curl, driving it in and out of the spaces between her fingers, making a ghastly groan with each slimy poke of his tongue.

This is so crude and depraved. Depraved or not, Milan couldn't help moaning blissfully. With tension building, she hopped up on the desk and hitched up her skirt. "Take my thong off."

Relieved to dispense with the handcuffs, Royce cracked a smile. "Unlock 'em. The key's in my pocket."

"No! Be creative." She slid toward the edge of the desk, leaned back, and rested on her elbows.

With hands cuffed behind his back, Royce rose unsteadily. He buried his face in Milan's crotch and began tearing at the lacy fabric with his teeth. "Hurry up!" she ordered.

Growling now, he savagely ripped away the delicate fabric and held the lacy thong between clenched teeth. With the torn lace dangling out of the side of his mouth, he looked disgusting and rabid.

Oooh, this is so freaky and wonderful! Milan felt like clapping with glee. Royce was behaving like an angry beast and she got shivers imagining his lengthy tongue lashing her cunt. She drew her legs up and clasped the back of her knees, spreading open her pussy and giving her cuffed captive ample access to her flooding tunnel.

He penetrated her lush lips, plunged inside, filling Milan with the unusual length and thickness of his tongue. She moaned as she humped his coarse appendage. His tongue scavenged inside her walls, scratching her itch and then scraping across her clit. She shuddered in pre-orgasmic pleasure.

Royce's tongue became still. Milan bristled. "Finish licking, I didn't tell you to stop!"

"Um...your juice is gushing, Ms. Walden. I was getting ready to suction it out for you," he explained.

"Well, get to it," she snapped.

"I was going to, but I noticed some gook sticking on your leg...I wasn't sure—"

"Royce! Your long, flexible tongue has many responsibilities. I expect you to take care of whatever needs to be done. Now, shut your trap before I march you down to the paddling room. I'll give you a severe spanking that you won't soon forget. Is that what you want?"

"No, Ms. Walden. Please," he muttered. "I don't want a spanking; I just wanted your opinion on what I should handle first."

Milan struggled upright and glared at Royce. "I didn't notice you asking my opinion when you unceremoniously escorted me off these premises last year," she said, reminding him of the humiliating day when she was fired from Pure Paradise.

"I'm sorry, Ms. Walden. It wasn't personal. I was simply doing my job."

"Well, do your job now." She leaned back, resuming a reclining position.

Royce stretched open his mouth and extended his elongated muscular organ. With forceful stokes, he lapped at the smeared passion that was congealing on her supple inner thigh. Using his tongue as a cleaning utensil, he swished and mopped the area until it was spotless. Then he attached puckered lips to Milan's heated entry, carefully sipping her juices, stimulating her, attempting to make her passion boil over.

Milan purred and arched her back as Royce slurped large puddles of lust. As she writhed on his tongue, he began to greedily guzzle her hot liquid. He made loud gurgling and slurping sounds, his audible swallowing heightening her arousal.

Skillfully, he once again curled his tongue and narrowed until it was pointed and firm. He drove it in and out, penetrating her center of paradise. Stretching his moist and erect tongue, he probed, flicking against her vaginal walls, sweeping the roof of her canal, urgently searching for her special spot.

Preparing for sharp pangs of pleasure, Milan gripped the sides of the desk and scrunched up her face as she waited for Royce to locate her hidden treasure. Royce was the only man who could hit Milan's G-spot with his tongue. She could feel tension building as his twisting appendage grew closer to the mark. Testing, he gave the pad of flesh he'd discovered a tentative touch with the tip of his tongue. Milan responded with a tiny yelp. Wanting more, she scooched closer, clamping her knees against Royce's jawbone.

"Are you ready, Ms. Walden?" His breath tickled and excited her. She tightened her knee-lock. Milan couldn't care less if she crushed Royce's jawbone.

Desperate to be free, Royce lathed the sensitive, raised skin. Milan squirmed and whimpered as her captive stroked her spot unrelentingly, licking the walls of her pussy without mercy.

A rush of heat filled her loins. Milan screamed and then squirted. Ejaculating like a man, she shot several hot blasts of cum into Royce's mouth.

CHAPTER 4

S he'd been waiting for fifteen minutes, biting her fingernails and shivering. Gnawing on a fingernail, she nervously peeled away opaque polish and then began nibbling
at the cuticle. Her wide blue eyes bobbed around the darkened,
foreboding room, taking in the fear-provoking sights: an oil
painting of a naked woman bent over the knee of an elegantly
attired man, his palm held menacingly high; an assortment of
paddles on top of a table, a standing metal cage, and a frighten-
ing wooden bench.

Hanging from hooks and resting on shelves were a wide
assortment of whips, floggers, riding crops, canes, and other
pain-yielding devices. But the most foreboding piece of equipment was the wooden whipping post with its platform base
and bondage ropes dangling down the sides. Though the menacing device dominated the room, the woman refused to look
at it. Her wide eyes roamed the room; she visibly cringed upon
recognition of each taboo torture item that was displayed.

Wearing a tailored jacket and skirt, she sat on the side of the
bed eyeing the door. She rocked and hugged herself, terrified
and embarrassed knowing that the eye of a camera was capturing and recording her every move.

Twenty minutes later, the door burst open. She gasped when she saw her punisher, a powerhouse of a man with a metal chain vest draping his massive chest. He slammed the door and ominously flexed his bulging biceps. A torturer's hood, the exact shade as his onyx-colored skin, added to his menacing appearance. One mighty hand was bare and the other was covered with a black leather studded glove.

"Have you cheated on your spouse?" His voice, a rich and commanding baritone with a Caribbean accent, boomed inside the quiet, darkened room.

"Yes," she whimpered, shrinking back, retreating until she bumped into the headboard. Though his commanding tone informed her that resistance was futile, she squirmed and wriggled and raised her hands up defensively.

"I'm here to punish you for your adulterous activities. Do you understand?" He stroked the studs on the glove that covered his right hand.

Gnawing on her ragged fingernail, she nodded with her head hung low. Somehow, the hooded black man had managed to arouse her, making the threat of a painful punishment sound sensual and appealing.

"Remove your jacket," he ordered.

Obeying, she tugged off her jacket.

"Get rid of the blouse!"

"My...blouse?" she stammered, feeling modest, arms crossing her chest.

"Take it off!" he growled.

She jumped and then quickly unbuttoned her blouse.

"Your bra, too," the hooded man commanded.

Unwilling to further rile the man who was hired to spank her, she unclasped her bra, revealing creamy white breasts and rose-colored nipples, peaked from fear. Perspiration trickled down her neck; the droplets of moisture congregated on her breasts until they were soaked with sweat.

His penetrating eyes inspected her, traveling her shivering frame from head to toe. Then, without warning, the sadistic tyrant stalked toward her. Startled, she let out a sharp scream. He grabbed her by the neck with the gloved hand, the studs burrowing into her skin. She fought, trying to break his hold. With his bare hand he yanked her away from the headboard, pushed her on her back, and promptly stuffed her mouth with a rubber gag ball.

The woman choked and coughed from the oral intrusion. Tears burned her eyes. With her cries silenced, her torturer pulled her by her hair, dragging her to the foot of the bed.

Kicking and scratching, she fought valiantly, but was easily overpowered by the man commissioned to dispense punishment. Forcibly, he brought her arms down in front of her and methodically began to bind her wrists with black bondage tape. She struggled against the tape, but realizing her struggle was futile, she became still with solemn acceptance. She was captured. She was his.

He sank down on the bed and turned Mrs. Tamburro over his knees. She moaned with renewed terror. Her head dangled, her blonde hair swept the floor as blood rushed to her face, turning it beet red.

With one brawny forearm, he kept her pinned in place. He squeezed her breasts with his free hand, twisted them, soaking his palm with her sweat, and then he raised his hand and smacked her ass. She flinched and wriggled, making muffled

screaming noises as a succession of wet stinging slaps reverberated inside the paddling room.

He flattened his palm against the small of her back, mois-
tening it as he ran it down her sweat-sodden spine. And again,
he spanked her wriggling rump with a wet hand, stinging her
ass badly and leaving overlapping reddened handprints on each
pale buttock.

⇜⇝

Seated behind her luxurious desk, Milan watched the spanking from a monitor mounted on a wall. Literally sitting on the
edge of her seat, Milan was riveted by the kinky footage. The
anonymous punisher—recommended by Mistress Veronique,
whose consultant services Sumi had successfully secured—was
ripped. Bulging muscles and big veins covered his body. He
had boulder shoulders, bulging biceps; the muscles of his huge
thighs were visible through his tight leather pants. He had to
be on steroids with a body like that. He was truly huge all over,
like a Mr. Olympia winner.

Watching the masked man spank the roofer's naughty wife
made Milan's clit throb. Luckily, Royce was on hand, crouched
on the floor beneath her desk with his chin resting on the
leather seat, his head situated between her legs. With his outstretched, oversized, and resourceful tongue, he collected each
droplet of her lust.

But she strained and gyrated, unable to concentrate on the
tongue fuck she was getting while gazing at Mrs. Tamburro's
fiery red ass. Instead of getting down to business, Royce was
teasing her pussy. Frustrated, she stood up. "Stop fucking around.

Find my spot, dammit. I need to get my daily erotic release."

Royce mopped at his lips with the back of his hand. "Oh, I'm sorry. I thought you wanted me to prolong it until that sadist finished whipping that white chick's ass."

"How long have you been eating my cunt?"

He scratched his head. "About a year or so?"

"That's right. And by now, you should be able to read my body language. Didn't you feel me straining against your tongue?"

"Yeah, but—"

"But nothing!" She pushed the chair away, the wheels at the bottom of the chair rolling over the panties she'd flung to the floor. "I want you to get up and march yourself to the front of my desk."

With Milan on his heels, a repentant Royce rose from the floor and walked to the other side of the custom desk.

"Pull down your pants and bend over," she ordered, her pussy more moist than ever, her vaginal walls contracting so violently, she doubted if she could discipline Royce without cumming all over herself.

Royce gawked at her. "Now, I've been doing everything I could to make up for what happened last year, but I'm not gonna bend over your desk and let you spank me like I'm a child."

"Remove your gun, loosen your belt, and drop your fucking pants," she hissed.

"This ain't right, Ms. Walden. I didn't do anything to—"

"I own you," she reminded him, brushing her fingertips against her tightening nipples.

"I know you own me. I signed the paperwork. But my contract says I'm a sex slave, not your whipping boy. I didn't agree to nothing like that." He pointed to the monitor where Mrs.

Tamburro's spanking had come to an end. Her tormentor pulled her panties up and removed the gag ball from her mouth. Curled in a fetal knot, Mrs. Tamburro trembled and wept.

"Okay, Royce. Have it your way. Go back to your post." Milan made a dismissive gesture.

Royce didn't move. "Are you mad at me, Ms. Walden? I didn't deliberately try to get you upset."

"Upset?" Milan laughed maliciously. "I'm livid!"

Royce looked nervously at the clock. His shift would be over in another ten minutes. Royce sighed and reluctantly placed his gun on top of the desk. It was best to let Milan have her way. He doubted if she was strong enough to do any real physical harm. Slowly, he undid his belt and lowered his pants. Keeping his job and the extra perks she gave him for delivering his unique brand of cunnilingus was worth a bruised ego and a chunk of manhood.

CHAPTER 5

Milan and Sumi strolled through the corridors of Pure Paradise. They were conducting an impromptu walk-through intended to rattle the nerves of slacking employees and incite admiring glances from clients who were waiting for a beauty treatment that they hoped would give them a smidgeon of Milan's glamour and panache and Sumi's undeniable natural beauty.

Milan wasn't beautiful. Her mother had drilled that fact into her head at a very early age. She went through great pains to achieve her current look and the end result was stunning and well worth the painful Pilates, face peels, and hair processing twice a month.

During promotional interviews, she suppressed the urge to burst into giggles when an interviewer referred to her as "the beautiful Milan Walden." She definitely didn't believe the hype, but was proud to have literally pulled the wool over so many pairs of eyes.

She could imagine her mom shouting at the TV screen, "Milan's a fake; she's not pretty. She piles on globs of makeup just to look presentable. But you should see her sister, Sweetie. Sweetie's the real beauty in our family!"

Ha! Milan had the last laugh. She gloated briefly, and then her lips turned down. Despite her financial success and achievements, her mother and Sweetie still thought she was missing out on the joys of life because she remained single and without children.

They're just jealous! she assured herself.

Milan had style, a slender, toned body, a phenomenal hairstylist, and a killer wardrobe. From the time she sank her hooks into billionaire Maxwell Torrance, she no longer wasted time trekking to New York during Fashion Week. She now flew to Paris on Maxwell's private jet and sat in the front row watching models walk the runway in the Chanel haute couture show. She absolutely loved high fashion and enjoyed wearing numerous designers. But no one compared to Chanel. She got goosebumps and clit quivers whenever she slipped on anything by Chanel.

She was a statuesque, stunning woman. Her wealth and good taste had placed her in the "beautiful" category. And she milked it for all it was worth.

"Who was that hooded guy? What's his name?" she asked Sumi.

"His name is BodySlam."

"You're kidding."

"I kid you not."

"Mmm. I'd like him to slam my body."

Sumi arched a brow. "You're not serious. You love being in control."

"I don't mind switching roles. Breaks up the monotony." Milan smiled devilishly.

Sumi stopped walking. She put a hand on her hip. "So why do you give me so much grief when I try to take control?"

"The key word is *try*. Either you have control or you don't. BodySlam is a master at his craft. I wanna fuck him. Set it up."

Sumi looked worried. "I'm not sure if that's possible."

"Why not? I'll double his fee."

"He works with Veronique. They're like a team. I think they're in a relationship—a couple."

Milan shrugged, annoyed. "And...?"

"She loaned him out as a favor. I told her that I was in a bind and needed a dominant man for, like, a one-time occasion."

Milan let out an exasperated sigh. "What's the big deal? I like how he works. I was thinking about adding anonymous spanking to our list of services. You tell that Mistress Veronique that I want BodySlam to work for me, starting immediately. Get her on the phone and tell her if he doesn't show up for work tomorrow at ten o'clock sharp, I'll have her measly little dungeon shut down just like that." Milan snapped her fingers.

"How are you going to do that?"

"Maxwell Torrance."

"He's out of town," Sumi reminded her.

"He doesn't have to be in town to handle a hostile takeover."

"But...Mr. Torrance buys big companies. Mistress Veronique has a private practice. She operates her business from her apartment!"

"I don't care where she works from; I'm going to have her shut down if BodySlam doesn't come to work for me."

Sumi shook her head. "I'm confused." She looked off in thought. "Isn't it a conflict of interest for an employee to spank the boss?"

"Spank me! I didn't say I wanted him to give me a spanking. No, I want to watch him spank our clients and after he finishes,

I want to feel his hot-looking body slamming against mine. Mmm!" Milan gave a visible shiver.

"We don't have any clients requesting spankings. The paddling room is used by consenting couples. Mrs. Tamburro was an isolated case."

"I see you're incapable of thinking outside the box. Okay, obviously I'll have to personally take care of this matter." Milan turned on her heels and started walking in the opposite direction. Sumi raced behind her.

Inside her office, Milan pointed to the chair on the other side of her desk, indicating that Sumi should sit.

Sumi positioned herself provocatively, giving Milan a peep show, trying to coax her into a better mood.

"Close your legs. Stop trying to distract me."

Huffily, Sumi pressed her thighs together.

Milan tented her fingers. "I've been doing some thinking. You're obviously in over your head. I'm expanding and you don't seem to be able to keep up."

Sumi opened her mouth in wide protest.

Milan held up her hand. "Let me finish." She took a deep breath. "My mind is made up. I need another assistant."

Sumi gasped, pressed her hand against her chest.

"Relax. You're not getting canned."

"Thank God." Sumi blew out a calming breath and tried to collect herself.

"But you're in over your head, Sumi. You lack vision and I can't leg you drag the company down."

"How can you say—"

"I want you to hire two additional assistants. Female. Fashion-conscious."

"Any particular race...complexion...hair color?" Sumi said sarcastically.

"No. Just make sure they're pretty." Milan clapped her hands. "Get up and get to it!"

Sumi stormed toward the door. "Sumi!" Milan shouted.

She'd been pushed too far. Angry and humiliated, Sumi swung around, prepared to go toe to toe with Milan. "What!" she shouted, her face tinged red with fury.

Milan smiled, disarming Sumi with what appeared to be an unspoken apology. Then, the warmth left her eyes. "Make it abundantly clear to every applicant that the position requires lots of ass kissing and pussy licking."

Sumi gawked at Milan, dumbfounded, before walking out and slamming the door behind her.

≈§≈

Later that day, outside Pure Paradise, Hilton Dorsey opened the back door of the Rolls Royce for Milan. "Good evening, Ms. Walden," he said, extending professional courtesy.

Hilton was a big hunk of masculine perfection with a solid frame, defined muscles, a wide back, broad shoulders, V-shaped torso, tight abs, large hands, long limbs, and thick thighs and calves—an athlete's physique. A strong jaw, chiseled features, and neat, close cropped hair added to the man's physical magnificence. But his personality sucked. Milan couldn't stand him. It agitated her to no end, the way he so easily assumed a professional persona, acting aloof as if they hadn't fucked like dogs in heat since the day she inherited him as her driver.

Running a business was stressful and she'd had a hell of a

rough day. Royce had to be called to the carpet again, this time for arriving to work ten minutes late. Dispensing corporal punishment first thing in the morning had taxed her strength and ruined her day. She needed Hilton to be particularly attentive tonight. Long, tender lovemaking was what she needed to bring her stressful day to a pleasant end.

"Would it kill you to greet me with a smile and inquire about my day?"

Now in the driver's seat, Hilton looked over his shoulder and smirked. "What's good, baby? You feelin' all right?" he asked, deliberately slipping into slang, knowing it irked her.

Milan made a chastising, *tsking* sound and rolled her eyes. "Never mind. You're so crude. I should have fired you a year ago."

Chuckling to himself, Hilton drove Milan to her luxurious home. Off the main road, he cruised past the opened gate and up the circular driveway of gray paving stones. He eased to a stop when he reached the front door of her chateau. "Do you want me to park the Rolls in the garage?"

"No, leave it out here." She made a sweeping gesture, indicating the spacious courtyard. "Aren't you coming in?" There was a hint of panic in her voice.

"Not tonight." His dark sparkly eyes became hard. His playful mood switched to moody and tense.

"Why not?" Milan monitored her tone, careful to not sound too desperate.

"I have to get up early. Gotta hit the gym."

"That's ridiculous. Why go to a smelly fitness center when I have a private, fully equipped personal gym right here?" She was aware that she was starting to sound pushy, but being slightly aggressive was preferable to sounding desperate, she decided.

"I like working out in smelly gyms. It's manly." He laughed.

Milan didn't share the merriment. She glared at him.

"I can't stay over tonight, Milan. I have things to do." He got out of the idling Rolls and opened the back door.

Defiant, Milan didn't budge.

Irritated, Hilton sighed, shifted his feet, and folded his arms. He looked over at his black SUV that was parked in the courtyard. Adamant about going home, he aimed his keypad and pressed down. The headlights of the SUV flicked on and the doors unlocked.

Wearing a sour expression, Milan reluctantly eased out of the backseat. Hilton stood outside the Rolls, waiting for her to go inside the large and empty home. She took a few steps and then stopped. "Can you be honest with me?"

"Whaddup?"

She tsked again. "Are you seeing anyone?"

Hilton leaned back, scowling. "You shouldn't concern yourself with how I spend my spare time or who I'm seeing. It's not your business."

"Don't take that tone with me. I pay your salary and don't you forget it."

Unflinching, he met her gaze and then frowned down at his watch. When he looked up, his eyes were lit with amused arrogance. "I'm off the clock, baby," he scoffed. "That means I'm no longer attached to your invisible leash."

Ah, so he was still afraid of succumbing, of becoming one of her playthings. His fears were ridiculous. He was so willful, so proud, and so damn sexy, she'd given up on the idea of controlling him a long time ago. She enjoyed fucking him. She also enjoyed snuggling up in his arms, but she'd never let the cocky bastard know.

"So what!" she spat. "Just because you're off the clock doesn't mean you can speak to me with disrespect." She realized she'd been unconsciously cutting her eye at the area that stored his thick manhood. She caught herself and forced her hungry eyes to narrow in disapproval at his entirely too casual attire: cargo pants, T-shirt, and sneakers. "You look so unprofessional," she pointed out. "Really sloppy!" She turned up her nose. "My driver should look crisp and professional."

She flipped her hair off her shoulders for emphasis. "I have an image to uphold. Be sure to wear your formal uniform tomorrow." She arched a brow, waiting for him to balk at her demand. He didn't, giving her no choice but to throw in more sarcasm. "Obviously, fucking the boss has gone to your head and caused you to forget who really calls the shots. Well, let me remind you, you work for me." Milan gave him another long look. Knowing how much he hated wearing the unflattering and demeaning chauffeur's uniform, she gave him a few moments to change his mind.

He slouched against the Rolls insolently and stared daggers at Milan. She stood seething and returned his stare.

But the yearning that knotted her stomach made her eyes blink. Desire had her close to crying in surrender and screaming out loud. She could hardly restrain herself from yanking his belt loose and ripping open his fly. She needed some dick—and not any ordinary dick. She wanted that thick, big-headed penis that he was deliberately withholding for no reason other than being ornery—making her yearn for him.

Hilton took a toothpick out of his shirt pocket. Milan's gaze wandered to his hand and watched his thick long fingers travel slowly to his luscious lips. He chewed on the toothpick. *He wants me!* Milan could tell by the slow and sensual movement of his lips. He wanted her as desperately as she wanted him.

Then he allowed the toothpick to dangle disrespectfully on his bottom lip, a convincingly rude affirmation that Milan had not broken his steely resolve.

Giving up, she exhaled harshly.

"Have a pleasant evening, Ms. Walden."

Taunted by his formal farewell, she whirled away from him. Three hurried strides and she was at her front door. She glanced back briefly and then rushed inside.

CHAPTER 6

Milan was tired, but troubling thoughts denied her the peace of precious slumber. She picked up the latest copy of *Vogue*, leafed through a couple pages, and then snapped the magazine closed. She eyed the bedside clock and wondered what time it was in Japan. She shrugged irritably. Did she really give a shit if she disturbed Maxwell at an inappropriate time? *Hell, no!*

Billionaire business tycoon Maxwell Torrance, her benefactor and personal possession, was in Japan on business. Enforcing her power, she snatched the phone from its base and speed-dialed his number, confident in the knowledge that even if he was in a coma-like sleep, or in the midst of critical negotiations, or teeing off on the golf course, or dining with an important client, it didn't matter, Maxwell Torrance was at Milan's beck and call and when her ring tone chimed, he was required to pick up. Immediately. Or suffer her wrath.

"Yes," Maxwell whispered on the other end.

"Don't you mean 'Yes, Mistress'?" Milan snarled.

Maxwell cleared his throat. "This isn't a good time. Uh… I'll…uh, call you back in five minutes," he stammered, his vocal level barely audible.

Seething, Milan clicked off the line and slammed the phone back into the base. Nothing was going her way. She thought about calling her sister, Sweetie, to confide her feelings for Hilton. *Bad idea.* Sweetie would try to lecture her and all Milan wanted was a listening ear and some loving and useful advice. Her mother crossed her mind. *Now, that's a laugh*, she thought with a sardonic chuckle. Her mother didn't know the meaning of the word loving—not when it came to Milan.

Through the kindness of her heart, she'd taken Sweetie and her family out of the 'hood and put them in a nice home in Willow Grove, Pennsylvania. Generously, she'd also bought a charming one-level home for her mother that was right around the corner from Sweetie's. But her mother wasn't grateful for anything Milan had done for her. She still found reason to criticize, insisting Milan would never know true happiness until she got herself hitched and saddled with a couple of snot-nosed kids. Ugh!

She thought of Hilton. Being his wife. She released a blissful sigh, her mouth arched into a pleasant smile. *Oh God, I'm whipped!* She shuddered. The last time she'd lost her mind over a man, she'd ended up crawling on all fours, kissing his feet, trying to impress him with her willingness to submit. Milan shook her head, recalling her days as a submissive. Gerard, her former trainer and the man who had controlled her, had never fucked her, never sucked her, and had never even allowed her to please him with oral sex. In retrospect, she decided that Gerard was nothing more than a dick-teasing, latent homosexual.

But Hilton! Mmm. What a man! Her pulse raced and her lashes fluttered dreamily. Snapping out of that sickening romantic state, she reminded herself, *Hilton is nothing more than a fuck buddy. An unappreciative one at that.* It was time to cut him off and hold him to the same standards she held all her employees. Yes, that was exactly what she intended to do! Feeling vindicated, Milan curled up and drifted off to sleep.

But the blaring telephone woke her up, yanking her out of the sweetest dream. "Hello," she muttered, her voice scratchy with annoyance.

"Mistress, forgive me," said Maxwell in a trembling voice.

"Are you out of your goddamn mind, waking me up at this hour, talkin' that 'Mistress' bullshit?" Milan exploded, unconsciously resorting to the way she spoke before she'd polished and redefined herself. "Kiss my ass!"

"Gladly, Mistress. I'll gladly kiss your ass."

The lust in his voice made her nauseous.

Milan wasn't a trained dominatrix. She was an imposter and had tricked Maxwell into believing she could keep him in line. Maxwell was really trying her patience, pushing her to her limit, attempting to coax her into disciplining him more severely.

Apparently, uttering insults and forcing him into sexual submission wasn't enough. Milan frowned. If she wanted to keep her cash cow satisfied, she'd have to start dressing the part and dispensing harsh corporal punishment before he started looking elsewhere for the severe discipline he craved.

Oh, the very thought of someone stealing her wealthy property gave her the shivers. Luckily, she'd seen this coming and had prepared herself by practicing on Royce. She was getting quite good at paddling, but she'd have to get serious, buckle down and consult with Mistress Veronique. Take lessons. Really learn the craft. Her financial future depended on it.

CHAPTER 7

"I'd like to put BodySlam on my payroll," Milan informed Mistress Veronique.

"BodySlam is not for sale. Not now. Not ever." Veronique's voice was grating, coarse, and scratchy as if she smoked ten packs of cigarettes a day and constantly guzzled hard liquor. Ugh!

Obviously the woman didn't realize whom she was dealing with. "I beg your pardon," Milan said, giving her a moment to rethink her position.

Without flinching, Mistress Veronique met Milan's discontented gaze and stared at her with hard, cold eyes, maintaining her refusal.

Milan flinched at the nerve of the dominatrix. The woman sitting on the other side of her desk was a hellish sight. She wasn't at all what Milan had expected. She was dressed entirely in black, but there was nothing glamorous or sexy about her. Disheveled, with pasty white skin, her stringy black hair covered with a black leather cap, Mistress Veronique looked more like a rebellious biker bitch than a sexy dominatrix. With her stick-straight, spaghetti-thin figure, she had some nerve commanding men to grovel at her feet.

Before the unappealing dominatrix had taken a seat, Milan

had noticed that her posture was terrible. She was a hideous disgrace with slouching shoulders, a flat ass, and as skinny as she was, she had the nerve to have a pronounced potbelly that her worn-looking corset couldn't conceal. Milan really couldn't imagine why men paid large sums of money to grovel at this hag's feet. Milan had done her research and knew for a fact that Veronique had a large and loyal clientele. *What does she do with her money?* Milan wondered. She surely didn't give a crap about investing in a decent wardrobe.

Milan was disappointed and let it show by giving the hag a reproachful look. The ol' crone had the audacity to return Milan's look with a sneer, which emphasized her unappealing facial features: pasty pale skin, beady eyes, hooked nose, elongated chin, and lips that were thin, dry, and chapped. The red lipstick that covered her chapped lips resembled chipped paint.

With her expression twisted in a scowl, Veronique instantly morphed from crude biker bitch to a goth-looking Satan worshiper. Milan felt a chill run over her. The hag gave her the creeps.

Shrewdly, Milan had insisted that a secret entrance to the building be constructed for abominations such as Veronique and BodySlam, keeping them and all the other fetishists away from the sensitive eyes of her hoity-toity clientele who were upstairs enjoying the posh amenities that Pure Paradise offered.

"I'm trying to be civilized and offer you a reasonable deal, but this can get ugly." *As ugly as you*, she refrained from adding. "If that's what you prefer." Milan sighed heavily and closed her eyes, shutting out the image of the vexing and unsightly Mistress Veronique.

Veronique snorted. "I don't scare easily."

The ugly crone needed an attitude adjustment and a strong dose of discipline. Milan would pay good money to watch BodySlam get this slut in line. *Hmm*. She'd love to watch that powdery white ass turn a blazing red. "Listen, I was trying to reason with you, but you leave me no choice. I want you to turn over your business records within two days. I'll be drawing up new contracts for you and BodySlam." Milan tore the old contracts in half and placed the ripped pages in the shredder.

"Hey, you can't do that. Those were valid consultant's contracts," Veronique said in a rush of surprise.

Milan decided that Veronique's expression of shock was even more unsightly than her perpetual scowl.

"Those were meaningless words signed by my assistant, who has no authority to speak for me. The next contract you sign with me will be a thick legal document with my signature affixed."

Veronique's scabby red lips tightened. She pushed the chair back and stood. "You're out of your mind. I don't have to work for anyone and neither does BodySlam."

The woman was butt ugly and Milan would relish having her taken in hand, turned over BodySlam's knees, and thoroughly reprimanded. Whatever hold Veronique had over that gorgeous modern-day gladiator, she could kiss good-bye. BodySlam would soon belong to Milan. Maxwell Torrance would see to that.

Milan smirked. "I guess we'll see about that."

With her colorless face twisted in anger, Veronique left the modest, lower-level office.

And Milan returned to her well-appointed office suite on the top floor.

Now sitting behind her luxurious desk, she picked up the phone and summoned Sumi. Looking harried, Sumi materialized in moments.

"You look like shit," Milan said casually.

"Thanks," Sumi muttered with weary sarcasm. "I've been interviewing assistants all morning and I've narrowed the search down to two candidates."

"Are they educated?"

"Yes, of course."

"Pretty?"

"Yes, and with great sense of fashion."

Milan swirled in her chair, grinning. "And are they highly skilled in cunnilingus?"

Sumi gave a slight smile. "Yes."

"And you know this because…?"

"I insisted that all the applicants go down on me. That's why I look like shit. I'm exhausted and my cunt is sore." She shifted from one foot to the other, waiting for Milan to dismiss her or offer her a seat.

"You're always whining. Never satisfied. Why do you think I'm willing to pay two extra salaries? Duh! I'm trying to lessen your load. So can you please try to limit your complaints?" Milan looked at Sumi with mild disdain before cocking her head in curiosity. "Did you have to coerce them or did they suck your pussy eagerly?"

"Eagerly. They're both freaks."

"How freaky?" Milan raised her brow suspiciously.

"They were competing with each other. Both tried to lick my snatch clean. After I came twice, I told the two freaks to pleasure each other. They quickly worked their lovely bodies into a sixty-nine position and went at it. The performance was impressive. Both are multi-orgasmic." Sumi brushed back her hair wearily. "Do you want to meet them?"

"No, I don't have time for that today. Tell them they're hired and that their job training starts tomorrow."

"Okay." Sumi turned to leave.

"I'm not finished." She motioned Sumi over. "Sit down. There's something else we need to discuss."

Sumi slid into the chair positioned on the opposite side of Milan's enormous desk. Donning a serious expression that suggested interest in Milan's every word, Sumi pulled the chair even closer to the desk. But there was a something in Sumi's eyes that Milan found disturbing. Was it suppressed rage or was it—God forbid—insanity? Sumi fluttered her lengthy lashes and the weird look was gone. Milan chose to ignore what she'd thought she'd seen, chalking it off as a bout of uncharacteristic guilt for treating her smart and pretty assistant like a sex toy and an unworthy lackey. Oh well, it was her duty to keep her assistant in her place. If she didn't, who knew what liberties Sumi would take?

"My vision for Pure Paradise is not being realized." Milan gave a loud sigh of dissatisfaction.

Sumi scowled. "What do you mean?"

"It's boring."

"The salon is running fabulously and with the new couples' fantasy themes downstairs, what's lacking?"

"Excitement. The salon is beautiful, but it's run of the mill. I promised myself that Pure Paradise would be a cutting-edge salon. Unparalleled by others." She shook her head. "And it isn't. It's just ordinary."

In silent contemplation, Sumi sat with her chin resting in her hands. Milan picked up a Pure Paradise brochure and tapped it against her own chin, thinking. "I have an idea!" she suddenly exclaimed. "I want you and your assistants—"

"*My* assistants!" Sumi's doe-shaped eyes sparkled. "You're giving the new assistants to me?"

"Yes. I don't have the patience to deal with two more employees. So I'm putting them in your hands. Their duties will be multifaceted and ever changing. In other words, I want them trained to handle a variety of situations." Tapping on her slender fingers to count, Milan rattled off a list of responsibilities: meeting with couples during the initial screening process, maintaining the adult website, and drumming up more business. "Once the couples' theme business picks up downstairs, your assistants will have to schedule sessions and coordinate the flow of heavy traffic. It's of paramount importance that our clients do not bump into each other. Our freaky clients must be assured that their privacy is protected while indulging their fantasies."

Lost in her own thoughts, Sumi blurted, "Can I get a bigger office?"

"No, your office is large enough. But I'm giving you a hefty salary increase and I'm changing your job title to..." Milan looked up at the ceiling in thought. "Senior marketing executive. How does that sound?"

Sumi screeched in excited approval.

"That's quite a climb for a former secretary who could barely type."

Sumi's expression soured at the insult. "I have other qualifications."

"Yes, you have a talented snatch that earned you the privilege of sleeping with the boss."

"I don't know why you feel the need to tarnish our relationship when you know my feelings for you go beyond sex."

Milan sucked her teeth. "Our sex life has nothing to do with work. I have to expand this company and I'm hoping I can rely on you to make it happen." Milan paused, tapping a finger on her desk. "Can I?"

"Of course, but uh, we didn't discuss my raise, Milan."

"We'll have to negotiate later. Now, did you listen to one word I said?"

"Yes, you want me to teach my assistants how to conduct interviews and schedule sessions and run the adult website." Sumi pushed back her chair, eager to bark orders at her new assistants.

"I'm not finished. There's more."

Disappointment registered on Sumi's face. "Yes?" she said with a sigh, settling herself into the chair.

"I want you and your assistants to comb this city—check out male exotic dancers, male models, go to gyms, and solicit body-builders. Take your search anywhere that you think beautiful buff men might convene."

Curious, Sumi crinkled her brow. "Because…"

"Because I have a brilliant idea that will increase business upstairs."

"Business is booming upstairs."

"Like I said, we're not doing anything out of the ordinary. I want to offer my upscale clientele an incomparable, ultimate spa experience—a sensual full-body massage that includes nipple kneading, pussy petal parting, finger probing, and clitoral stimulation."

Sumi gasped. "Is that legal?"

"Perfectly."

"Aren't you worried that those chiseled men might lure your clients away?"

Milan shrugged. "Not particularly. I'm going to make Pure Paradise such an appealing pleasure parlor, it would be silly for a patron to risk exposing a lurid encounter outside the safe haven that I provide here. I'll offer an array of beautiful men of various ethnicities in a soothing clinical environment. Pure Paradise will have something for everyone. Fetishism downstairs and kinky, freaky side orders upstairs." Milan inhaled and rushed on with exuberance. "For example, the licensed manicurists can do all the nail clipping, cuticle snipping, and the scouring and scraping of dead skin off the soles of the clientele's feet, but I want a gorgeous man to take over and provide a sensual foot massage that includes toe sucking and foot kissing before he even begins applying the polish to their toenails."

Overcome by a rush of sexual excitement, Milan shivered. Her first impulse was to have Sumi do some pussy tricks on her clit, but she changed her mind. Sumi had work to do.

"I want your assistants to start working on this immediately." Milan clapped her hands.

Dismissed, Sumi pushed to her feet and left.

Maxwell Torrance had returned from his trip to Japan and Milan was not pleased with him. She imagined various forms of punishment that she'd dispense upon her disobedient sex slave and was so excited by a wickedly sexy idea that she released an outpour of liquid warmth that saturated her panty crotch. The sticky secretions flowed abundantly, soaking through the cotton liner and dribbling onto the seat of the chair, demanding immediate attention.

She stabbed the emergency button, pulled off her panties and let them drop to the floor. She swept every article off her desk, climbed atop it, and spread her long legs wide. With her eyes fixed on the wall clock, she counted the seconds that ticked as she waited for Royce to burst through her office door, panting and with his tongue lolling outside his mouth as he was trained to do.

CHAPTER 8

Aside from wearing casual golf apparel, business mogul Maxwell Torrance was never seen in public without his armor: a custom-tailored business suit, an expensive designer tie, high-end shoes, and a luxury leather briefcase.

But tonight, in keeping with Milan's orders, he was inexplicably dressed in a brightly-colored, logo-enhanced T-shirt; sneakers; baggy jeans; and a belt with a rhinestone encrusted buckle—clothing that looked as outlandish and foreign on Maxwell as would a Scottish kilt with knee-high ribbed hose.

Flaunting a black Chanel sheath with a cascade of white pearls and very sexy black satin heels, Milan, on the other hand, was the picture of good taste and high fashion. With her flawless mocha complexion, coiffed hair, and toned, slender body, she resembled a sleek black goddess, while the wealthy Caucasian tycoon looked tacky and crass.

The oddly paired couple entered Maxwell's favorite restaurant—a swanky establishment with a strict dress code, where Maxwell was so highly regarded the renowned chef had created a menu just for him.

"Good evening, Ms. Walden and Mr. Torrance," the hostess greeted them, eyelids fluttering as she fought to hold back a puzzled look. Finally, she forced a wide, ingratiating smile that assured Maxwell Torrance that his outlandish attire would be overlooked—his immense wealth and prominent status entitled him to dress in any manner that pleased him.

Milan snickered to herself, wondering if Maxwell could feel the burn of humiliation that was showing on his face.

"Your table is ready," the hostess said and then led the couple past a succession of linen-draped tables adorned with flickering candlelight and shimmering white china. The elegantly clad patrons, who were seated at the attractively adorned tables, couldn't believe their eyes. They gawked and did a series of double takes, then quickly raised crystal goblets to their lips, taking in generous, head-steadying sips of wine.

Yet, despite looking like a crazy, spiraled-down version of himself, Maxwell made his way to his table with his chin up, seeming the ever-scoffing elitist despite his unattractive and disturbing attire. With their eyes fixed on his peculiar wardrobe choice, the onlookers missed the telltale perspiration beads gathered at his temples, his nervously bobbing Adam's apple, and the thin collar around his neck.

The hostess seated Maxwell and Milan. She gave a nervous smile and then quickly departed. Had the hostess been bold enough to openly scrutinize the indecently casual fashion victim, she would have noticed the collar looped around his neck. And if she had dared to ask why he was wearing it, Maxwell would have been obliged to divulge that he, a billionaire and ruthless business tycoon, wore the collar as a symbol of ownership. Prior to their dinner date, Milan had insisted that if anyone inquired about the collar, he was to fess up and admit that he was indeed the property of Milan Walden. Thankfully, for

Maxwell's sake, the hostess hadn't asked. Nor did the maître d' when he took their order.

Milan placed her palm lightly upon his hand, briefly enjoying the color contrast and the symbolism of her mocha-colored hand on top of his pale white skin. "How are you feeling tonight?" The concern in her tone did not match the wicked glimmer in her eyes. When he didn't respond quickly enough, she pressed down, crushing his palm into the table, grinding it until he winced in pain.

"I feel awkward," he admitted miserably.

She removed her hand. "And…"

"And I feel vulnerable," he added quickly.

"You look ridiculous—like a complete fool. I'm embarrassed to be with you," she taunted, even though he was dressed in clothing selected by her.

Face flushed, he lowered his head. "I know. I'm so sorry."

Milan glanced around the ornate dining area. "All eyes are on you," she reported. "People are so curious, they can't concentrate on their overpriced cuisine." She gave a spiteful giggle.

A waiter appeared, presenting a six-hundred-dollar bottle of wine. Milan nodded; the waiter uncorked and began pouring the wine.

"Have you been faithful?" Milan did not bother to monitor her tone.

The waiter paused, curious to hear the billionaire's response.

The red color in Maxwell's cheeks deepened. "Of course I've been faithful."

Milan swirled the wine around in her glass, sniffed, and then tasted it. "Mmm. Very good," she said with a smile, though she actually hated the taste of expensive wine.

The waiter looked at Maxwell. Maxwell didn't meet his gaze. The waiter cleared his throat. "Mr. Torrance?" he said, obviously uncomfortable as he waited for Maxwell's approval.

"I said it's very good." Milan sneered in Maxwell's direction. "His opinion doesn't matter," she added tersely, making it clear that she was the central player at the table.

"Enjoy," the waiter said, backing away while darting a confused eye at the uncharacteristically docile tycoon.

"So..." Milan began with a smirk. "You claim you've been faithful."

"Absolutely."

"I'm not referring to dalliances with other women. I know you wouldn't dream of cheating on me. What I mean is, have you kept your hands to yourself?"

Lacking understanding, Maxwell frowned.

"I don't like that expression," she admonished. "It's unbecoming."

He quickly lowered his head as if in penance. "I'm sorry, Mistress. I don't understand the question. Are you asking if I've used my hand to grope someone?"

"No, that's not what I'm asking." She clucked her tongue in disgust.

"I've kept my hands to myself and I've been faithful," he said, voice low and miserable.

"Have you masturbated during my absence?"

"Yes, I...I've relieved myself..."

"So, you lied. You haven't kept your hands to yourself. You've been fondling your cock without permission."

"Mistress, you never expressed any objection to manual release when you're not around."

"I don't like it," she said sulkily. "You should have asked permission."

"I'm sorry. It won't happen again."

"What's done is done," Milan pointed out. "You have to be punished."

He scowled down at his unsightly attire. "You've humiliated me...disgraced me in front of my friends and business associates. Isn't this punishment enough?"

Milan shook her head grimly. "No, Maxwell. It isn't enough. I have a little business problem and I want you to take care of it."

Relief washed over him. "Of course. Anything. Whatever you want, consider it yours," Maxwell assured her.

Gesturing excessively with her long, slender hands, her brow furrowed in displeasure, Milan told Maxwell about her meeting with the arrogant Veronique and how the ghoulish woman refused to cooperate with her vision for Pure Paradise.

Maxwell stroked his chin. "Do you want to take over her dungeon?"

"Yes, shut it down. Have her evicted. And after that, I want you to persuade her and her male counterpart, BodySlam, to work for me. How soon can you make that happen?"

The powerful deal maker was accustomed to flying around the globe purchasing major corporations. At her request, he'd easily shut down her former nemesis, Mistress Ming's, establishment—a sex den disguised as a fitness center. To obliterate a home-based dungeon would be as uncomplicated for Maxwell as squashing a bug.

Now assuming the demeanor of a self-assured billionaire, his eyes glowed with confidence, his slumped shoulders lifted and squared, and his thin lips turned down smugly. "What time would you like the woman and her partner to show up for work?"

Milan glared at Maxwell. "Wipe that self-satisfied look off your face!"

Maxwell instantly humbled himself. He dropped his head and stroked the dog tag that dangled from his collar. "I apologize for my arrogance. I am at your service, Mistress. Always."

"That's better." Milan threw her head back and downed her glass of wine. "Hungry?" she asked sweetly.

"Starving," he responded.

"Then let's get out of here. You're going on a liquid diet tonight and your dinner is hot and swirling between my legs."

Milan picked up her purse. Maxwell rushed over to pull back her chair. She remained seated and handed him a cloth napkin. "There's a smudge on my shoe."

A look of misery covered his face. Taking the white cloth in hand, Maxwell looked around self-consciously and then lowered himself beneath the table and began wiping Milan's shoe.

Conversations ceased and mouths gaped as the astonished diners witnessed the billionaire groveling on the floor. Milan tossed the crowd a baffled look that quickly transformed into beaming pride. *I'm as shocked as all of you. I guess he's pretty smitten*, her smile suggested.

Beneath the tablecloth, his face hidden from view, Maxwell's tongue darted out and gave Milan's shoe a swift, surreptitious lick.

CHAPTER 9

Maxwell could not eat pussy worth shit. He did a much better job of spit-polishing her footwear, but that was so very boring, Milan could only bear a few minutes of his tongue sliding up and down the soles of her shoes.

After receiving a lackluster tongue job that garnered her only two tiny orgasms and a great deal of disgust, she called her driver and sent the mogul to a squalid, rented room in the Nicetown section of North Philly. Maxwell needed a timeout to contemplate a more skillful cunnilingus performance. He didn't deserve to ponder inside the splendor of his vast and extravagant estate in Chadds Ford, Pennsylvania. And his performance certainly didn't merit jetting off to his Mediterranean-style mansion in Florida or any of his other magnificent estates located around the world.

But he did need a few necessary items to properly conduct business on her behalf, so she allowed him his briefcase, BlackBerry, and laptop to get the job done.

Her phone rang. She eyed the caller ID. It was Hilton. He'd been given explicit orders to let her know when he'd dropped Maxwell off at the dreary abode, which was located on a dangerous corner where thugs and drug dealers loitered.

Milan wasn't concerned about Maxwell's well-being. She'd paid a security firm a hefty price to ensure his safety. No way would she allow her cash cow to fall into harm's way. But Maxwell had no way of knowing that. She relished the idea of him shivering and shaking with fear and humiliation, looking over his shoulder while he talked tough as he wheeled and dealed with the haggard Veronique.

"Good evening, Ms. Walden," Hilton said, using a professional tone that both annoyed and aroused Milan. "Mr. Torrance is settled inside his room. The security team is in position inside and outside the boarding house."

"Good. Thank you, Hilton." Milan used a soft tone. Hilton had been withholding his good dick long enough; it was time for her to make amends.

"Will that be all, Ms. Walden?" His voice oozed the confidence of a well-endowed man who knew how to use his masculine tool. Hilton was too damn sexy for his own good. *Cocky bastard!*

"Actually, I did have something else in mind," she said, sounding sultry, even though desperation threatened to squeak out between the words.

"What's good? Whatchu got on your mind?" Hilton switched to jargon, making Milan's pussy pulse. Oh hell, anything her driver did or said made her kitty meow, real loud.

"I was thinking about dinner for two."

"Oh yeah? You gon' cook something? You gon' gimme a grub?"

She giggled and then covered her mouth to stifle the ridiculously girlish sound. "Stop teasing me. You know I'm not talking about that kind of food."

"Oh! I got it—you miss me?"

She swallowed. "Yeah, I really do."

"Whatchu miss about me?"

"Everything," she uttered. Her words were so true.

"Nah, you're not getting off that easy. Break it down. Tell me whatchu miss."

Squirming, Milan began listing everything she'd missed: "Your lips, your taste, your kiss."

"Uh-huh. What else. Whatchu miss the most?"

"You know," she said, blushing. "Stop teasing me, Hilton," she whined, though the lilt in her voice was a clear admission that her heart desired him as much as her pussy did. And that was fucked up. She couldn't and wouldn't allow herself to consider Hilton to be anything more than he was—a good fuck. *Shit! Sexy-ass motherfucker!*

"Tell me," he insisted.

"I miss Big Hammer," she whispered, using the nickname she'd given the head of his dick, which was a humongous and bulbous part of his thick pleasuring instrument.

"How's my lil' Na-Na?" His voice grew husky with lust when he spoke the pet name for her vagina.

"She's in distress. Going through withdrawal." Her voice cracked.

"Big Hammer's leaking right now, baby. Feenin'! My man needs to get between Na-Na's cute little lips."

"Mmm." That was the only sound Milan could make. Hilton was talking dirty and he had her Na-Na in a terrible uproar, had her squeezing her thighs together, trying not to open the floodgates, holding back a splashing hot eruption.

Hilton chuckled and the sound had a mocking tone.

"What's so funny?" Insecurity wrapped around her like a

tattered hand-me-down coat from her childhood. The feeling, a reminder of the old Milan, seemed too close for comfort. She gave a shudder as if shaking off the raggedy old coat.

"Nothing, baby." There was lingering amusement in his voice. "You got your game tight, Milan. You can turn the sexy charm on and off like water. But when you're ready to step into your Miss Boss Lady role…" He paused and laughed again. "You know how to bring it—full force. Lucky for me, I played football."

"Yeah, so what?" Anger crept into her tone. Hilton was starting to annoy her. He always managed to bring football into a conversation as if his former profession made him wise…a demigod of sorts.

"I know how to focus," he explained. "I studied your moves and I'm all over it."

"Meaning…" She didn't bother to conceal her irritation. She knew exactly what he was talking about. Hilton was saying that she couldn't play him the way she played the rest of her staff nor could she control him the way she controlled his former boss, Maxwell Torrance.

But he switched tactics, softened his tone. "If we were on the football field, I'd be knocking players out the way, snapping necks if I had to…keeping mofos from getting too close…protecting my lil' Na-Na, keeping my baby safe."

Feeling briefly flattered, a quick smile appeared and then vanished from her face. Milan reviewed Hilton's words. He'd guard the pussy but he didn't mention a word about protecting her. Oh well. What did she expect? Her relationship with Hilton was all about sex.

"The door is unlocked. I'll be upstairs in my bedroom. Don't make me wait too long," she said, using an authoritative tone.

It was best to play along with Hilton's perception of her as a sexually insatiable, heartless bitch. Revealing that he possessed the key that could unlock the steel cage protecting her sensitive heart could send her on a downward spiral. Unlike a cat, Milan didn't have nine lives. She couldn't risk taking another hard fall.

≈§≈

Sitting in front of her vanity, Milan leaned in and gave her image an approving wink. Her recently waxed brows were arched to perfection. Her unblemished dark brown skin gave off a glow and had the look of smooth velvet. With the help of facials, expensive skin care products, and tons of expensive makeup she had drastically improved her appearance. Personal hairstylists and manicurists employed by Pure Paradise were at her beck and call, keeping her hair and nails flawless. With a killer wardrobe and a body toned and sculpted by painful Pilates, Milan had redefined her ordinary looks into supermodel perfection. None of her sex partners—not Hilton, Sumi, Maxwell, or even Royce, had ever caught a glimpse of her unpainted face.

And they never would. Milan would prefer walking down Broad Street naked at high noon before granting anyone other than her cosmeticians a glimpse of her natural, unpainted, scrubbed mug.

It seemed like eons ago that she was a gangly, unattractive kid in grade school, a bookworm considered too corny to get an invitation to a sleepover or to join in on jump rope or other fun games the kids around the neighborhood played. Her older sister, Sweetie, ran with a gang of fast-behind girls. Sweetie and her girls ran the 'hood as well as the elementary school. The tough crowd used profanity without inhibition, carried loose cigarettes in their backpacks, and engaged in malicious girl fights.

Due to Sweetie's ruthless rep, Milan was spared numerous beat-downs from the cruel kids who taunted her. Then Sweetie told Milan it was time for her to stand up for herself, and taught her how to defend herself and how to fight dirty if she didn't think she could whip her opponent's ass. Milan became a ruthless terror to anyone who fucked with her. She was a weirdo loner who'd throw her book down and jump up swinging at anyone who looked at her the wrong way or murmured an unkind word.

Returning from her trip down memory lane, Milan reassessed her image, nodded, and finished her look with a shiny coating of lip gloss on her bronze-tinted lips.

"Hey, beautiful!"

She winked at her makeup-enhanced reflection and smiled. The smile remained in place as she spritzed her wrist with a new perfume—something Maxwell had brought back from Japan. She sniffed her pulse point. The scent was spicy, exotic...very sensual.

Suddenly interested, she examined the frosted glass container, caressed the smooth surface. Impressive. From an abstract perspective, the bottle looked phallic and suggested sex. But not everyday, ordinary sex; this bottle implied the wearer would get erotic, exotic, hot, multi-orgasmic sex.

She spritzed her other wrist and her neck. Oh, she had to have more of this erotic product. She couldn't make out the name of the fragrance or anything else written on the outside packaging. Every word was written in Japanese. Milan shrugged.

It didn't matter; she'd ask Maxwell to translate. Having conducted business abroad for years, the man was fluent in numerous languages.

The scent was intoxicating. She sniffed again, filling her lungs with the fragrance. *Mmm, divine!* Her clients would love the scent and as an entrepreneur she'd be remiss if she didn't offer her patrons an opportunity to purchase the product. Of course, she'd raise the price four times its actual value. After all, a good businesswoman had to turn a profit.

First thing in the morning, she'd instruct Maxwell to have the company send her cases of the sexy stuff. For free, of course. Or else! Milan beamed with the knowledge that Maxwell's pit-bull tactics and unscrupulous reputation preceded him. He'd get her the fragrance and accessories: lotion, bath gel, and any other frills that accompanied the Japanese scent.

She hadn't heard him enter or climb the stairs and his sudden appearance in her mirror was startling. Out of uniform, Hilton stood filling the doorway of Milan's vast bedroom wearing loose-fitting shorts, an unbuttoned shirt that exposed a massive concrete chest, and washboard abs, and a cocky smile.

"Where's your uniform?" she kidded him.

"Oh, you changed the game. Now you expect me to wear that thing on my free time?"

"The uniform looks good on you. Makes you look stately," she teased.

"I'll have to remember that the next time you invite me over. But can I keep the jacket unbuttoned, so I can show off my abs?" He stroked his washboard tummy. "You know I keep my body tight just for you, boo."

Milan's pussy perked up. Behaving like the slut that it was, her pussy didn't even pretend to be ladylike or demure. It started spitting and dripping the moment his sexy vocals filled the room and penetrated her ears. *Shit! Shit! Shit!* Hilton's instant effect on her pussy was a damned disgrace.

He swaggered into the bedroom, lips scrunched, brows furrowed. "What's that smell?"

"It's a Japanese fragrance." Her voice faltered. "What's wrong with it? Is it too strong?" Milan jerked her head toward him, waiting for his response.

"It's sexy. Smells good." Still frowning as if the Japanese fragrance gave Milan an unfair advantage, Hilton came up behind her, bent over, kissed her neck, and inhaled the distinct and sensual scent.

Milan closed her eyes, enjoying the feel of his strong embrace. There was a time when she wouldn't have been able to bear such romantic intimacy, but Hilton had changed that and she found herself taking pleasure in his unique touch.

"You look beautiful, baby. As usual," he added, nodding. He took her hand, pulling her to her feet. Hungry eyes gazed at her modest cleavage and trailed over the small swell of her hips, draped by a clingy, ice–blue, satin and lace ballet-length slip. His eyes sparkled in admiration. "Damn, Shawty's a ten," he complimented, reverting playfully to another street colloquialism. He gave her a smile that was a mixture of appreciation and desire.

And something else. *Love?* No, Milan knew better. Their relationship was strictly about sex. *Hilton is an employee who gets extra benefits*, she reminded herself.

"You look good, smell good…" He paused, his eyes roving downward. "I already know the poontang tastes good, but it's been a while, so you might have to let me whet my palate—let me sample it right quick."

Milan blushed something awful. Thank God her dark skin hid the blazing red from flaming across her cheeks. Hilton did not play fair. Damn shame the way he could break through her hard exterior with a few well-chosen words and a lingering gaze. She couldn't prevent her lips from spreading into a big, cheesy smile nor could she slow down her accelerated heart rate.

He had that effect on her. If she didn't watch herself, he could have her groveling at his feet, the way her ex-trainer, Gerard, had. Her submissive side was lying dormant, kept at bay and cloaked by her bravado and panache. She'd learned her lesson and vowed to keep that side of her persona heavily guarded and under lock and key.

Mentally, she gathered her wits and called on her inner strength. Mustering courage, she took a deep and revitalizing breath and then looked Hilton in the eye.

He turned her around and ran his hand over the mound of her small ass, trailed a thick finger down the satin fabric, creating a valley between her butt cheeks. He stroked the cloth-covered crevice and Milan trembled at his touch. He lifted the slip and rubbed her bare ass with his large palm, circularly rubbing on a buttock and then the other. She released an agonized gasp and turned around and faced him.

Invited by his open arms, she melted inside his embrace. Hilton's lips touched hers softly, and then he kissed Milan deeply. His tongue slipped between her lips. Probing. Wandering. Becoming reacquainted with her silky moistness. The sweet invasion of his wandering tongue told her that he'd missed the taste of her mouth and her lips.

Woozy from the devastating kiss, Milan pulled away, her hand pressed against her chest as she struggled to catch her breath. Showing no mercy, Hilton reclaimed her lips, absorbing her intoxicating nectar with hunger and urgency. She felt him harden against the blue satin that covered her sex. His phallus pulsed deeply with surges of need.

Incited, Milan joined in the conversation, her own tongue twisting and swirling as it danced with his. Soft moans and murmurs made the sensual music their bodies swayed to, grinding and undulating in an agonizing and desperate rhythm.

Without warning, Hilton's lips swept down to her neck, her weak spot. Milan squeezed her eyes closed and clenched her teeth. He kissed and then sucked the sensitive flesh, forcing the breath from her lungs.

Overwhelmed, her knees buckled, her body sagged. Hilton caught her. Instead of holding her upright, he gently eased her down to the floor.

CHAPTER 10

Just a few moments before, she'd been the picture of pampered elegance and femininity. Now her slim body was down on the floor, on her back, writhing like a snake, her newly shaven pussy a bare offering. Milan didn't want to fuck on the floor like a dog, but she was so damned worked up, her cunt, overwrought and in frenzy, was behaving as if in crisis mode.

Repetitious pussy clenching and pulsing had taken her strength. Realizing she was too weak to even crawl toward her beautiful, comfortable bed on the other side of the enormous room, she'd surrendered herself, hiked up her slip, and spread her legs.

Scowling, nostrils flaring like he'd already tackled Milan and was now about to finish her off by leaping on top of her ass, Hilton flung off his shirt. Next, he unsnapped his waistband and unzipped his fly, but his movements weren't fast enough for Milan. She reached for him.

"Hurry. Please," she muttered, voice cracking with yearning, as she urged him to join his hard body with hers.

With sexual tension rippling through the air, Hilton moved swiftly. He tugged off the cargo shorts, kicked them aside, and then crouched down.

Impatient and unwilling to wait another second, Milan sat up and grabbed his hand the moment his fingers touched the elastic band of his boxers. She caught a glimpse of his hard muscled thighs and her eyes lingered on his body—a work of art that demanded admiration. Briefly torn between stroking his quadriceps or his intimate manly muscle, she opted for the latter when Big Hammer jutted against the cotton fabric. She slipped her hand inside the opening of his boxers and seized his erect shaft.

"Oh, baby," she murmured appreciatively as she felt his cock gently pulse inside her fist. Possessively, she reclaimed the dick she'd missed, her grip growing tighter like a blood pressure cuff taking a reading.

She loosened her grasp and slid her cupped palm up and down his solid length. One hand cupped his taut scrotum, deftly rolling his testicles in her palm. Her thumb eased upward and began to trace the thick ridged flesh that bordered the crown. She caressed the smooth globe, using the warm liquid that oozed from the tiny hole in its center to give it a glossy shine.

Big Hammer was gleaming and spitting more liquid and it was an amazing, pussy-pulsating sight. Hilton whimpered when she applied feathery tongue flicks to the sensitive underside of his turgid shaft. Both Milan and Hilton were panting as if they were running a race. Overcome and about to lose all sense of reason, Milan decided to hell with foreplay, she wanted to fuck. Milan drew in a deep breath, prepared to push him on his back, straddle, aim, and thrust down.

But one look at Hilton's heavily hooded eyes, his slackened lips, encouraged Milan to prolong her control of the situation while she had it. It wasn't an everyday occurrence for the hot ex-NFL player to allow himself to be seduced.

Working fast, she continued the aggressive role, easing him into a prone position, but instead of connecting her pussy with his dick, she fastened her lips around Big Hammer. She pulled on it for a few seconds and then licked the thin fluid that trickled out. She dragged her tongue over the smooth flesh and polished the oversized glans. Hilton's toes curled, his eyes rolled into the back of his head as Milan licked Big Hammer lavishly, sending tingles to the many nerve endings of the sensitive area.

Concentrating on savoring the experience for as long as possible, Hilton gently pushed himself in deeper, giving a husky groan as Milan's lips wrapped tightly around his length. Her tongue sloshed against the tip of his dick, giving him dual stimulation and double pleasure, making it difficult for him to hold his load even though his thrusts were methodical and slow.

Milan's mouth was hot and entirely too moist. Unable to endure the heat, Hilton pulled his dick out. Hurt and bewildered, her mouth suddenly vacant, Milan frowned, her flicking tongue capturing traces of pre-cum and her expression asking, *What's wrong?*

"Come 'mere, baby." Hilton leaned forward and embraced Milan. He pressed her cheek against his broad, bare chest, patting her head and murmuring, "Lemme catch my breath. I have to get used to you again. Been away too long. I forgot how tight you are with your oral skills."

Hilton's chest heaved against Milan's face. He had no idea that his was the first and only dick she'd ever sucked. And what she did with her mouth had nothing to do with experience. It was all about love. God-dammit! There was no denying it—not even to herself. She loved Hilton Dorsey, but she knew he didn't love her back. Who could? According to her mother, she was ornery, selfish, and unlovable. Milan believed the hype, accepting that she was entitled to all the things that money could buy and granting herself permission to have everything but love.

‰

Hilton mounted and slowly entered her. Milan wrapped her legs around his back, binding him to her. Wantonly, she threw him the na-na, uttering raunchy sounds, making lewd gyrations as she did her best to mimic the loveless, uncommitted fucks she was accustomed to.

"Slow down, baby." Hilton slid his dick out of Milan's pussy. "What's up? Why are you trying to get me off so quickly?"

"I'm not. Na-Na misses her man," she replied, keeping her tone nonchalant.

"Na-Na's acting like she's trying to make me bust a quick nut." He unwound Milan's long limbs from around his back, leaned back on his haunches, and pulled her up. His big hands cupped her small, round ass. "Lil' Na-Na's getting out of control," he whispered as he aligned the head of his dick with her slippery opening. He pulled her close, gripping her buttocks so tight she couldn't move. "Tell Na-Na that I got this, I'm calling the plays," he muttered harshly in her ear and then hungrily nibbled at her neck, making her twist and squirm with pleasure.

His gigantic hands covered her ass, maneuvering her slim and limber body in every direction that best suited his carnal desires. He started off bouncing her ass up and down his lengthy pole. Next, he grabbed her waistline and began rotating her around his shaft. Then his hands palmed her buttocks again. This time, he dug his short nails into her delicate flesh, making her flinch at the unexpected pleasurable pain.

Without any show of affection, Hilton worked Milan, giving her the kind of fuck that was about expertise, proficiency, and control. He fucked her senseless and did not stop thrusting until he shot out violent spurts of fluid. She inched closer, keeping her body fastened to his, desperate to prolong the connection until she joined him in breathless ecstasy.

Depleted, his flaccid appendage slipped out, leaving Milan's na-na bruised and sore.

At some point they crawled into bed and while in the throes of slumber, Milan rolled over to Hilton's side of the bed. Half asleep and acting on pure instinct, she snuggled up, molding her body against his and draping her arm across his muscular frame, her hand hanging over his bicep. Swiftly sinking into a sound sleep, she didn't know Hilton's eyes had fluttered open when her body connected with his.

In a dreamlike state, she murmured contentedly when his lips brushed her dangling fingers. She inched closer, burying her face into his broad back. Now in a deep sleep, she didn't experience the warmth or feel the beating of his heart when he repositioned her hand, pressing her palm against his chest, keeping it close to his heart as he covered her slender hand with his own.

⚜

Milan was accustomed to waking up in an empty bed, but this morning she felt particularly alone and abandoned when she reached over and patted Hilton's side of the bed, finding it empty. There'd been no kiss on the cheek, no "Thank you, ma'am, for a fantastic fuck," no hastily scrawled, "See ya later," no nothing. He'd vanished at dawn, presumably to get in his daily workout. The twenty-nine-year-old ex-football star still had dreams of getting back into the game. He still envisioned himself taking his team to the Super Bowl.

Ha! Keep dreamin', Hilton!

Milan felt violated and angry. As usual, Hilton had fucked her and discarded her like he'd dispose of a used condom. Someone would have to pay for her bruised ego. In search of a victim, her mind did a quick scan. Maxwell? No, he was too easy a target and, quite frankly, she was beyond bored with the billionaire.

Royce? Ugh! She scrunched up her lips in revulsion. What a crude pig! She really had to be in a severe state of horniness to ride his gross, bumpy tongue.

Sumi? No way! Her assistant was lovesick, moping around the salon wearing her heart on her sleeve. Milan had no choice; it was for her own good that she wean herself off Sumi's snapping pussy. She recalled that crazed look that had briefly appeared in Sumi's eyes. Who knew what harm a hot-headed, love-obsessed martial arts expert was capable of inflicting? Milan flinched, unwilling to allow herself to even ponder the dire possibilities. Yes, Sumi would be handled with kid gloves from now on. Good thing she had new assistants to keep her busy. Milan hoped she fell in love with one of the girls because she was weary of being the object of Sumi's love.

CHAPTER 11

At precisely ten o'clock in the morning, Hilton called to let Milan know he was outside. Making him wait, she stepped outdoors a half-hour later.

Appropriately attired in his chauffeur's uniform, Hilton tipped the brim of his cap and gave her a broad smile, showing no sign that he was miffed at having to wait.

"Good morning, Ms. Walden," he greeted in an affected professional voice.

Milan sucked her teeth, looking as offended as if he'd just said, "'Sup, bitch!" Frowning excessively, she slid into the back of the car. "Where's Maxwell? Did his car pick him up this morning?" she asked, her voice sullen.

"Yes, the security team confirmed that he was picked up at seven a.m., on schedule."

"Where is he now?"

"I'm not sure."

Leaning forward, Milan released a derisive grunt. "You're not sure? What the hell does that mean?"

"You didn't ask the security team to tail Mr. Torrance. The detail was complete after he safely entered his car."

A horrible bout of panic made further inquiries catch in her throat. She coughed as if to clear it. "Did you call his driver?" she asked, finally finding her voice.

"Yes, Ms. Walden. I called his driver. No answer. In fact, I made numerous calls. Mr. Torrance is not at his estate and he's not at his office."

"Maybe he's out on the golf course."

"No. I contacted his country club. He's not expected there until Thursday."

Losing her patience, she blurted, "Hilton, did you speak directly to his secretary? Surely she knows his whereabouts; she schedules his appointments."

"I couldn't get through. I spoke to his secretary's assistant, and she acted real secretive, like she knew something but wasn't telling." Hilton looked at Milan in the rearview mirror. "What do you think Mr. Torrance is up to?" He waited for Milan to respond. She didn't. She sat in silent contemplation. "He probably has a major come-up for you...like a shopping spree in Paris," Hilton ventured optimistically.

Milan gave him a weak smile, but she was perplexed. Obviously, something had gone wrong. She'd pushed Maxwell too far, forcing him to spend the night in that squalid rooming house. *Where is he?* She shook her head, convinced Maxwell had finally had enough of her abuse and was now out for revenge. A terrible sense of doom engulfed her. When she noticed her hands beginning to shake, she clasped them together to still the terrible trembling.

Instead of sending a team of lawyers and a sheriff to shut down the dungeon and evict Veronique and BodySlam from their home as she'd instructed him to, Maxwell was probably holed up with lawyers scheming to take over Pure Paradise just for spite. He knew that would be the best way to really screw her over. Taking Pure Paradise from her would really bring the pain and hostile takeovers were Maxwell's specialty.

Nausea knotted her stomach. *How stupid can you get!* she chastised herself. The last person she needed to turn on her was the unscrupulous Maxwell Torrance. It was not a good idea to have him on your bad side.

She swallowed a lump of fear that formed in her throat. Foolishly, she'd allowed her kitty to get dick-whipped by Hilton, who was a few steps above being a pauper, while allowing a billionaire to slip from her grasp. She should have kept a close eye on Maxwell. Clearly, he thrived with hands-on discipline; he simply couldn't hold up under the strain of exile.

Stupid, stupid, stupid! Her desire to get a hot fuck from the driver Maxwell had bequeathed her was a bad business call. Now blaming Hilton for her predicament, she narrowed her eyes at the driver and then gave a loud, exasperated sigh.

"Why are you giving me the evil eye? I didn't lose your boy."

Here I go again, letting my heart get me in trouble. She rolled her eyes hard at Hilton, whose cool demeanor and unwillingness to love her was a callous reminder of her ordeal with Gerard. Refusing to give up easily, she picked up the car phone and called Maxwell's home.

"Mr. Torrance is away on business," his housekeeper informed her politely. Milan slammed down the phone. She looked off in thought and then called his cell, which went straight to voicemail. Aghast, she covered her mouth, unable to come to terms with the fact that she was in possible jeopardy of losing her generous benefactor. *What am I going to do?* "*Call his secretary,*" a tiny, insecure inner voice instructed. She'd always treated his secretary with disdain and disrespect; it would be so humiliating to have to resort to speaking to the woman in an undeserved civil tone. She snatched up the phone again. *A girl has to do what a girl has to do*, she reminded herself.

"Hi, Barb, how are you? This is Milan Walden. What's on Mr. Torrance's schedule today?" Milan asked crisply, removing all arrogance from her voice.

"Mr. Torrance's schedule is strictly confidential; I'm not at liberty to say," his secretary happily responded.

"Oh, fuck you, bitch," Milan spat and then banged the car phone inside its compartment.

A million scary thoughts flitted through her mind. Instant poverty was at the top of the list. She blamed Hilton and gave herself an inner warning to keep the chiseled hottie at bay until she had Maxwell securely back in her clutches. Good dick spelled nothing but trouble and she, of all people, should have known better than to put her heart on the line before she'd acquired a more substantial amount of Maxwell's assets.

⁓≋⁓

The mixture of citrus and woodsy scents wafting inside Pure Paradise normally put a smile on her face but today the smell seemed heavy and irritating, making her wrinkle her nose in annoyance the moment she entered the building.

"Good morning," Royce said politely.

Mad at the world, Milan wanted to say, "Oh, shut the fuck up!" but other staff members were within earshot. Keeping it professional, she returned a mumbled greeting accompanied by a sneer that she hoped conveyed her true feelings to her personal pussy licker. Striding toward the elevator, her hard clicking heels announced to anyone within earshot that she was not in a good mood. She exited the elevator on the top floor, thinking that there had better be a large container of cappuccino waiting on her desk or she was going to go ballistic.

Outside her office, in the reception area, Sumi sat on the plush white sofa. "Where's my cappuccino?" Milan barked.

"On your desk, of course," Sumi replied sweetly, but her smile was reminiscent of the cat that caught the canary.

"Why are you looking so smug?" Maxwell's mysterious disappearance had Milan's nerves frazzled. Seeing her assistant wearing a self-satisfied smile was the last thing she needed.

"I have great news," Sumi offered, rising to her feet as Milan wordlessly accepted a stack of mail from the receptionist. Sumi followed Milan into her office. "My new assistants, Lily and Harper, designed a new website last night and we have more requests for appointments than we can accommodate."

"Really?" Milan brightened. Then she frowned. If Pure Paradise became more lucrative, would it become an attractive acquisition if she were on Maxwell's hit list?

How had she allowed a casual fuck to turn her life upside down? She shook her head, thinking how much she hated Hilton for his part in making her future uncertain. As soon as she got this shit straight with Maxwell, she planned to fire Hilton. That's right. Business took precedence over pleasure. If she wanted to continue to succeed, she'd have to become more disciplined and tell that good dick goodbye and good riddance.

Milan clicked her keypad and brought up the Pure Paradise website. She tilted her head when she saw the current home page. "Where's the new design?"

Sumi hovered over Milan, pointing. "Look at the new link at the bottom of the page."

Milan's gaze moved downward. At the bottom of the page was the image of a menu with script that read: *Pure Paradise Specialties.* Her interest piqued, Milan clicked on the link and was taken to an open menu that listed items such as Double Chocolate massage, Spicy Asian pedicure, Caramel-Cream foot bath, Strawberry Soufflé body wrap.

"Nice concept, but why are people clamoring? I mean...we already provide these services without the sickeningly sweet stuff."

Wearing a smug smile, Sumi said, "Pick one."

Milan clicked on Spicy Asian pedicure. She gawked and fanned her face when she took a look at the rear view of a ripped Asian guy. His head was turned, giving a glimpse of his handsome profile. He had bulging meaty deltoids that Milan would love to fondle and squeeze.

"The client who selects that service will get her toenails polished by this hot Asian hunk," Sumi informed.

Her lust fired and her curiosity piqued, Milan quickly clicked all the selections. Double Chocolate were two fine-ass, dark-skinned brothers who'd obviously put in long and rigorous hours at the gym. Milan arched an eyebrow.

"They work together," Sumi explained. "After giving a client a hot chocolate massage, one licks chocolate from the back-door and the other works his magic on the punany."

"Oh, my!" Milan exclaimed, getting instant and stimulating visuals. Sumi's assistants had outdone themselves. Beneath the menu, Milan saw a single link that read Kaleidoscope Sunshine. She looked up at Sumi questioningly.

"Check him out." Sumi sounded more smug than ever.

Milan clicked on the link. Kaleidoscope Sunshine was a mean-looking, bald, white, biker-type. His buff body and even his bald head were covered with a rainbow of tattoos. Milan looked up, curious. "What's his specialty? And why add Sunshine to his moniker? He looks more like a thunderstorm than a ray of sunshine."

"After Mrs. Tamburro's session, I knew there had to be a shitload of women who needed discipline. You're having trouble prying BodySlam away from Mistress Veronique so I told the girls to find a qualified master. Hey, we can't discriminate against the B&D freaks."

Sumi had taken a liberty in assuming that Milan didn't have the power to make Veronique and BodySlam offers they couldn't refuse. However, being momentarily at a disadvantage with Maxwell MIA and all, she overlooked the fact that Sumi had seriously crossed a line.

"Again, why'd you add Sunshine to his name?" Milan repeated, irritated.

Sumi took in an enthused burst of air. "Well, he's going to do group sessions. He claims he's a master at transforming spoiled housewives into obedient and *happily* submissive housewives."

Memories of Gerard formed a cloud over Milan's face. "How's he going to achieve that lofty goal? I can't imagine a pampered housewife being eager to hand over her five-carat tennis bracelet in exchange for a pair of metal handcuffs."

"Well, you saw how BodySlam whipped Mrs. Tamburro into shape."

"That was different. Her husband forced her into that spanking session. That crackpot was holding a prenup over his wife's head." Having had firsthand experience, Milan knew the obscene lengths a woman could go to in order to get her hands on a rich man's money.

"Rich husbands are signing up their trophy wives for obedience training," Sumi clarified.

Milan shook away the bad memories of Gerard and her scoundrel of an ex-fiancé, Noah Brockington. She drew in a revitalized breath. "Sumi, this is great. Your assistants did all this in less than twenty-four hours?"

Sumi beamed. "Pretty amazing, huh?"

"I'm impressed." Milan tried to infuse cheer in her tone but her melancholy over Maxwell's disappearance seeped out.

Sumi's smile faded. "Are you okay?" Her beautiful eyes grew large with concern.

"I'm fine," Milan said tersely, unwilling to share her secret fear that she'd lost her power over her benefactor. Worse, was the trepidation that he was coming after Pure Paradise, guns drawn, salivating with revenge.

"I have the perfect remedy for what ails you." Sumi bestowed Milan with a radiant smile.

"You have nothing to offer me," Milan blurted, her voice dripping acid. Irritated by Sumi's uncomplicated existence, she spit more venom. "Why do you think your ancient Chinese remedies can resolve the complex issues in my life?"

"I'm not Chinese. I'm half Korean," Sumi fired back. "I don't appreciate the way you lump all Asians together. It's disrespectful and very ignorant," she ranted.

Before the fiery half-Asian got worked up enough to split Milan's beautiful desk in two, Milan quickly placated her. "I'm sorry, Sumi…that was rude of me. What exactly did you have in mind?"

Sumi's brightened eyes indicated that the storm had passed and all was forgiven. "As I've said, my assistants are not only business geniuses, they're both freaks. Lily can give you an orgasm in the most unusual way."

"I know she gives good head. You told me about the assistants' oral expertise when you hired them."

"Lily's freakier than Harper," Sumi added.

Milan was bored but indulged her assistant with a weak smile, half-heartedly encouraging Sumi to continue.

"If she wasn't such a great asset to business, I'd put Lily on the new Pure Paradise menu. I'm serious, Milan. Do you want her to give you a demonstration?"

Milan briefly considered the offer, but decided to decline. After the hard humping she'd gotten from Hilton last night, her libido was sluggish. "I don't feel like participating. I'll watch."

"Watch? That's it? I'm shocked because you're always horny," Sumi exclaimed, giving Milan a suspicious glance.

Sumi knew about Milan's sexual dalliances with Maxwell and Royce, but she didn't know that Milan was fucking her chauffeur. She believed that her boss hated the cocky former jock and that she only put up with his insubordinate behavior because she'd inherited him from Maxwell and had to honor Maxwell's promise to Hilton that he'd always have a job.

"I have a lot on my mind, Sumi. I'll meet Lily another time."

"Milan, Lily is the de-stressor that you need. Trust me on this," she urged. She winked at Milan and snapped her cell open. "Hi, Lily. I want you to join me in Ms. Walden's office—ASAP." Excitedly, she turned to Milan. "Take off your panties, Milan."

"No, I said I'm not in the mood. I'm willing to assume the role of voyeur, but that's it. Lily can demonstrate her talent on you."

"Okay. Have it your way. I could go for another big O. I was simply trying to save you the trouble of hastily struggling out of the panties that will, without a doubt, end up on the floor."

CHAPTER 12

With a devilish gleam in her eye, Sumi sat on the settee waiting for Lily to appear. Milan sat behind her desk hugging herself, something she did when she was tense. Her mind was on Maxwell and money. It had been a grievous error to loosen her grip on the man to whom she was financially beholden.

Sick with fear, Milan had no interest in viewing sex tricks, but hoped that the entertainment might distract her from her disturbing thoughts and keep her mind occupied until Maxwell resurfaced.

The desk phone rang. Milan grabbed it. Her heart sank further when the receptionist announced Lily's arrival instead of telling her that she had Maxwell Torrance on the line.

"Send her in," Milan said dryly.

Lily trotted in, quick and proud, like a prize-winning filly. She wore a skimpy tank top and tight jeans that were low-cut, showing off the youthfully taut skin of someone recently out of her teens. Milan gave her a quick, competitive sizing-up, panning from the dark tresses that fell in lustrous waves down her back and around her shoulders to her pointy-toed ankle boots.

Pilates kept Milan in shape but the nine- or ten-year difference between her and Lily was painfully apparent. Lily didn't have a drop of makeup on, yet her face was luminous and flawless, her heavy lashes ink black and fluttery. And unlike Milan's fake butterfly lashes, Lily's were real.

Lily was a self-assured, frisky little thing with a pretty, doll-like face, bow-shaped lips, pale porcelain skin, and large brilliant blue eyes. Slim and curvy, the hot little number was only about five feet tall with a tinier waistline than Sumi's, small rounded hips, and disproportionately large and jutting breasts. Stung by instant breast envy, Milan consoled herself with the fact that Lily's boobs looked like jugs—too large and totally unrealistic. The little bitch had probably been cursed with pitiful breasts as small as Milan's.

As if Milan and Sumi were paying patrons at a titty bar, the brazen little heifer pulled off her snug-fitting top without prompting and flung it to the lush carpeted floor. She was braless, yet her giant, pink-tipped, white torpedoes, needing no support, sat up high and proud. Apparently feeling that going topless was a sufficient exhibition, Lily kept on her jeans. Milan made a mental note to tell Sumi to inform her assistant that tank tops and jeans were not appropriate attire in the workplace.

Lily threw her head back, arched her back, and fondled her ample bosom. Sumi was drawn to her feet and moved toward her as if magnetized. Though also petite, Sumi was several inches taller than Lily. She ducked her head and softly brushed her lips against each rosy areola. She delivered a series of quick, moist kisses to the rosy tips and then, as if afraid of overindulging, she abruptly abandoned Lily's breasts for her lips.

The two women kissed, gently at first, and then with more

ardor. Their arms tightened around each other, their bodies swaying together, lips locked in a deep kiss.

Sumi and Lily obviously had the hots for each other. Milan wasn't jealous in the least, but she refused to be a captive audience to this lustful exhibition. Making her watch was most likely getting the two freaks off. Averting her gaze, she became lost in thought. Her mind began to wander until it found its way back to her miserable predicament. Maxwell! Who would have ever thought he'd be out to get her! She emitted a soft sigh. *Why, oh why, did I banish him? His fortune would be still within my grasp if I'd only allowed an hour or two of shoe-licking pleasure.*

A sudden shrill cry caught Milan's attention. No longer feisty, Lily looked like a fragile creature, standing still with her arms hanging helplessly at her sides, her head thrown back as if in ecstasy while Sumi viciously twisted her nipples until they became extremely elongated and hardened into fleshy cones.

Milan's mouth fell open and remained that way for several moments as she watched Lily come out of her trance and grasp Sumi by the shoulders, leading her backward toward the settee. Lying on her back with her knees spread and squirming, Sumi uttered anguished moans while Lily gripped one of her big pointy titties, crouched between Sumi's legs, and penetrated her with her unnaturally large and conical nipple. Like a big dick with a pointed glans, the firm, torpedo-sized breast glided in and out of Sumi's tight cunt.

It was an intriguing sight, sending a succession of shivers knifing through Milan's coochie. And as Sumi had warned, Milan's juices overflowed, soaking through her panty crotch and wetting the seat of her chair.

Her first impulse was to sound the alarm and call on Royce,

but Milan was so entranced her finger could not find its way
to the emergency button that would alert Royce and send him
rushing to her aid. Besides, she didn't want what Royce had to
offer. She wanted what Sumi was getting—a silicone titty fuck.
Before she made her needs known, Sumi helped Lily out of
her tight jeans and she and her assistant switched positions on
the settee.

Lily was now on her back with Sumi straddling her chest,
talking dirty in Korean, using her snapping pussy to nip at the
tip of Lily's coned breast. Extremely limber from years of
studying martial arts, Sumi reached behind her back. Without
missing a beat, she doubled Lily's pleasure, giving her a severe
finger-fuck, her probing finger working its way deeply inside
Lily's cunt. Meeting Sumi's finger thrust, Lily's hips jutted forward, her body undulating as though it was liquid. Meanwhile,
Sumi's tight little pussy bit and twisted Lily's flushed nipples,
giving her lucky new assistant immense pleasure.

None too pleased that she'd been left out, Milan squirmed
in sexual agitation as she swallowed the lump of yearning that
formed in her throat. She preferred another session with Hilton's
good dick but would settle for getting her kitty licked by her
security guard. Then it occurred to her that Royce's lumber-
ing ass would take forever to leave his post, ride the elevator,
and trudge down to her office to put out her fire. Desperate,
she started yanking open desk drawers, looking for a dildo, a
vibrator—something to masturbate with. All she found was
files and folders. In the middle drawer, she eyeballed a foot-
long ruler, gave a lingering glance to a plump pen, but refused
to stoop that low.

Then a light bulb went off inside her mind. She rooted through
her creamy tan leather handbag and located the phallic-shaped

bottle of Japanese perfume. French manicured fingers caressed the frosted glass and then she slid the container in and out of her vagina until she felt a familiar rush of heat.

Ever the businesswoman, though she was hanging at the edge of an orgasm, Milan reminded herself to tout the dual appeal of the heady Japanese fragrance to her patrons...the marvelous scent and the convenient fuckability of the phallic-like container.

Aiming upward, Milan located her hidden spot and pressed the smooth rounded perfume cap against her G-spot until she felt the big bang. One right after the other, the three women climaxed. A medley of high-pitched sounds denoting feminine release filled the executive office. Sucking in a shivering gasp of air, Milan dropped her head, resting it on the desk.

With sexual relief came a soft peacefulness. A clear mind came next. And then enlightenment, so luminous it caused Milan's head to jerk up. She looked around her office. Lily and Sumi were gone, having left behind the heavy aroma of pussy and a whisper of perfume. Milan was grateful for the solitude. Her revelation required privacy.

Call it feminine intuition, gut instinct, or clairvoyance, but it was suddenly crystal clear that Maxwell had made a personal visit to Veronique's dungeon. Milan knew with certainty that within a brief matter of minutes, the seasoned dominatrix had sized Maxwell up. The pasty ghoul smelled money and recognized prey. With her twisted and sadistic mind, Veronique had lured Maxwell into the type of captivity his warped heart had been longing for.

Sure, Milan had treated him miserably, abused him in the

only way she knew how, dispensing verbal and emotional humiliation on a regular basis. In hindsight, Maxwell's impertinence had gotten out of hand. He'd been silently pleading to be taken to task. But she was not a trained dominatrix and admittedly, she'd grown lazy, never bothering to improve her performance or dress in an appropriate dominatrix wardrobe. She owned no sexy leather lingerie, no zippered latex, and no intimidating chains dangled from her body, clinking and clanging, announcing her menacing approach.

She'd never reprimanded Maxwell with heavy lashes from a cane or whip, nor had she bothered to learn how to skillfully utilize the metal torture devices that she kept on hand and displayed on the lower level, role-playing fantasy room. The numerous devices were merely for show, promising pain and heightening the torture chamber ambience. Sure she'd practiced paddling Royce, but it was more to humiliate him and keep him humbled than to actually cause pain. She was a fraudulent mistress and had been bullshitting Maxwell all along. But now that he'd had a taste of the real thing, how could Milan compete? She wrung her hands in despair.

Holding her chin up, she vowed that the gaunt and ghastly Veronique would not win her prize. She'd rack her brains until she figured out a way get her billionaire out of the hands of that vicious, ugly, and undeserving hag. Pronto!

CHAPTER 13

Though she would have preferred to order her dominatrix wardrobe online, there really wasn't time. Maxwell was prime chattel and it was imperative that she retrieve her valuable possession from the gnarled hands of Veronique, an undeserving and horribly unattractive shrew. Milan would have to act fast if she expected to regain custody of her wayward slave.

Inside a dimly lit sex paraphernalia shop on Walnut Street in downtown Philly, Milan tried on quite a few outfits: a lace-up leather corset, a very revealing leather-strapped teddy, a ribbon-trimmed spandex bustier, a studded leather thong and matching pushup bra, black lace-topped fishnet stockings, stilettos, and thigh-length rubber boots.

Feeling vampish in a black and pink plastic outfit with full-length gloves, Milan sauntered up to the counter and plopped the other items on the glass countertop.

"Need some props? A whip…cat o' nine tails?" the creepy-looking, elephant-eared clerk asked, his eyes twinkling with sexual mischief as they darted toward a display of whipping devices.

"No, I don't need any of that." She had more than enough

flogging implements in the paddling room at Pure Paradise.

"How about a paddle? A lot of fellas enjoy the sting of a good paddling," the salesclerk recommended, practically frothing at the mouth, his big ears seeming to flap with excitement.

Refusing to be to be lured into fulfilling the creep's lust for dirty talk, Milan wrinkled her nose as if something stank. Pulling out a credit card, she scrunched up her lips, intensifying her expression of disgust. *Pervert!*

Loaded down with six bags of new dominatrix gear including a studded leather glove the creepy clerk had coerced her into purchasing, she exited the shop wearing a pair of "you know you want to fuck me" heels and the shiny, pink-cupped, black plastic dress.

On point and professional, Hilton got out of the Rolls and relieved her of her bags. He didn't bat an eye at her brazen and outlandish attire.

"Where to?" he asked, closing the back door and returning to the driver's seat.

Veronique's so-called "dungeon" was actually housed inside a plush downtown loft. Calling it a "lair" would have been more appropriate. "Eighteenth and Arch," she absently instructed as she flipped through the pages of *Dominatrix for Dullards*, a yellow-covered, quickie how-to guide. She could have kicked herself for not reading the manual and mastering the techniques back when she first acquired Maxwell.

At that very moment, Sumi, Lily, and Harper were orchestrating the transformation of Milan's basement into a fully equipped dungeon. Milan had considered taking an online crash course in dominatrix training, but changed her mind. She'd rely on her rage and fury to persuade her into cracking a whip

across Maxwell's ass. His reckless disappearing act had jeopard-
ized her sense of financial security and for that transgression,
Maxwell would be shown no mercy.

There was nothing like the fear of losing one's assets to get
the creative juices flowing. At least a dozen devious ways to
inflict pain flitted across Milan's mind. Once her runaway sex
slave was back in her grasp, Milan intended to flog and torture
him for hours.

"Mr. Torrance is in apartment 1224. Tell him his true mistress
is waiting inside the car," Milan told Hilton. "If he's hesitant
about leaving, inform him that he's displeased me and—" she
groped for harsh and threatening words— "tell him I said to
get his ass downstairs, immediately." She'd worked herself up
and her nostrils flared as she heaved in angry breaths of air.

"Yes, Ms. Walden."

Milan made a mental note to give Hilton a raise after she'd
reclaimed her goods. His humble and professional behavior was
greatly appreciated during this very tense and critical time.
She felt charmed that he could forgo his cockiness and put her
interests first. But then again, Hilton wasn't stupid. His own
survival instincts had kicked in, alerting him that Milan's loss
would affect his lifestyle as well. A two-to-three-hour-a-day job
that paid the salary of a ten-hour day, with sexual perks, was
nothing to sneer at.

Her desire for Hilton was simmering and not boiling over.
The threat of losing money kept her libido in check.

Only Hilton could look stately in a chauffeur's uniform and
cap. Striding proudly, he proceeded to the entrance of Mistress
Veronique's high-rise building and then disappeared inside.

"Please don't let me be too late," Milan whispered as if in

prayer. For all she knew, Mistress Veronique could have seduced and tortured Maxwell into transferring his entire fortune to a Swiss bank account in her name. Oh God! She felt so vulnerable. And feeling helpless made her mad as hell.

Milan swore to herself that if she got her slave back, she'd stop being lazy. No more Ms. Nice Guy. Her insults, public humiliation, and insistence that he service her with his tongue were far too tame, not nearly severe enough punishment for such a despicably deceitful slave.

As much as she dreaded the inconvenience, there was no other way around the task. She'd have to work up enough stamina and develop creative scenarios while dispensing cruel and harsh physical discipline. Oh, God. Her life had been so carefree…cursing at him, belittling him, and demanding that her shoes and pussy get licked was the extent of the effort she'd put into being a mistress. Now she had to work for Maxwell's devotion. It was so not fair. Damn that horrible Veronique. The woman had ruined her cushy lifestyle.

Anxiety ridden, she lowered the window and craned her neck, peering inside the building. She could see Hilton. She shook her head in apprehension. Usually, looking at Hilton made Milan's stomach tighten with yearning, but not now. That he was still yakking on the phone and hadn't yet made it up to the loft was making her tummy flip with fear.

What the hell was the problem? From her vantage point, Hilton appeared to be scowling in frustration and gesturing frantically, like he was having a hard time getting Veronique or her sidekick to be reasonable. *Shit. Shit. Shit.* The operation was not going well at all. Unable to bear witnessing Hilton return to the car in defeat, she rolled up the window, closed her eyes, and imagined the kind of torture she'd put Maxwell through if she was fortunate enough to get him back in her clutches.

That damn Maxwell was going to pay dearly for causing her such a high degree of agitation. Red hot anger engulfed her. At that moment, she was furious enough to do Maxwell the kind of harm that could put him in the hospital…or kill him. *Hmm.* Getting hit with a murder charge was not a pleasant thought. She took a deep, refreshing breath and decided she wouldn't lay a hand on Maxwell until her some of her rage dissipated.

Antsy, Milan checked her watch and peeked at her cell phone. It was a simple mission. Capture and seize! Why was Hilton taking so long? Biting her bottom lip, she imagined Hilton barging in the loft and Veronique and her muscular cohort, BodySlam, overpowering him, killing Hilton, or enslaving him for life. People committed lesser crimes for less money. With billions at stake, who knew the lengths Veronique would go to.

Unable to concentrate, she put down the training manual and then took a deep breath, trying to relax in the well-cushioned back seat of the Rolls. She couldn't. On pins and needles, she leaned forward, eyes riveted to the brightly lit lobby. With her fingers and toes crossed, she waited anxiously for Hilton to deliver her benefactor. Hopefully, Maxwell would return with his financial status intact.

Five minutes later, a grim-faced Hilton returned to the car. "I spoke over the intercom to a man and asked to speak to Veronique. He told me that she wasn't available. Then I asked to speak to Maxwell Torrance and he put a woman on the phone." Hilton took a deep breath.

"And?"

"I demanded that she let me speak to Mr. Torrance. The woman burst into laughter and said that Mr. Torrance was tied up." Obviously distressed, Hilton rubbed his chin. "Think we should call the police and report that Mr. Torrance has been kidnapped?"

"No. I'll handle this," Milan insisted, sounding bolder than she actually felt. Opening the back door herself, she stepped out of the Rolls. Hilton opened the driver's side door, but Milan motioned for him to stay inside the car.

Despite a feeling of panic and foreboding, she swept inside the building like she owned the place. She approached the lobby phone and picked it up. Ignoring the anxiety that coursed through her, she took a deep breath and then pushed in Veronique's apartment number.

"Hello!" Veronique chortled.

Milan winced. There was triumphant laughter in the bitch's despicable gravelly voice.

"You have something that belongs to me," Milan stated calmly. "And I want it back."

The threatening tone in her voice was unmistakable and very real. She suddenly realized that if Veronique didn't release Maxwell, she'd have to get ghetto on that ass and take her property back. Apparently Veronique didn't know who she was messing with. Milan could fight and she didn't need any manmade paraphernalia; she'd whip that bitch's so-called dominant ass the good old-fashioned way. She'd forget about keeping up appearances and resort to her housing project days. Yes, Milan was ready to handle her business. If she got close to Veronique, Milan was prepared to kick off her stilettos, snatch off her earrings, slather some Vaseline on her face, and commence to whipping some Goth ass.

Better yet, she'd keep her heels on and stick a size ten stiletto up that flat ass. She could imagine herself scratching up Veronique's pasty face with her long acrylic nails, and then she'd bite the mound of the hag's dowager's hump with her full set of healthy teeth. Yeah, she'd get real ghetto up in Veronique's loft if she didn't quickly turn over Milan's personal possession.

"He's my property now, he offered himself to me," Veronique said contemptuously.

"You're misinformed. Maxwell Torrance serves only me. Look at the collar he's wearing. It clearly states that he is my property!"

The crude woman coughed into the phone—a horrible, hacking cough. Finally, she cleared her throat. "He gave himself to me," Veronique said. Her voice was so grating, it made Milan wince.

"That man you're holding hostage belongs to me! There's a collar around his neck that bears my name."

"Not anymore."

Milan gasped in shock. "What do you mean? No one can remove his collar. It's locked. I have the key."

"Like I said, he's not wearing any collar. My man BodySlam's pretty handy. All it took was a pair of wire cutters to free Torrance from your flimsy bondage."

Milan bristled, hating having to hear Veronique's nasally voice refer to her wealthy human property by name.

"He's been whipped, fucked in the ass, and at the moment he's resting…strapped down. Bound and gagged." Veronique gave a wheezy sigh. "He looks happily miserable as he attempts to develop a tolerance for pain and my special brand of punishment," she taunted. "So take your fake-dominatrix ass back to your vanilla world of fantasy dungeons and delightfully playful torture toys. People like you make a mockery of a very serious lifestyle."

"You're right," Milan conceded. "And if you're the superior dominatrix you claim to be, then you won't mind allowing Maxwell to tell me to my face that he prefers you over me?"

Veronique wheezed into the phone for a few unpleasant moments and then abruptly hung up. A buzzer sounded, granting Milan entry to the other side of the locked glass door. Her mind racing as she crafted numerous seizure scenarios, Milan stepped inside the elevator and rode to the twelfth floor.

BodySlam opened the door. Big, bald, and virile, he was even more imposing in person than when she'd viewed him on the monitor. Watching him spank Mrs. Tamburro from the safe confines of her cushy office was...um, sexy. Standing face-to-face with the sadistic brute was terrifying.

Milan gulped. "I'm here to see Veronique." Surprisingly, her voice came out strong and steady.

He gave a snort, loud and threatening, challenging her to run as fast as she could to the safety of her waiting car. But the thought of bungling her mission and leaving empty-handed encouraged Milan to stand tall, boldly matching BodySlam's scathing gaze.

BodySlam's suspicious eyes gave her a quick once over, rapidly scanning Milan from head to toe. After a final grunt of displeasure, he stepped aside and allowed her admittance inside the loft.

Milan interpreted BodySlam's throaty utterance as defeat. *Aha!* She'd made the cut. She'd impressed him with her sneer, her hot-pink and black plastic dress, and her ultra-sexy boots. She wanted to give herself a big fat kiss for pulling off the look and demeanor of an authentic dominatrix. Strutting with a newfound sense of power, she followed BodySlam into the main room, which had the customary furnishings of a typical home: sofa, chairs, tables, lamps, tasteful art adorning the walls. No whipping posts, blood spatters, or any signs of torture and brutality.

Veronique, milk white and ugly, sat in a black leather chair watching a game show on TV. Her long, skinny legs were outstretched, her body language crude and masculine. Severely vexed at having her show interrupted, the hag glowered at Milan.

Milan's eyes wandered back and forth, inquisitively. Which of the two had introduced Maxwell to anal sex, BodySlam or Veronique? Veronique looked mannish enough to strap on a dick. But even with all his muscles and seeming virility, it was quite possible that BodySlam was a down-low brother. It was a hard call. Milan shrugged. Maybe they were a tag team, taking turns butt-fucking the traitorous billionaire. For his treachery against her, Maxwell deserved far worse than a bloody asshole.

Veronique took note of Milan's outfit. Standing tall and proud, Milan stared her down, forcing the woman to blink.

"He's in the back room," Veronique told her; then she rose.

She and BodySlam escorted a confident and boldly strutting Milan down a corridor. Unflinching, Milan strode into the torture room, rolled her eyes at the many dungeon-devices. The chink in the armor had been detected when she made Veronique blink.

Naked and bruised, Maxwell lay shackled to a padded table with a gag ball inside his mouth. At the sight of Milan, his eyes widened in surprise.

Milan smiled at her slave. Her curving lips, beautifully wicked, promised to deliver a thrashing that he wouldn't soon forget.

Enthralled by the unspoken pledge, Maxwell trembled with

delight, informing Milan that he was eager to endure harsh and relenting punishment for his rebellious behavior.

Veronique cleared her throat and shifted her feet uncomfortably. The haggard dominatrix wasn't looking quite as smug, Milan noted with amusement.

Milan smoothed Maxwell's tousled hair and chuckled, "You've been a very naughty boy." She frowned up at Veronique. "I believe there's been a misunderstanding. My slave has been playing a prank on you and me." She leaned down to her naked and helpless slave. "Your discipline will be severe and unrelenting."

Veronique parted her lips in protest.

"Don't worry," Milan cut in before the woman could utter a word. "You'll be compensated for your time."

"Let's get something straight—" Veronique's voice shook. She looked upward anxiously as if she were witnessing billions of dollars sprouting wings and swirling out of her reach.

Rubbing her victory in Veronique's face, Milan beamed down at Maxwell. "For the record...to whom do you belong?"

Maxwell's eyes fixed on Milan's face. Unable to speak, he groaned deeply, conveying his devotion. Milan plucked the ball gag from his mouth. "Tell her." She nodded toward Veronique.

Veronique's upper lip curled in disgust as she and BodySlam stared down at Maxwell curiously.

"I belong to you, Mistress Milan. I'll do anything to get back in your good graces," he said, his voice raspy with regret.

"You piece of crap. You dirty scumbag!" Veronique spoke through clenched teeth. She raised her hand menacingly. Maxwell flinched, but BodySlam grabbed Veronique's arm before she could strike the billionaire.

"My, my. You're such a sore loser and it's quite unattractive."

"Fuck you!" Veronique bellowed.

Milan pursed her lips and wrinkled her nose in disgust. "You really ought to work on developing some dignity and grace in the face of defeat." Smirking, she glanced at her watch and then glared at Veronique. "Look, I don't have all day. Unbind my slave!" She sucked her teeth and began tapping her foot impatiently.

Veronique hovered over Maxwell. She brought her angry face close to his. "You ingrate. You wasted my time. I worked all day whipping you into shape—"

"Let him go, Veronique. We'll get another..." BodySlam stopped, leaving out the words *rich man*.

BodySlam wedged himself in front of Veronique and undid the leather straps that bound Maxwell's upper and lower limbs. The billionaire sat up and rubbed his tender wrists.

Furious and unable to witness her great loss, Veronique stomped out of the room, leaving BodySlam behind.

Milan pressed her lips close to BodySlam's ear. The heavily muscled bald man folded his massive arms and then nodded a reply.

CHAPTER 14

"Good evening, Hilton," Maxwell said sheepishly as he followed Milan into the backseat of the car.

Milan shot Maxwell an admonishing look. "Did I give you permission to speak?"

Contrite, he lowered his head. "I'm sorry, Mistress."

"Save your apology. You can't begin to imagine how sorry you're going to be for your impudence. Your utter gall," she added, shaking her head in disbelief.

"I know I don't deserve you, Mistress. I beg you to please accept my humble apology. Please! I promise to be your obedient and faithful servant for the rest of my life."

Hilton turned the key in the ignition. "Should I drive Mr. Torrance home?"

Milan could tell by his voice that her chauffeur was uncomfortable. It embarrassed him to hear his former boss beg and grovel. Putting on a show for Hilton, she thrust her hand between Maxwell's legs and squeezed his balls. Maxwell grunted in genuine pain.

"That's just the beginning," she warned.

"I understand, Mistress," he whimpered, rubbing his aching balls.

"Actually, you don't understand. But I'm sure we'll see eye-to-eye after you've been properly trained." She gave his scrotum another squeeze and a sharp twist.

"Ahh!" he gasped in shock and then uttered incoherent, pain-filled sounds.

Hilton grimaced, unsure of what Milan was doing to Mr. Torrance, but his instincts, as well as the volume of his ex-boss's screams, gave him a fairly good indication.

Looking at the driver in the rearview mirror, Milan gave him a wink. "Don't pay Maxwell any attention. He's full of theatrics."

Maxwell's breathing came in short gasps, but he finally stopped whimpering. Milan kept her eyes on Hilton's face. She noticed that a hint of amusement, a trace of a smile, had appeared on Hilton's lips after Maxwell quieted down.

And there was something else. She continued to peer at her driver in the rearview mirror. He gazed at her, raw desire in his eyes. She felt her breath catch, and her mouth watered. She wanted to do Hilton right there in the car. White passion oozed between her legs.

She was on fire and would have gladly opened her legs and welcomed him inside her hot hole, but business before pleasure, she reminded herself. Exercising control, she closed her legs tightly. Only a thrill seeker or a hopelessly addicted gambler would put a fabulously wealthy lifestyle on the line for another night of lust.

For the sake of her financial future, she focused her undivided attention on her slave. There were marks on his face, his neck, and his arms. Scars left by Veronique, and reminders of his flagrant disobedience.

Infuriated, Milan whispered tauntingly, "I heard you're a

sissy." Milan placed her lips near Maxwell's ears. "How come you never mentioned that you liked taking it up the ass?"

"I don't. Those people are animals. They violated me."

"Is your little butt-hole burning?" She giggled.

Humiliated, Maxwell dropped his head, covering his face with his hands and murmured, "Yes, Mistress, I'm in a great deal of pain."

"So you were sodomized and kidnapped, is that what you're saying?"

"Exactly."

She patted his hand. "Don't worry. They're not going to get away with what they did to you." She tapped Hilton on the shoulder. "Take us to the closest police station."

"Yes, Ms. Walden. Right away," Hilton responded. He slowed down and made a right turn.

"Why…why did you tell him to do that?" Maxwell asked, his eyes suddenly filled with terror.

"Are you questioning my judgment?"

"No." He wiped droplets of sweat from his forehead.

"We're going to press charges, Maxwell. Those criminals should be held accountable for what they did to you. I don't take kindly to having my property kidnapped and defiled." Scrunching up her lips, she scrutinized him and winced. "Look at all the marks they left on you. I'm personally offended. I want justice. Don't you?"

"No!" Maxwell begged. "I can't allow that type of information to leak to the press. It'll ruin me." He began shaking his head adamantly.

"Let me get this straight." Milan gripped his chin, and turned his face toward hers, forcing him to look her in the eye. "You were held captive and you were brutally assaulted by sadists who had no justification for putting their hands on you and you're saying that you don't want to see your tormentors punished?"

"No, I don't. I'm sorry, Mistress, but I can't afford that kind of publicity." His blue eyes welled. "My image would be tarnished. I'd be a laughingstock. I'd have to move to some remote corner of the world."

"I see," she said bitterly and then shoved his head against the back of the leather seat. "Forget the police station, Hilton. Drive me and this sissy to my home."

"Okay." Once again, Hilton changed the direction of the car.

Milan set rage-filled eyes on Maxwell. "You can crush corporations but you can't shut down a home-based dungeon? You're pathetic," she spat.

"I'll shut them down. I promise you."

"Your promises aren't worth shit."

"I made a mistake, Mistress. I should have never personally delivered the news that the dungeon had to be shut down."

"You were supposed to have your people handle Veronique. I didn't tell you to make a personal visit."

"I wanted to inform her that she had two days to tie up her affairs."

"That's ridiculous. Since when do you give a heads up to a company you intend to squash?"

"You didn't say you wanted to take over the dungeon. You told me to shut it down."

"You're mincing words and I'm losing my patience," she hissed. "Be honest."

Resolute, Maxwell sighed. "I let my curiosity get the best of me. I wanted to see the inner workings of an S&M establishment."

"You're disgusting and unworthy of my attention. In fact, you're beyond unworthy; you're total scum."

"Yes, I agree. I'm scum."

"You disobeyed me and look where it got you."

"You're right. I disobeyed you and I suffered greatly."

"By the way…?"

"Yes, Mistress?"

"Why did you allow yourself to be strapped to Veronique's table?"

"She invited me to take a tour. I…I…," he stammered. "I found myself excited by all the dungeon equipment and the idea of bondage. Veronique noticed my…uh…erection and offered to cuff me. Just for fun. Then she took advantage of me."

"Your dick got hard for another woman?" Milan slapped him across the face. "You're a dirty whore, Maxwell. You belong to me; you're my property and yet you permitted that hideous hunchback to strap you down, beat you, fuck you, and worst of all, you allowed her to remove your collar."

Maxwell rubbed the handprint left on his face. "I'm so sorry, Mistress. I told her that I belonged to you, but she wouldn't listen. After I'd allowed her to strap me to the table, she told me that after she introduced me to the pleasure of pain, I would have to relinquish myself to her."

"And you believed that crap? Jeez, how did I get saddled with such a dumb, disgusting sub?"

"I was shackled. There was nothing I could do. I couldn't stop that big brute from cutting off my collar. Do you realize that I was violated in the most depraved way?"

"Are you blaming Veronique and BodySlam?"

"Yes!" His face reddened with rage. "I was victimized. I'm innocent."

"You're a liar."

Maxwell reached for Milan's hand and showered it with sloppy kisses. "I love you and only you. I'm completely devoted. Sowing my wild oats came with a great cost. I'll never stray again. I promise you."

"Shut up. You were disloyal and disobedient. You thought you could get away with cheating on me. But you got caught." Milan pointed her finger in Maxwell's face. "You're going to pay."

❧❦❧

"Good night, Ms. Walden," Hilton said, holding open the back door of the Rolls.

Milan gave Maxwell a hard shove after he exited the car. The tycoon took a few stumbling steps before steadying himself.

"Why are you so friggin' clumsy?" Milan poked him in the back.

"I apologize, Mistress," Maxwell mumbled in embarrassment.

She looked over her shoulder at Hilton and sighed at the injustice of being laden with such a klutz. Hilton wore a stoic expression.

Knocking Maxwell around in full view of her chauffeur was making her pussy twitch. She wondered if her mistreatment of her slave was giving Hilton an uncomfortable hard-on.

"Get in there," she hissed at Maxwell and gave him a swift kick in the shin after pointing a remote to unlock the front door. Obeying her, Maxwell quickly limped inside.

Milan studied Hilton's face, looking for a sign that he wanted some na-na before he hit the road. All he had to do was say the word and she'd strip naked and splay her lean body on the backseat of the Rolls. Hell, she'd get down and dirty and let him hump her in back of the house on the lawn, against the oak tree, or they could stay where they were and do the nasty on the friggin' hood of the car.

Other than the almost imperceptible tension in Hilton's face, his expression remained unchanged. And what did that look indicate? Was he fighting back passion? Struggling against the fervor of coursing blood that rushed to his loins? Milan leaned against the door, studying Hilton's face.

"Have a pleasant evening, Ms. Walden," he said, dashing her hopes as he got inside the Rolls.

With hunger in her eyes, Milan stared as Hilton parked the Rolls, willing his straining dick to lead him back to her.

Business before pleasure? What a laugh. She was in heat and nothing else mattered. Maxwell had a small pecker, not nearly enough dick to satisfy her needs. She wanted Hilton. She wanted his big hammer, dammit!

But apparently Hilton didn't want her. He climbed inside his SUV and pulled off. Milan's heart sank at the sight of the tail-lights. That she had to watch good dick drive away, leaving her with a tingling vagina that didn't bode well for Maxwell Torrance.

She waited a few moments longer, giving Hilton some time to come to his senses. She envisioned him speeding up the driveway with his pants unzipped to release the strain from his aching loins. Stroking his dick, he'd rush toward her, prepared to pummel her na-na until it caved in.

But Hilton didn't return. She yanked the front door open. Maxwell assumed a submissive position down on the floor, placing fervent kisses upon her shoes. There'd been times when such ardent worship could induce intense arousal, making her juices flow like water, but tonight Maxwell's wishy-washy adulation provoked intense loathing.

Had she read her dominatrix training book or taken lessons from a pro, she would have known how to handle Maxwell. She'd be attaching a leash to a collar around his neck and walking his sorry rich ass down the basement stairs to torture and terrorize him. But under the circumstances, she'd have to curb her curiosity and venture down to the dungeon at another time to inspect the torture mechanisms that Sumi had hired a crew to install.

Milan often admired the ominous devices at Pure Paradise but didn't have any idea how any of them worked. She'd never bothered to find out. In fact, no one used the menacing furniture. They were mere props set up to enhance the mood for freaky couples.

She kicked Maxwell out of her way and sauntered across the room. Waiting for her instruction, Maxwell remained in homage position.

Milan sat down on a high-backed chair. "Crawl to me," she said sternly. He crawled and when he reached her feet, she ordered him to stand. "What's the name of that fragrance you brought me back from Japan?"

Maxwell looked puzzled.

"Do I have to beat the information out of you?"

"No, no. I was trying to think."

"Well, hurry up."

Maxwell frowned in concentration. Impatiently, Milan groped inside her purse and pulled out the attractive bottle of perfume.

"Oh! It's called Kimochi. It's a Japanese word that's used to conveys inner feelings such as gratitude, joy, friendship, love, and apology."

"I guess now would be a good time for you to express your *kimochi*—apologize!"

"I'm so sorry, Mistress."

Milan sucked her teeth. "That's not the kind of apology I was thinking of."

"How can I show you my deep regret and my sincere remorse for running out on you?"

She stood and took a couple steps forward. "You can have the manufacturers of Kimochi deliver tons of the stuff to my salon. I'm not paying one nickel, so you better figure out how you're going to make that happen. I want the perfume, the Eau de parfum, the Eau de toilette, the cologne, the body splash, body lotion, bath gel, and any other accoutrements. Got it?" She pushed her face so close to his, she could see her lovely reflection in his anxious eyes.

"Yes, yes," he agreed hastily. "Consider it done. I'll have a large shipment delivered the day after tomorrow."

"Tomorrow!" Milan insisted, unreasonably, considering the business day in the States was over. She didn't know or give a damn what time it was in Japan. All she knew was that she wanted truckloads of Kimochi, immediately.

"Certainly. You'll have the shipment tomorrow, Mistress."

"Good, now show me some real *kimochi* and take down your pants!"

From her open purse, she withdrew the metal-studded leather glove and pulled it over her hand. Maxwell swallowed hard and did as he was commanded. With a combination of dread and excitement in his eyes, he lowered his pants.

"Over my lap, you cheating slut." Her voice was razor sharp; she sounded like a true dom. Good thing she'd been practicing spankings on Royce because she'd need to read a few more chapters of *Dominatrix for Dullards* before she was qualified to inflict a more severe and complicated punishment on Maxwell.

CHAPTER 15

Ellen, the licensed manicurist, soaked and dried the client's feet, sloughed off rough skin from the bottoms, clipped her toenails, trimmed the cuticles, and buffed her toenails to a nice smooth shine. Her component of the procedure was complete. Wearing a gratuitous smile, the manicurist accepted a tip and exited the room.

Sitting behind her desk, Milan sipped cappuccino as she stared at the monitor. As if waiting for the next scene in a titillating film, she leaned forward, eyes glued to the screen.

Moments later, Shin, a handsome young Asian, came into view. Shirtless and flaunting a heavily muscled torso, he bedazzled the client with dancing, flirty eyes and then bestowed her with a gleaming smile that any fool should have been able to interpret as insincere and practiced.

Despite their differences in age, physical attractiveness, and muscle mass, the client—a stalking, middle-aged "cougar"—was flattered and ready to pounce. She patted her stiff, newly coifed hair as if she possessed some indefinable inner sexy that Shin would find irresistible.

Kneeling before her, he took her foot in his strong hands. Reverently, he gazed at the arched upper part of her foot and then kissed the smooth sole. Shin squeezed lotion into the palm of his hand and began to massage the client's foot, seductively inserting a lotion-covered finger in the spaces between her toes, creating a squishy sound that mimicked sex.

The fortunate beneficiary of the erotic foot massage appeared to be sliding out of the chair in ecstasy.

Seated across from Milan, Sumi beamed. "Well?"

"I'm impressed. Remind me to start hanging out in China Town."

"Shin is Korean!" Sumi was fired up, her small nostrils flared. "You're so narrow-minded. All Asians are not Chinese."

Milan sighed. She hadn't deliberately dissed the Koreans, but how the hell was she supposed to tell the difference? One of these days she was going to tell Sumi that her flaring nostrils was totally unattractive and her sensitivity regarding the Asian half of her heritage was turning her into a terrible bore. But not right now. Sumi was too angry to be reasonable and something hot was occurring on the monitor.

Simultaneously, Milan's mouth and that of the client, who'd been getting her foot massaged, dropped open. Milan was gaping in shock, and the client was taking Shin's dick inside hers.

"What the hell is going on? Are you trying to sabotage my business? As you well know, sexual acts between a client and a member of my staff is considered prostitution!"

"Not in this instance," Sumi said, pointing to the screen.

"She's sucking his dick and that is not acceptable. Go in there and put a stop to it right now!"

"Calm down, Milan. There's been no money exchanged between Shin and the client. She tipped Phoebe. He's a magnificent male specimen and you can't blame her for wanting a taste of his virility."

"Oh my God!" Milan covered her mouth in shock as she witnessed Shin swiftly extract his cock from between the client's collagen-filled lips. Aiming downward, he spurted cum all over both her feet, then continued giving the foot massage, now working his semen between the woman's curling toes.

"Kinky, huh?" Sumi smiled widely, obviously no longer feeling the sting of Milan's racial slur. "We're touting Shin's semen as a natural skin softener," she added proudly. "He'll be assisting with facials." Sumi giggled. "He'll also be helping the shampoo girl out."

Milan held up her hand. "Don't tell me…Shin provides hair conditioning as well?"

Sumi nodded. "He's multi-talented."

"You didn't mention the many uses of his cum when you displayed the new Pure Paradise specialties. That's sort of underhanded, Sumi. I don't appreciate being left out of the loop," Milan said, cutting an eye at the monitor.

"I wasn't being underhanded. When I showed you the new website, I wasn't aware of Shin's many abilities. You haven't been exactly accessible lately," Sumi said accusingly and then folded her arms.

"You're right," Milan conceded. "I've been going through a major issue with Maxwell."

Knowing Maxwell was the money man behind Pure Paradise, Sumi's eyes narrowed warily.

"The problem's been resolved," Milan assured her. Bored with Shin's shenanigans, she clicked off the monitor.

"Thank goodness. Listen," Sumi went on, "since we posted the specialties on the website, we've attracted more clients than staff can accommodate."

"Really?"

"Uh-huh. There's a long waiting list."

"That's not good." Milan shook her head.

"Why not? We're in demand. How's that not good?"

Milan pondered briefly. "I don't like the idea of losing money. Tell your assistants that they weren't hired to sit on their asses all day." Milan shot Sumi an evil look. "Nor were they hired to titty fuck during working hours. This is not a non-profit organization. Tell those two bitches to pound the pavements and find me some more good men."

"Okay, I'll have them get on it ASAP." Suddenly, Sumi's dark eyes lit with glee. "So, how'd you like it?"

"Like what?" Milan asked, now distracted by thoughts of Hilton.

He'd given her a quick sideways glance when she stepped outside, swathed in French couture. That look spoke volumes. It assured her that she looked more stunning than ever, but most important, there was hunger in his furtive gaze. He missed her na-na and could no longer fake it. That tough guy routine last night had been merely an act. *Ha!* He couldn't wait to get in her bed. Tonight, she intended to fuck him senseless. On top, she would ride him like he was a wild stallion, humping him hard and fast until the back of his head banged against the headboard.

Spanking Maxwell last night had given her a hell of a rush. She felt powerful. So very dominant.

Hilton didn't know who he was dealing with. Showing him no mercy, she would fuck him into a state of semi-consciousness. Milan felt a mild quiver as butterflies tickled her insides.

"Earth calling Milan," Sumi said, waving her hand in front of Milan's face.

Snatched out of her wonderful reverie, Milan's eyes bore into Sumi's. "What?" she snapped.

"How'd you like the dungeon?"

Milan twisted her face in annoyance. "I didn't look at it yet."

"You told me that you needed it right away. I worked like a damn mule, finding all that equipment and then tracking down workers to set it up with such short notice."

Milan shrugged indifferently. "I'll look at it tonight. And by the way, I'm going to need a competent person to show me how the stuff works."

"Can't Veronique—"

She flung Sumi a contemptuous look, cutting her off. "Don't mention that hunchback bitch's name ever again. Now, tell your assistants to get to work."

Sumi rose. Surprisingly, she didn't sulk. Gathering her purse and notepad, she showed no signs of hurt feelings. In fact, she looked visibly relieved.

Sumi claimed her affection for Milan was true and deep. "I love you, Milan," she'd proclaimed numerous times. Once, she even went so far as to suggest that they fly to Vermont or Massachusetts and join hands in same-sex marriage. Now, Milan suspected that Sumi had an emotional connection with Lily, but pretended the relationship was purely sexual.

Fuck you, you cheating whore. Go ahead, rush out of here so that silicone bitch can give you a titty fuck.

What a deceitful slut Sumi had turned out to be. She deserved to be suspended from her work duties, demoted, or fired! She'd deal with Sumi's unfaithfulness at a later date. Preoccupied with thoughts of getting Hilton back in her bed, Milan was forced to push thoughts of revenge aside.

⌘

Milan checked the time. 4:15. She turned the monitor on and clicked to the spanking room and there she was; Mrs. Tamburro, the cheating spouse, pacing nervously. Her stupid husband would have been better off taking her over his knee. A spanking from his loving hand, rather than bringing out her inner freak, may have filled her with outrage and curbed her adulterous affairs.

But her session with BodySlam had introduced her to her submissive side and had kindled a passion she hadn't known she possessed. Now, she wanted more. Behind her husband's back, she'd been calling Pure Paradise daily, pleading for a secret session with BodySlam.

Feeling no loyalty toward a client who was too cowardly to whip his own wife, and not being one to turn down money, Milan had finally gotten the opportunity to whisper in Body-Slam's ear. She'd made him an offer that he couldn't refuse.

"Come work for me or I'll have you deported. You'll find yourself on the first boat back to Haiti."

If Veronique had planned on keeping BodySlam joined at her hip, she should have married the illegal alien and made him a citizen of the United States.

Dressed in her usual business suit, sensible pumps, and up-sweep hair-do, Mrs. Tamburro was rocking the sexy librarian look. Wringing her hands and biting her bottom lip, Mrs. Tamburro looked terror-stricken.

From her own experience with Gerard, Milan knew all too well that fear was part of the turn-on for a woman who enjoyed being submissive.

CHAPTER 16

The door burst open and banged against the wall. Mrs. Tamburro flinched at the sound. Also startled, Milan nearly jumped out of her chair. "Damn!" she muttered as she reached for the remote and then turned the volume down.

BodySlam was not wearing the leather executioner's hood. This time, he arrived with tribal paint smeared across his face, his shaved head adorned with an ostrich-feathered headdress. Wearing a buckskin loincloth, leather wristbands, and a saber-toothed neckpiece dangling at his chest, BodySlam looked like an African warrior, ferocious and primitive.

He gave Mrs. Tamburro a cold smile and then yanked her toward him. She screeched as he swept her up into his bulging, muscled arms and stalked over to a majestic purple leather gothic throne. He situated himself on the seat of the throne and then released his captive.

Mrs. Tamburro tumbled out of his arms.

Milan winced at the sound of the woman's slight body as it hit the floor. She peered intently at the screen, afraid the poor woman who lay in a tiny heap was injured. She doubted if incurring broken bones or open wounds would encourage Mrs. Tamburro to continue writing checks to Pure Paradise.

Milan wondered if he resented being snatched from Veronique. She shrugged indifferently, deciding he was just being true to his sadistic nature.

BodySlam reached down and grabbed a handful of blond hair, undoing the neatly pinned hairstyle as he wrenched her head upward. Mrs. Tamburro's gleaming eyes did not indicate pain and Milan's fear of losing her client's business was quickly assuaged.

"So, you want BodySlam to discipline you with another spanking?" he growled.

Milan typically sneered at anyone who referred to himself in third person but somehow BodySlam pulled it off, effectively making his staged alter ego a credible, fear-invoking, and separate sadistic entity.

"Yes," Mrs. Tamburro whimpered. Her body trembled, her blue eyes widened with fear.

"Do you want more of my fancy artwork imprinted on your ass?"

"Oh, yes, that's exactly what I want," Mrs. Tamburro said in a voice that was husky with lust.

BodySlam tightened his grasp on the tuft of disheveled hair, giving her head a hard shake and causing her to give a small cry of pain. "This time, you'll have to earn it," he said in his lilting accent. He pulled his loincloth to the side, revealing a full, dark scrotum. "Lick," he ordered, wrenching Mrs. Tamburro's head upward.

Her eyes warily flicked from BodySlam's frowning face to his crotch. Her pink tongue slipped past her thin lips and then brushed against his hairy sac, tentatively at first and then with ardor, lavishly licking as if his ebony flesh held the tasty richness of Haitian cocoa. Loud tongue lashes made Milan squirm in her seat, overcome with a strong and sudden sexual yearning.

With his balls sufficiently licked, BodySlam pulled the cloth back farther, freeing his long, hard member from the confining loin cloth.

Milan sucked in air. Her heartbeat quickened. BodySlam had a monster-sized dick. It was a gorgeous sight, but much too big to suck or fuck without great discomfort. Milan stared at the screen intently. Mrs. Tamburro stretched her mouth open and sucked in the head of the coal-black sex organ. BodySlam held the back of her head and rammed in several inches of dick.

Mrs. Tamburro's blue eyes watered and she made choking sounds as he mercilessly pumped his impossibly large dick deeply inside her mouth. With her eyes now squeezed shut, her head flung back, she opened her mouth as wide as she could, trying to accommodate his impossible girth and length. BodySlam grasped the sides of her flushed cheeks as he pumped his huge midnight cock into her gaping mouth.

"Suck it," he growled.

Mrs. Tamburro attempted to pucker up, but her thin lips were stretched taut.

"I said, suck it!" BodySlam rose from the throne, clutching Mrs. Tamburro's head and holding it pressed into his crotch. Her body sagged like a rag doll, her eyes bulged pitifully as he thrust and shoved his thickness as far as it would go, making her gag and heave.

Milan's eyes were glued to the monitor. *Oh!* Unable to bear much more of the torturously sexy image of Mrs. Tamburro's mouth being plundered with BodySlam's big, brutal penis, Milan opened a desk drawer, scrounging around in search of a vibrator or dildo. She came up empty. Where the hell were her sex toys?

Her eyes darted back to the screen; she rocked back and forth in her seat, trying to soothe her sexual yearning.

BodySlam's outrageously big dick disappeared inside Mrs. Tamburro's mouth. The crown of his dick pushed into her throat while his nut sac knocked against her chin.

"I'm coming, bitch. You better swallow every drop," he growled, humping hard and causing tears to fill her eyes and slide down her cheeks. Unfortunately, the tears that trailed down intermingled with the white lust that spilled from the corners of her mouth.

Furious that she'd disobeyed, BodySlam pulled his throbbing cock from her lips, held it firmly, and aimed it like a weapon toward her face. His body jerked as he shot out the remaining jets of jism into Mrs. Tamburro's horrified face.

He grabbed her by the arm and flopped down in the seat of the throne, then turned her over his lap, yanking up her skirt so violently Milan could hear it ripping at the seams.

Frightened by the intensity of his anger, Mrs. Tamburro instinctively put up a fight, trying to wrench herself free. But pinned down by his powerful hold, she went limp in defeat, whimpering pitifully as he slowly pulled her panties down.

Gently, he placed a huge hand on her small white rump. His hand was so big, it completely covered her ass. He fondled and caressed her buttocks, rubbing soft circles on each cheek. Teasingly, he trailed a thick finger down the crack of her ass and wriggled it inside the crevice. He tickled her anus, giving her visible shivers, making her moan with pleasure. Then, quite suddenly, he gave her ass a painful twisting squeeze. Her lithe lower body squirmed and bucked. The more Mrs. Tamburro struggled, the angrier BodySlam became.

Finally, the pain-seeking adulteress took a deep steadying breath as she awaited the next powerful impact of his hand of steel connecting with her tenderized ass.

He applied a flurry of sharp smacks to Mrs. Tamburro's behind, intensifying the blows until his palm prints completely decorated her ass. Twisting and screaming, kicking her feet in desperation, Mrs. Tamburro appeared to be trying to swim away from the pain. Milan noted with interest that the white flesh of the client's thighs was a stark contrast to her fiery red ass.

"I want you to thank me," BodySlam commanded irrationally.

Milan shifted her position, leaning forward, riveted to the screen.

"Thank you," Mrs. Tamburro quickly responded.

Milan gasped when she noticed BodySlam's big hand reaching for a cane that was conveniently propped against the wall near the throne. She held her breath as if waiting for the next scene in a horror movie.

Taking charge of his victim, he held her in place with a large strong hand and then swiftly brought the cane crashing down onto her cutely rounded and welt-ridden derriere.

"Ahhh! Oh my God. Please stop," Mrs. Tamburro screamed.

"That wasn't a proper show of gratitude," he said in an icy tone.

"What should I say?" Mrs. Tamburro asked, crying and shaking. "Tell me. I'll say whatever you want me to."

"You must always say, 'Thank you, Master,' with every whipping. Do you understand?" He twisted his lips into a cruel smile before delivering another brutal blow.

"Thank you, Master," she shouted. Thrashing in anguish,

she struggled to free herself from his pitiless hold, but couldn't.

"Don't fight me," he growled. "Take the pain. Learn to love it."

"I caaaaaan't," she screamed. Somehow, she managed to raise her torso and was able to turn her head. Spotting the object of her torture, she shrank back in horror. She gawked at the wooden flogging instrument and then gasped in shock that he'd been using a crude cane to beat her ass. "I beg you, Master. Please don't hit me again with that thing. It's too painful. I can't bear it. I came to you for a regular spanking. You're going to kill me with that thing." She squirmed and writhed uncontrollably.

Simultaneously, Milan writhed in sexual agony. Mrs. Tamburro's pain and fear was making her pussy too hot to ignore. Without conscious planning, her longest finger worked its way into her feminine opening, snaking and winding, seeking to provide sexual pleasure.

Milan hadn't realized that her clenched inner thighs were smeared white and sticky. She yearned for an orgasm. Requiring immediate assistance, she reached for the phone to call Sumi. *Oh fuck that.* She retracted her hand. Sumi's pussy snaps were pleasurable to her clit, but right now she needed something really hard inside her soaking wet cunt.

Royce? Sure, his wide tongue curled into a thick, dick-like structure; it probed deeply and could reach the right spot, but her pussy needed a good ramming with something much more solid and with more girth.

Lily! Oh, yeah, she could get into a seriously freaky situation with that talented and well-endowed little freak.

She snatched up the receiver and pushed a button. "Sumi," she said breathlessly, "send Lily to my office." She realized that her gasping breath communicated her sexual excitement but she couldn't help it.

"Lily?" Sumi asked nervously.

"Mmm-hmm," Milan moaned.

She's...." Sumi paused. "Uh, Lily's working on..." she stammered, trying to delay the inevitable surrender of her new sex toy.

"I want her," Milan hissed. "Do you understand me?"

"But—"

"But, nothing. Tell her I said to get her ass in my office, fake titty in hand."

"Okay, I'll send her," Sumi mumbled helplessly. Then she gulped. "I really like her, Milan. You...you're not going to keep her for yourself, are you?"

"I'm the one who pays Lily's salary. So stop meddling in my affairs. Like I said, send her to my office right now! I'm horny, dammit!"

⚜

Milan lay on the settee with her legs spread. Lily kneeled and considerately lowered her mouth over Milan's vagina, prepared to provide oral lubrication before inserting her big, flexible boob.

Grunting and writhing with need, Milan inched up, opening her legs even wider, giving the assistant better access to her opened cunt. Lily's tongue flicked out. A look of surprise came over her face when she realized Milan was already wet. She licked between Milan's legs, hungrily lapping the tasty glob of stickiness that had been pooling ever since BodySlam had commenced to smacking Mrs. Tamburro's ass.

No wonder Sumi was hooked on Lily. The girl was a phenomenal pussy eater, and she murmured endearingly as she sipped in streams of Milan's hot passion.

"I want this to be special," Lily mewed, and cupped and squeezed one of her breasts.

Taken completely off guard, Milan watched in shocked fascination as Lily began rubbing her boob between both hands, molding the pliant flesh until it became elongated like a bulky cock. Milan thought she'd died and gone to heaven when Lily smoothed out her nipple and sculpted her large areola into a sloping contour that was an exact replica of Big Hammer, the crown of Hilton's enormous dick.

Lily stroked Milan's mons. She felt herself ripen at the young assistant's touch. Pussy juice drizzled as Lily rubbed the firm tip of her titty up and down the soft flesh between Milan's plump feminine lips. She felt Lily's nipple begin to harden and knot as it teased the opening of her vagina. Milan shuddered and moaned with pleasure when Lily's areola crossed the threshold of her inner chamber, followed by her phallic breast, which she plunged inside Milan as far as it would go.

Responding wantonly to the unexpected sensation of the superb titty-fuck, Milan made guttural sounds, winding her hips to meet Lily's hand-held deep thrusts.

"Oh, yes. Fuck me, bitch. Tear this pussy up. Go deeper, baby. Get all up in it. Give me some more of that long, big-ass titty-dick. Goddamn, goddamn. Girl, you fuck like a man." She spread her lean legs wider, making her vaginal depth more accessible.

Lily pushed her breast in to the hilt and then slid in and out at a sensual, rhythmic pace. "Feel good?" Lily asked unnecessarily as she worked Milan over.

"Yes!" Milan shouted. "Damn right. You know your shit is

good. It's better than dick," Milan proclaimed and then felt slightly embarrassed at that admission. Was Lily really fucking her better than Hilton? *No!* But fuck it, the titty was so good, it had her talking shit that she didn't mean.

No wonder Sumi was so possessive. Lily had her cussing lewdly, and bucking upward as she met that big titty thrust for thrust. Her fingers splayed and then curled, groping thin air. The assistant was giving it to her so good, Milan threw her legs around Lily's back, pulled her closer, taking in the nipple and total breast, grinding feverishly against Lily's chest as she readied herself to bust a big-ass nut.

Deep in the throes of an orgasm, she screamed in passion. Forgetting what or who she was fucking, she drew Lily closer as if trying to squeeze the very life out of the young woman.

"Oh, God!" Lily cried, her high-pitched voice reminding Milan that she was fucking a woman.

But in her mindless and depraved state, Milan didn't think about the unfeasible act of warm cum squirting out of a woman's boob and filling her cunt. Nothing mattered; nothing made sense. "Yeah, cum for me, baby," Milan urged, gyrating lewdly against Lily's chest.

"Let me go!" Lily fought to pull out, but Milan wouldn't let her go. She couldn't. Her pussy was still clenching and needed to remain filled with titty-dick as her massive climax reached its peak.

Finally, spent, Milan unclenched her legs. Lily bolted upright, holding an injured and limp tit.

Milan looked at Lily in horror. "What the hell happened?" She grimaced at Lily's flattened breast. It looked horrible and lifeless, like a deflated basketball.

Tears spilled down Lily's face. "You were too rough! You ruptured my implant; it's leaking," she cried.

Shocked, Milan covered her mouth. "Eew!" Appalled, she looked down at her thighs, expecting to see a weird-looking liquid substance dripping down her thigh.

"Nothing splattered on you. It's leaking inside me," Lily explained tearfully as she cradled her droopy boob.

Milan pointed to the door. "Get out, you nasty, freakish bitch."

Still cupping her deflated breast, Lily stared at Milan in disbelief. "My boob job was incredibly expensive. Who's gonna pay for this?" Lily looked down at her damaged tit.

Milan frowned at her pussy, disgusted that she'd allowed Lily to penetrate it with her weird, torpedo tit. She slipped a finger inside, irrationally searching for traces of gooey, silicone leakage. Wearing a horrible grimace and with her legs widely gapped, she waddled toward her private bathroom, convinced that at any moment, disgusting silicone gook would ooze out of her vagina and smear her inner thighs.

"Don't make me call security. Get out," she yelled from inside her private bathroom. She yanked a washcloth off a crystal rack and then turned the faucets on full force.

"How can you fire me when you're the one responsible for this? You ruptured my implant!"

"Send me the bill. Now, get your nasty ass out of here, Lily, and don't come back. Your position has been terminated," Milan shouted. Though there wasn't a trace of evidence to support her fear, she dabbed between her legs and ran the washcloth down her thighs, her lips pursed in revulsion.

Needing to confront the horrible culprit face-to-face once more, she marched to the doorway of the bathroom, still holding the dripping washcloth. "You leaked that nasty shit inside my vagina. Who knows what kind of diseases you're carrying. Eew!" Milan raved again.

"I don't have a disease. I told you the silicone is leaking inside my breast. I can't believe you're trying to terminate me when you're responsible for this mess." She put her top on but continued to protectively cup her injured breast.

"I'm not *trying* to terminate you!" Milan shrieked. "I own this place and apparently you don't understand English." Milan stretched her mouth open as wide as possible and bellowed as she shook the soggy washcloth for emphasis. "You're fired! How many different ways to do I have to say it? Now, go! Get out of my sight."

Lily appeared in the doorway of Milan's bathroom, breathing hard and holding her hanging breast. "I'm going to need surgery to repair this and you're going to pay for it." Near tears, Lily's voice quivered.

"Not a problem. Get an estimate and send me the bill. Whatever." Wrinkling her nose as if the young assistant smelled bad, Milan waved her off. "Do you understand English? Get off the premises. Leave, Lily. Please."

Her face beet red, and her shoulders slumped in defeat, Lily finally turned and hurried away.

CHAPTER 17

Her gynecologist was on vacation; she had to make an emergency appointment with the physician who was filling in. Her own GYN knew Milan was a sexual deviant but was never judgmental and somehow managed to keep a straight face whenever Milan came to the office, freaked out over the possibility of an STD or something worse. Despite her doctor's warnings to be careful and use condoms, Milan continued to lead a reckless sex life.

How was she supposed to tell a total stranger that she'd had an absurd and unprotected titty-fuck and was terrified at the possibility that she'd contracted something unknown? And incurable? *Oh, God!*

As if things couldn't get any worse, her secretary told her that her sister, Sweetie, was on the line.

"What!" Milan yelled, unable to hide her irritation.

"Damn, what bug crawled up your ass?"

Milan shuddered at the word *bug*. "Why would you say something like that?"

"Something like what?"

"Why would you insinuate that I've contracted something? How can you be so insensitive?" Milan asked irrationally.

Stunned silent, Sweetie finally asked, "Should I hang up and call again, because you're trippin'."

"What is it, Sweetie? What do you want?"

"Don't be talking down to me. I'm not one of your peon workers. I'll slap the shit out of you in a heartbeat, Milan. So don't get it twisted, because I'm not the one."

Milan fell silent, grateful she was many miles out of her sister's reach. Sweetie was the older sister and had taught Milan how to defend herself in a fight. She'd give Milan a beatdown in a hot minute if Milan got in her face.

She'd grown so accustomed to barking orders at staff; Milan forgot that there were two people in the world who didn't take her shit...her mother and her sister.

"I'm sorry, Sweetie." Milan carefully monitored her tone. "There's so much going on here today. You don't understand how hard it is to run a business."

"Whatever! Look, I didn't call to hear you bitch about the trials and tribulations of living the glamorous life. I called because Mommy wanted me to talk to you."

Milan closed her eyes wearily and gave a sigh. "Talk to me about what?"

"She said you're not helping her out. And she's right, Milan," Sweetie said, sounding indignant.

"Whoa! You're kidding, right?" Milan took a few deep breaths, gathering her wits. "I bought both of you brand-new houses, so what's her beef?"

"Mommy's getting up in her years and she can't be pulling out weeds, trimming hedges, and doing all that yard work. She wants you to hire a gardener or sell the house and put her in a condo or someplace where she doesn't have to worry about taking care of shrubbery and shit. I bet you have a gardener for your big-ass, chateau-style home."

"Of course, I have a gardener; my home is sitting on three and a half acres. But Mommy doesn't need a gardener for that tiny plot of grass in her backyard, and that skimpy cluster of bushes and shrubs in the front of her house doesn't require much maintenance. They only need to be trimmed every now and then. Can't she hire a neighborhood handyman to trim her hedges and mow her miniscule lawn?"

"She feels you should have taken her lawn care into account when you put her in that fancy house."

"I didn't force her to move in that house. She asked me to buy it and I did. I bought both your houses—paid for them in full," Milan exploded.

"Milan. Damn, don't shoot the messenger," Sweetie said, peeved. "I'm not complaining; I appreciate all you've done for my family. I'm speaking on Mommy's behalf. She said it's hard for her to talk to you."

"Oh, really. I wonder why?" Milan felt old resentments resurfacing.

"Why don't you send your gardener over her house every other week? That would satisfy her," Sweetie suggested.

Milan went silent in amazement. "My gardener would think I've lost my freakin' mind if I sent him to work on Mommy's non-existent lawn. No, I can't send him there. Absolutely not."

"If you can't spare your precious gardener, then move Mommy into a condo so she won't have to worry about getting her grass cut and shit like that."

"I refuse."

"You refuse what?"

"I refuse to lift a finger to do anything else for such an unappreciative mother."

"Come on, Milan. You know you ain't right. You can afford it. Why you hatin' on your own mother?"

"I'm not hatin' on her," Milan said, reverting back to the vernacular of her youth. "But I'm seriously getting sick and tired of Mommy's abuse and I'm not buying her a condo."

"Abuse!" Sweetie gasped, clearly appalled. "Our mother never laid a hand on me or you."

"You're right, but I'm emotionally abused," Milan whined, near tears. "She loves you, Sweetie. She always has. But she hates me."

Sweetie sighed. "Oh, damn. Here we go again with that 'Mommy never loved me' mess. You're so dramatic. Look, Milan, I have to go pick the boys up from day care. What do you want me to tell Mommy? Are you going to buy her a condo or what?"

"The housing market is terrible right now. I won't be able to find a buyer for her house."

"Can't you ask your boyfriend...um, Maxwell, to help you come up with a solution?"

"Maxwell is not my boyfriend; he's my slave."

"Whatever." Sweetie couldn't mask her disgust. "He's well-connected. Can't he help Mommy out?"

"No, he can't! Listen, I'm not trying to sell her home or buy her another one," Milan said stubbornly. "She's going to have to learn to love the home she's got. I've done everything I could to make her proud of me, but all I get in return is scorn and ridicule. I'm sick of the way she treats me and I'm through with trying to buy her love. I really am, Sweetie. So, call *your* mother and tell her what I said."

"You gotta be tripping if you think I'm gon' tell Mommy all that bullshit you're kickin'. Obviously, you're going through something…so, I'll give you a call in a couple of days."

Yes, she was going through a lot. Being unloved by her own mother was most likely the root of her problem. Milan hung up the phone, dropped her head on her custom-made desk, and cried.

⇴⇵

A few hours later, Milan left the GYN's office feeling as if she'd been given a new lease on life. She'd been too embarrassed to explain to the new physician that she had a creepy feeling that some silicone may have squirted into her vagina, so she didn't mention it. It wasn't the nosey doctor's business. She said she was there for a complete checkup. After undergoing a series of tests, she was told she was A-okay—no infections. *Yea!*

She dreaded having to deal with Maxwell. But he enriched her life with all the wonderful trappings that money could buy and she'd do whatever she had to do to keep the money flowing. Beating his ass regularly would seriously cut into her free time. But a girl had to do…

Arriving home, Milan sighed heavily as she took the wooden stairs that led to the lower level of her home to investigate her remodeled basement. She flicked on the light and gawked in astonishment. Her S&M dungeon was superb. Leather and highly polished chrome and stainless steel bondage furniture and torture devices were spaced around the large basement.

Milan felt total appreciation for Sumi. Her assistant had done an outstanding job. From the hexagonal cage and the bondage bed to the steel jail cell, every item was top-notch and designed to provide the physical distress that Maxwell deserved.

The S&M mood was enhanced by a collection of shiny dom-inatrix outfits. Thigh-high boots and stilettos were visible through the partially opened doorway of a cedar closet. A highly polished chrome bondage head cage was prominently set on a shelf, ankle and wrist cuffs hung from hooks as well as a butt plug harness, a suede paddle, a stainless steel ball crusher, a leather ball separator, and an assortment of painful-looking sex toys.

For extreme bondage, there was gauze-like wrapping for mummification along with an instruction guide that was propped up with the front cover facing outward. Milan nodded. Maxwell could probably benefit greatly from being tightly bound and having his movement completely restricted. She made a mental note to flip through the pages of the mummi-fication guide after she finished the dominatrix manual. Jeez, being a mistress certainly required a lot of reading. Maxwell had some nerve, getting bored with licking her shoes and lap-ping her cunt.

She glanced around at all the complicated equipment and frowned. Just imaging herself struggling with the numerous intricate buckles, straps, chains, and complicated locks exhausted her. Maxwell's desire to live in erotic servitude was going to be time-consuming and physically exhausting for her. Lucky for him, his massive wealth left Milan no choice but to settle down and study the art of discipline.

She picked up and examined an odd-looking leather penis cage. The lower straps could be tightened to inflict pain in the scrotum while the many buckles kept the penis confined—a male chastity belt.

She set it down. A feeling of uneasiness came over her. Maxwell was a shrewd player. He'd upped the stakes, silently threatening to give his money and devotion to another if she couldn't meet his demands. Sure, Milan was mean as a snake. The challenges she'd faced in life had left her with no choice but to strike first. But Milan was not a physically violent person. Her vicious ways came in the form of verbal assaults and money swindling. She could dole out humiliating emotional cruelty without batting an eye. And yes, she could handle a light paddling quite easily. But to actually progress to the extreme domination that Maxwell now craved did not sit well with her. She wasn't into using whips and other torture devices that caused tearing of skin and bloodshed. It was a nauseating thought.

She got hot from exerting power, not dispensing brutal beatings. So, what was she going to do? She flopped down on the bondage bed and pulled the yellow dominatrix training manual out of her handbag.

CHAPTER 18

His driver delivered him. Under Milan's orders, Sumi and Harper were to prepare the slave for his first night of debauchery. Clad in black masks, black latex corsets, and thigh-high boots, Sumi and Harper were waiting for him in the foyer. Without uttering a sound, the two women took charge, taking his hands and walking him through the vast house and toward the narrow stairs that led down to the dungeon.

Maxwell was of average height, about five ten or so, while Sumi and Harper were tiny little things, and standing between them he seemed much taller than his actual height. The excitement of being dominated by the two petite women whom he should have been able to easily overpower made his palms sweat and had him trembling with anticipation.

"I bet his little pecker is hard," Harper muttered.

"It better not be. His mistress is extremely jealous and she won't be pleased if she finds out that he's been aroused by anyone other then her." Though Sumi's voice was low, the threat in her tone was loud and unmistakably deadly.

A rush of pleasure pulsed through Maxwell so violently, his knees almost gave out. Mistaking his faltering steps for defiance,

Sumi gave his arm a hard yank. "It's too late for a change of heart. Your fate is sealed, cunt."

Maxwell let out an aroused whimper. He dragged his feet across the shiny hardwood floor, barely able to walk with his penis hardening and quivering inside his pants.

Harper swatted his backside in a most disrespectful way. "Pick up your feet. Move it!" she commanded, sounding like a prison guard. And Maxwell felt like a captive. For a man who toppled corporations and put fear in the highest paid CEOs, relinquishing his power and allowing himself to be controlled by a woman was the ultimate sexual high. He hadn't anticipated being deprived of liberty by two anonymous females and judging by the way he was wriggling with excitement, it was obvious to him that tonight he would reach a level of erotic pleasure never experienced before.

Eager to begin the adventure, he obediently kept pace with his captors. The sound of their heels clicking against the dark parquet floors was at once ominous and tantalizing, triggering an erection so severe that he struggled against an explosive release.

Down in the dark dungeon, Maxwell's hands were released. He waited patiently for his captors to turn on the light. Suddenly, music, loud and irritating, filled the room. At the same time, overwhelmingly bright light, practically blinded him. His head spun as he attempted to take in the sights—the two shapely masked women, the numerous disciplining devices—with eyes that were squinted as he tried to adjust to the blinding, sharp light.

"Dance for us," Harper said dispassionately.

"What?" Maxwell gawked at the masked woman, whom he noted had succulent red lips.

"Are you defying me?"

Though she hissed the words through angry curled lips, he found himself transfixed by her curvy figure and didn't respond as quickly as was expected.

"Answer me!" Contempt flashed in Harper's hazel eyes and Maxwell became deeply aroused by her anger.

Sumi detected the bulge in front of his pants and gave him a sneering smile. She stalked across the room, yanked a whip off a rack, and prodded him in his chest with the handle. "Dance, bitch," she snarled.

"I... I'm not very good—"

Thwack! The tails of the whip flashed across his thighs, bringing stinging pain along with burning humiliation. She turned the whip around and again used the handle, this time giving him a hard jab in his side.

"Ow! Hey, not so hard. You could damage—"

Harper slapped him across his face. "Shut your mouth or I'll shut it for you."

She was serious. Her glinting eyes dared him to give her a reason to do him more bodily harm.

"Show us your dance moves." Sumi stroked the tails of the whip menacingly.

He swallowed and closed his eyes in shame.

"Shake your ass, you moron!" Harper confronted him, standing on her toes, her face so close to his, he could feel the warmth of her breath. Titillated by her lovely cruelty, he fought to control the urge to kiss her glossy red lips.

Reminding him of the order he'd been given, Sumi struck his expensive leather shoes with the hard handle of the whip. Following the order to dance, he swiped his left foot to the side and repeated the stupid movement with his right foot.

"Put your ass in it. Dance like a bitch." Sumi rolled her dark eyes.

Desiring to please the exasperated woman who normally treated him with the utmost respect, he wiggled slightly as he moved his feet. He was without rhythm and completely out of step with the hip-hop music that poured loudly from the speakers.

Shaking her head, Harper gave a loud sigh of exasperation. "I can't watch this."

"Milan wants him to dance," Sumi insisted.

Wearing a ridiculous expression of utter shame, Maxwell continued his choppy movements, not daring to stop unless instructed to do so.

"Can't we move on to the next thing on the list? I feel like I'm the one being tortured if I have to keep looking at this jackass trying to dance."

Sumi snickered. "You're right. His dance skills are terrible."

"And very hard on the eyes," Harper pointed out. Both girls began giggling, nudging each other as they pointed out his flaws. "Shake that ass!" they chorused and laughed even harder as he danced badly with his eyes focused on his shoes.

Maxwell's face was crimson with shame but his privates were enflamed with desire. Their jeering was giving him a powerful hard-on.

The laughter suddenly halted. Maxwell's eyes shot upward in alarm at the very moment Harper's open palm slammed across his face. "Who gave you permission to stop shaking your ass?"

The sudden slap had practically knocked him off his feet. Stunned silent and trying to regain his composure, he couldn't think of a quick response.

"Oh, so the cat has your tongue?"

After a series of smacks on both sides of his face, words finally tumbled out.

"No one gave me permission," he blurted. "I didn't realize I'd stopped. I'm sorry," he said. With his lips set in a firm, determined line, he danced faster and shook his ass horribly. Tears brimmed in his eyes from the harsh face slapping he'd taken. He wiped his eyes and gave his tormentors a weak smile of apology.

"Okay, he looks creepy. That's enough dancing. Seriously, Sumi, what's next on the list?"

"She didn't write out instructions."

"Well, what else does she want us to do to him?"

Sumi shrugged. "I guess it's time for an inspection."

Harper grabbed him roughly by the front of his crisp shirt. "Stop dancing." As if by magic, the earsplitting music ceased to play. Tugging him by his Versace tie, Harper yanked him over to a leather-covered bench. "Take down your pants."

He bit his lip as he unbuckled his belt, terrified of what would happen next. He lowered his pants, revealing a pair of white briefs.

Harper grimaced. "Ugh! What are you, gay or something? Only a flaming fag would prance around in tight underwear."

Maxwell nodded in agreement just in case Harper was poised to slap him around again. Her small hand had done enough damage to make his cheeks chafed and sore.

"Pull down those tightie-whities, bend over, and spread your ass, you panty-slut."

He hesitated for a millisecond and then, completely humiliating himself, he bent over as he was told, pulled down his underwear, and separated his buttocks.

Harper moved behind him. "Press your forehead against the bench and keep it there."

Sumi strolled to the rack of whips and replaced the one she'd been carrying. "I don't like that whip," she said aloud but was clearly talking to herself. Her heels clicked threateningly as she strolled back and forth, perusing the collection of whips.

Maxwell gasped. Harper was rubbing something cold and moist into his quivering butt hole. "Loosen up, tight ass," she snapped. His anus clenched in apprehension.

"Oh, here's the perfect whip," Sumi murmured delightedly. With his forehead positioned on the bench, Maxwell could only see her boots and thighs. The weapon she wielded and snapped in the air was out of his view, but the terrifying sounds made his scrotum tighten and his cock rise. He craved the suspense and the fear but dreaded the pain that Milan's minions were all too happy to provide.

Something was eased inside his ass. It hurt a little, but it was a mild probing when compared to the harsh ramming he'd taken from Mistress Veronique. She'd strapped on a monstrous cock that her black boyfriend, BodySlam, had lubed, helping to prepare it for their newly acquired slave. Maxwell had watched in fear as she tested her big greasy dick by thrusting it in and out of BodySlam's hand. Terror-stricken, Maxwell had instantly changed his mind about giving himself over to the crazed pair. But he was gagged and couldn't scream out in protest as BodySlam's strong hands pried open Maxwell's trembling buttocks, allowing Mistress Veronique complete access to jam her huge shaft up Maxwell's virgin ass. She'd thrust with such violence and seeming hatred, Maxwell had actually shed tears. Throughout the horrible rape that had caused his ass to bleed, the sadistic couple had kissed each other passionately.

His asshole had just started to heal.

"You took that like a champ," Harper whispered, bending down to his level, her arms draped across his shoulders, her mouth close to his ear. Unfortunately, a raspy moan escaped his lips when he felt her pert breasts pressing into his back.

She bolted upright and made a gasping sound that broadcast her displeasure. "You stinking pervert! Look at your little wiener sticking out!" She pointed accusingly at his smallish erection.

"It was an accident. I couldn't help it. I'm sorry. Please forgive me!" he shouted, raising his head to better plead his case. His eyes landed on Sumi's whip, a brutal-looking cat o' nine tails. The sight of it made him slightly nauseous.

Like a tender lover, Sumi massaged the back of his neck, while Harper yanked out the butt plug, mumbling in complaint that it was too small. Sadly, he presumed that Mistress Veronique's violent intrusion had stretched out his anus.

"Take off your tie," Sumi said sweetly. Maxwell stood and removed his tie. She flung it over her shoulder.

"And your shirt," she uttered in the same soft voice, even though her actions and sneering expression contradicted her tone.

Slowly, he unbuttoned his shirt, took it off, and handed it to Sumi. She dropped the expensive shirt on the floor and ground it with her boot.

"Get that forehead back down on the bench," Harper barked from behind.

"Better do as you're told, she can get rough." Sumi gave him a mean smile.

He resumed the position, his forehead down, his ass pointed upward.

"Spread your cheeks and keep them open," Harper demanded.

Though it was an uncomfortable position, he obeyed, amazed at how each unkind word and every assault sent shockwaves of pleasure through his body. This time Harper wasn't gentle. She introduced a larger object inside his anus with a great shove. He yelled, the roaring sound a mixture of pain and pleasure.

"Be quiet." Sumi cracked the whip across his back. He screamed, his hands fell to his sides. With the larger butt plug inserted in his anus, Harper smacked his ass with a paddle while Sumi viciously delivered whip lashes. He was dizzy with sexual pleasure. His penis bobbed up and down.

Hard footsteps were heard stomping down the basement steps. "Is he ready?" Milan's voice echoed inside the dungeon.

"Not quite," Sumi responded. There was trepidation in her voice.

Maxwell had to maintain his position as he listened to Milan's footsteps growing nearer. Only inches away, he could smell the scent of the fragrance he'd brought her from Japan. It was lovely. And strong. So strong, it overpowered his senses, making him woozy with adoration for his mistress. He'd been dishonorable, unfaithful, and he deserved her cruel punishment.

She grabbed him by his hair and yanked his head up. "Cheating on me again, huh?"

"No, Mistress. I'd never do that again. I've learned my lesson."

"Oh, really?" Milan gave his head another yank, pulling some of his hair out at the roots. "Liar! Your dick is hard." She shot a glance at Sumi. "Chain him up!"

Sumi and Harper quickly complied, shackling his wrists with the restraints that were attached to the bondage bench.

"Look at me," Milan demanded. He lifted his head and looked at her. Her beauty astounded him. She was naked, wearing five-inch heels and strapped with a shimmering black appendage. Not as large as Mistress Veronique's, but large enough to do him harm.

"How do I look?" she asked, proudly stroking her appendage.

"Seductive and beautiful," he whispered as she glided closer, her phallus pointing at his lips.

"Do you like sucking dick?" The spark in her eyes challenged and mocked him.

"Yes, Mistress." Maxwell closed his eyes, ashamed.

"Good answer. Okay, then. Open your mouth and show me how a worthless cocksucker gives head."

And he did. His lips wrapped around the plastic phallus and he sucked greedily.

Meanwhile, Harper probed his anus with a vibrating dildo.

Sumi knelt beneath him, her long fingernails raking across his scrotum.

Unable to hold out any longer, he shot out a load of cum. Milan pulled her dick out of his mouth and shot him a look that informed him that there would be hell to pay.

CHAPTER 19

Business had more than quadrupled with the Specialties menu added to the list of services provided at Pure Paradise. Initially, there were minor glitches, but it appeared that the business boom was more than the staff could handle. Today, it seemed like all hell was breaking loose.

Since Milan's arrival at work this morning, Sumi had been in and out of her office, delivering one piece of bad news after another. Dressed today in her typical conservative fashion: sensible pumps; a black-and-pink pinstriped fitted jacket, buttoned with a hint of silk fuchsia scoop-neck top showing; and a matching pinstriped pencil skirt that fell tastefully just below the knee, and her long hair pulled back into a tight and perfect bun; Sumi looked professional and polished. Though pretty as ever, Sumi was overworked. Milan could see the weariness in her assistant's large doe-shaped eyes. *Oh, well!* Sumi wanted to be second in command and hard work came with the job title.

It would be hard to believe that last night, Sumi, such a remarkably professional woman, had been stomping around in thigh-high boots, tight-fitting Lycra, and wielding a nasty whip that she enjoyed cracking.

Sumi's performance had gone beyond role-playing. She'd been

genuinely angry. Though Milan was sure Maxwell enjoyed the scene, she still felt that Sumi had gotten out of hand; her harsh treatment of Maxwell was really uncalled for. Milan had witnessed Sumi go into numerous tantrums and tirades, but never had she known her to fly into such an uncontrollable fit of rage as she had after Maxwell accidentally climaxed. The way Sumi reacted, you would have thought Maxwell had deliberately peed on the floor. She'd whipped him with a frighteningly long-tailed whip and didn't stop until she'd shed the man's blood. When she thought about it, Sumi and that girl, Harper, were both really malicious and if Milan hadn't intervened, she might have ended up with a dead body on her hands. Suddenly, her mouth turned downward. Imagining such an unspeakable crime made her shudder.

She gave Sumi a long, curious look, now wondering if last night's violence was somehow subconsciously directed at her. Sumi had several reasons to be furious with Milan. First, preferring to spend her at-home time with Hilton, Milan only used Sumi's pussy snaps there at the office, making the overly sensitive girl feel more and more like a personal sex toy. Secondly, after Sumi found someone who satisfied her in bed, Milan had broken her girlfriend's fake boob and then given her the boot. Oh, well. No way could Milan have allowed that nasty, leaking heifer to continue prancing around Pure Paradise. Her propensity to spring a leak was not good for the salon's image.

Milan's thoughts traveled back to Sumi and she decided that her assistant could very likely be harboring ill feelings toward her. Milan made a mental note to keep an eye on Sumi and be on the lookout for any unusual or abhorrent behavior.

Looking on the bright side...Sumi and Harper were a wonderful opening act. They did all the yucky hard work and all Milan had to do was pump dick in Maxwell's mouth.

She smiled, loving the fact that once again, she'd gotten over. Reading that dominance manual felt like doing homework, which she'd always hated. She'd tried flipping through the pages but she really couldn't get into it. She'd make Sumi read it and instruct her to provide the highlights of what she'd read. She could pretend she was giving the girl a pop quiz, when all the while she'd be shrewdly getting the information she needed. Milan smiled, proud of her ability to so cunningly maneuver in life.

Meanwhile, Sumi and Harper would continue to "prepare" Maxwell for her. No one, not even Maxwell, would be the wiser. Case closed. Satisfied, Milan leaned back in her chair.

She was about to launch into a pleasant daydream that involved her and Hilton doing something normal, like... hmm. Her mind raced, trying to summon a couple of scenarios, but she came up blank because she'd never had a boyfriend and had never been on a regular date. *A date!* Maybe she'd invite Hilton out to dinner. Yeah, it would be nice to sit and chat and act like a normal couple. A warm feeling oozed through her.

But the good feeling was interrupted by Sumi, tapping on her door. Back again, her expression grim.

Milan didn't bother to hide her irritation. She frowned excessively. "What is it now?" she asked the annoying messenger of doom.

"The Double Chocolate twins didn't show up for work."

"The who?"

"The two new guys who work together as a team."

"Oh, I didn't realize they were actually twins—"

"They're not; that's their nickname around here."

"I see," Milan said dryly.

She didn't consort with the help and had no way of knowing their nicknames. Other than Body-Slam and Sumi's assistants, Milan hadn't bothered introducing herself to any of the new staff. They were all too sordid for her to ever get up close and personal with. *Never say never,* she reminded herself. Who knew which of the new specialty services she'd require in the event of a sexual emergency.

"We're in the midst of a serious crisis. Ms. Warminster is not happy. She's threatening to revoke her membership."

Milan gasped at the thought of the free-spending and very wealthy Ms. Warminster taking her business elsewhere.

"I reminded her that if she broke her contract, she'd be slapped with a significant penalty."

"I hope you said that with tact." She sucked her teeth. Sumi sure had nerve, speaking to her clients discourteously.

"Of course." Sumi sounded offended.

"So, what was her response?"

"She says she doesn't care about any silly penalties."

Milan flinched. "Refresh my memory. What's got her panties all twisted?"

"About a week ago she came in for the chocolate treatment…"

Milan's brow furrowed as she tried to recall what the hell the chocolate treatment was all about. Sumi and her assistants had made so many changes, she couldn't keep up with them all.

"They position the client on the massage table on her hands and knees. Then the guys double team her, massaging warm chocolate into both ends, letting her cum on their sticky fingers, if that's what she prefers." Sumi sighed. "Ms. Warminster was given the deluxe treatment. After the sensual massage, the twins licked the chocolate out of her cunt and her asshole at the same time."

"Oh, my. Sounds scrumptious. No wonder she's all in a tizzy."

"Yes, and she's seriously craving more chocolate."

Milan told herself to make sure she had the monitor on the next time the chocolate brothers administered to a client. "So what excuse do those chocolate twins have for not showing up for work?"

"They didn't give an excuse." Sumi shrugged. "No call; no show."

"What!" Milan screeched. "As much money as I'm paying them, they have the audacity to shuck their responsibilities without giving me so much as the common courtesy of a phone call?"

"Looks that way."

"Where'd you find them?"

"A male strip club."

Milan shook her head. "No wonder. Stripper assholes don't have any work ethic."

"What are we going to do about Ms. Warminster? She's fuming because she booked extra time with the twins and she's blaming the salon for not calling to cancel her appointment. She says she's a busy woman and her schedule has been thrown off completely. She was putting up such a fuss, I had to escort her into my office."

Milan turned up her lip. "Lucky you," she said sarcastically.

"Exactly! So, what are we going to do? I've got to get her out of my office. She's all puffed up and red in the face and I promise you, it's not a pretty sight. She seems to be taking their absence personally, carrying on like a jilted lover."

Pondering the situation, Milan leaned back and tented her fingers.

"Why didn't you cancel her appointment?" Milan's voice was icy, accusing.

Sumi glared at her. She narrowed her eyes menacingly. Speaking though teeth that were clenched, she hissed, "My boss had me working overtime last night. There were a million things to attend to this morning." She drew in a deep breath. "In case you forgot, I only have one assistant. She worked late too and she won't be in until noon." Sumi's shoulders heaved with fury.

Whoa! Milan did not think it wise to fuck with Sumi right now. The girl was looking like a cornered rat and there was no telling what she might do.

Sumi cut an angry glance that seemed to linger on Milan's beloved custom desk, which had taken six months to be designed, constructed, and delivered. *Oh, Lord! Please don't let this lunatic leap into the air and come down with a karate chop that splits my beautiful desk in two.*

"Focus, Sumi. Focus." Milan gestured with both hands. "What else can we offer Ms. Warminster?" Milan twirled her computer monitor in her direction, clicked keys, and brought the specialties menu onto the screen. Squinting, she leaned forward. "Double Chocolate massage, Spicy Asian pedicure, Caramel-Cream foot bath, Strawberry Soufflé body wrap," she murmured to herself. "Hmm. Ask Ms. Warminster if she'd like to try the Spicy Asian pedicure." I can vouch for that treatment. I watched that gorgeous Asian guy squirting cum all over a client's feet and the visuals had me practically cumming in my chair."

"Oh, really? If memory serves me, wasn't that the day you summoned Lily to your office to sexually harass her, mutilate her, and then callously throw her out on her ass without so much as severance pay!"

Milan chose to ignore her assistant's biting sarcasm. Obviously Sumi was holding a grudge and Milan would have to figure out a way to placate her, but right now, she had to get Ms. Warminster hooked up with a sensual service and placed in a better frame of mind.

"Oh, this looks good," Milan said cheerily, changing the subject.

"What?" Sumi muttered, still peeved.

"The Strawberry Soufflé body wrap!"

"Read my lips, Milan. Ms. Warminster wants chocolate. Nothing else will do."

Milan bristled. "I don't know who you think you're talking to, but you need to watch your mouth." She rotated her neck as she worked herself up. "You don't run this place, I do. I pay your salary, so don't use that tone of voice with me."

Milan had had enough of Sumi's belligerence. That dominatrix routine she'd allowed her to play was obviously going to her head. Fuck the martial arts and any other tricks she might have had up her sleeve. Milan was about to kick off her heels and get ghetto on Sumi's ass.

"Sorry," Sumi muttered. But she wasn't; there wasn't a trace of remorse in her voice. She was up to something. But Milan couldn't put her finger on it. Maybe she'd replaced Lily's titty-dick with one of Harper's circus tricks. She recalled the gusto with which Harper had fucked Maxwell last night. Hmm. Most likely Sumi was pussy snapping Harper's twat while

Harper was giving Sumi multiple O's with her big-ass strap on. Good dick—real or fake—had a way of making some women act uppity.

Actually, Milan was glad to have Sumi shift her moony-eyed, love-hungry gaze to someone else's face.

"Apology accepted," Milan said with a secret, good-riddance smile. "Now, let's get down to business. We have to get Ms. Warminster some chocolate."

"BodySlam is the only chocolate we can offer her." Sumi gave a mirthless chuckle. "I doubt if she'd enjoy his repertoire of pain."

"Don't be so sure about that."

Sumi looked perplexed.

"I want you to go back to your office and use your powers of persuasion to tell that old bat that she needs to fully explore her sexuality. She should take advantage of all our wonderful services instead of limiting herself to dual tongue penetration. I want you to gently but forcibly introduce her to the idea of having a session with BodySlam."

Sumi grimaced. "BodySlam! Milan," Sumi whined. "Body-Slam's name alone is enough to scare the crap out of Ms. Warminster and anyone else in their right mind. How am I supposed to convince a woman who wants an orgasm from two brawny men, that she'll get just as much pleasure from a chain-wearing weirdo spanking her ass until it's burning and red?"

"Look, I don't have time to mince words with you. If she leaves this salon, I'm holding you responsible. And believe me, Sumi, I can get another assistant, but can you get another job like this?"

Aiming the remote toward the overhead monitor, Milan checked on BodySlam. He had a plump brunette over his knee, spanking her with one hand as he finger-fucked her with the other.

"Oh, I see BodySlam has enhanced his routine. Perfect! Get him some warm chocolate and tell him to give Ms. Warminster a light spanking and afterward, he can dip his middle fingers in the gooey mess and give it to her in both ends." Milan gave a self-satisfied sigh.

"She paid for the deluxe treatment; she's going to want to be licked."

"BodySlam is a master. He won't do that and you know it," Milan shouted and then contemplated the dilemma. "Who else licks and sucks around here?"

"The guy who does the Strawberry Soufflé body wrap does."

"Great. After that bitch gets her chocolate finger-fuck, I want BodySlam to put a blindfold on her. Tell him to murmur something in his sexy dialect about the blindfold enhancing her experience. Then, let the Strawberry dude come in and finish her up. Ms. Warminster will be none the wiser. She'll think she's getting double chocolate."

Sumi nodded and turned to leave.

"And get those two male exotic dancers on the phone," Milan said snippily. "Tell them to get back to work. Make sure they know I intend to follow them to the gates of hell and I'll have every club they shake their asses in shut down!"

Nostrils slightly flared, Sumi took a few steps forward, closing the gap of space between them. When she reached the chair across from Milan, she gave it a quick glance but didn't take a seat. Instead, she paused in front of the desk and braced her hands on the shiny wood, leaning in as if she were about to give Milan a piece of her mind.

Don't fuck with me, girl. Milan arched a brow and pursed her lips confrontationally.

Sumi gulped, swallowing down whatever she had intended to say. "I'll share your sentiments with the chocolate twins." Wisely, Sumi hurried out of Milan's office.

Sumi was trippin'. What the hell was going on with her? Did she miss that big-titty Lily so much, she was willing to pick a fight and deliberately get her name added to Milan's shit list?

CHAPTER 20

Milan gave a sigh of relief after Sumi left. If it wasn't one thing, it was another. Why did she always have to come up with the solutions? What the hell did she pay Sumi for when she always had to end up putting out all the fires? No one cared about Pure Paradise as much as Milan did.

There was no one to share her burdens with at the end of a long day. She shook her head sadly. It had always been Milan against the world and she supposed that was the way it would always be.

Gripping her forehead in despair, she cut an eye at the time. Eleven in the morning and already her energy was dwindling fast. Mentally exhausted, she needed a quick pick-me-up. *Royce?*

Hell, no! She needed something else. Her pussy could definitely use some action, but in her current state of fatigue, what she really needed most was an emotional healing. She yearned for someone to console her, reassure her that everything would be all right. She hated to admit it, but it was her heart and not her pussy that needed emergency treatment.

She checked the time again. A few minutes after eleven. Where was he? The gym? No, he worked out early in the morning.

She pondered a few moments. Most likely, he was at the Sports Medicine Center. Hilton was delusional, still holding on to the hope that his bum knee would heal and someday he would resume his football career. Milan didn't know jack shit about the rules of football but common sense told her that it wasn't likely that a twenty-nine-year-old former player, who had experienced such a major, career-stopping injury, would ever again hear the roar of the crowd as he charged across a football field.

And that was a good thing. Milan didn't want Hilton traipsing around the country. She wanted him in the Philadelphia area and under her thumb. She wanted him to remain on call, a devoted chauffeur. *Devoted? Yeah, right.* Hilton was about as devoted to her as she was to Maxwell. But every now and then, she sensed that beneath their casual, no-strings-attached sexual relationship lay deep feelings—an emotional bond between them. She smiled wistfully, then chastised herself. *Keep dreaming!*

She called his number. Feeling awkward and vulnerable, she listened to his cell ring, her pulse pounding erratically in a combination of anticipation and anxiety. When the call was picked up by his voicemail, Milan breathed a sigh of relief. Under the circumstances—dealing with such a severe case of the jitters—she preferred to talk to a machine.

"Hi. Um…Hi, uh, this is Milan. It's Milan," she said again, stammering. She could have kicked herself for sounding like such a tongue-tied jerk. "Give me a call, when you get a minute." *Much better.* Now her words were coming out clear and concise. "This isn't a business call. If you aren't busy tonight, I'd like to take you out to dinner." She paused and nervously cleared her throat. The sound was deafening, a blaring indication of awkwardness. *I'm definitely not on top of my game,* she silently berated herself. *Shit!*

"Give me a call when you get a chance. I'm at work." She ended the call. *Duh! As if he doesn't know where I am.* "He dropped you off, stupid," she said out loud. God, she hated it when her old insecure, graceless persona resurfaced. She should have practiced what she was going to say to him before she picked up the phone. Humiliated, she slumped over, buried her face in her hands. *Damn, damn, damn!*

A few moments later, she jerked up, removed her hands, and peeked at the time again. Five minutes had elapsed. She wondered impatiently how long it would take for Hilton to return her call. Indignant, and refusing to wait around for Hilton the way she used to wait for Gerard to call, she decided to redirect her attention. *To what?*

Her mouth curled into a wicked smile as she picked up the remote and pointed it toward the overhead monitor. The click of a button produced an image of the spanking room. Apparently, Sumi had been persuasive because there was Ms. Warminster on the screen, looking tense as she removed her pearls and then her totally dignified attire.

BodySlam's island lilt seeped from the speakers. "Hurry! My time is valuable. There are many others craving my chocolate."

Hmm. Milan switched the angle of the camera and panned in on BodySlam, who was lounging on his throne. Instead of sitting up straight in his customary proud and aristocratic manner, he was kicked back in a relaxed and irritatingly arrogant position. His muscular legs were gaped and outstretched; his long dark cock jutting outward and dripping with chocolate syrup. Leeringly, he gazed at Ms. Warminster. "Come quickly, while the chocolate is still warm."

Naked, Ms. Warminster took a few faltering steps. The old bat had the nerve to have a nicely toned body, Milan noted grudgingly.

"No, that won't do," BodySlam said, shaking his head disapprovingly. "I am your master. You must crawl to me."

Obediently, Ms. Warminster lowered herself to the floor.

"Not so fast."

Ms. Warminster rose quickly.

"When I give you an order, I expect you to say, 'Yes, Master.'"

"Yes, Master," she whispered, her face bright red and stinging with shame.

Triumph lit BodySlam's eyes. "Now, get back down on your knees and crawl to me quickly."

"Yes, Master."

Ms. Warminster dropped to the floor and crawled across the room speedily. Within seconds, BodySlam was guiding her head toward his big chocolate cock, urging her to suck. Tentatively, she licked, catching chocolate drops before they fell to the floor, and, in no time, the aging socialite was slurping chocolate off BodySlam's big dick, making greedy sucking sounds that loudly proclaimed that her chocolate craving was being satisfied.

Totally fascinated with BodySlam's capacity to so quickly turn an incorrigible snob into a docile slave, Milan folded her arms and studied the depraved activity. A true master was at work and she needed to be taking notes.

Then she got angry. Sure, the man had skills worth watching, but she'd laid out guidelines, a specific script that she expected to be followed. She rolled her eyes. Sumi's obstinate refusal to do as she was told was working Milan's nerves. Perhaps a two- or three-day suspension was in order. While mulling it over, the buzzer on her desk console interrupted her thoughts. She jerked her head toward the annoyance, then yanked the phone out of the cradle, ready to spew venom at her secretary.

Between Sumi's intrusive visits and her dingbat secretary bothering her with nonsense that she should be able to figure out for herself, Milan would never get any work done. "What is it?" she bellowed.

"Your driver is on the line, Ms. Walden."

"Oh!" Milan said, her voice lowered. Unconsciously, she began smoothing her hair into place. "Put him through."

"Right away, Ms. Walden," the secretary replied.

"Wait!" Milan needed time to get herself together.

"'Sup, Ms. Walden," Hilton crooned in his silky voice.

Too late! "Hi," she replied breathily. Too breathily. Anxiety caused the corner of her mouth to twitch. *Aw, shit!* She knew he was quietly waiting for her to expound on the message she'd left, but how the hell was she supposed to communicate with her lips quivering and teeth clenched tight to prevent them from chattering?

"You mentioned something about dinner?" he asked, mercifully filling the silence.

"Yes, I wanted to thank you for helping me recapture Maxwell." She laughed and the sound was convincingly playful. Flirty, yet indifferent. *Whew!* She had her swagger back!

"Oh!" There was disappointment in his tone. "Nah, I'm straight. Look, you don't owe me dinner for that. All I did was drive. Besides, I doubt that I'd enjoy celebrating another man's captivity, you know what I mean?" He chuckled.

Milan was speechless. She'd gone out on a ledge. She'd swallowed her pride and invited this unappreciative bastard out to dinner. And based on some antiquated, old-boy, macho bullshit, Hilton had rudely turned her down.

"How about a drink?" she cajoled.

"Do you miss me?" he said, cutting to the chase.

Yes! "A little bit—I guess."

"I appreciate the offer, but we both know you're not the wine and dine type. How about we just cut through the bull-shit. I'll stop over tonight and tighten that thing up. That's what you really want, right?" There was amusement in his tone.

Though deeply offended, she laughed on cue as if his perception of her needs was right on target. Her laughter, shrill and false, was as close as she could come to actually screaming and crying. "You are absolutely right! Wine and dine? *Moi?* Never! I'll see you tonight, and make sure you drink a protein shake because you're going to need it." She laughed again, trying to save face by resorting to her typical sassiness.

"Oh, I got something for you and I don't need a protein shake, Red Bull, or any stimulants. I'm *au natural*; you should know that about me."

And she did. Unfortunately, she knew a lot about him. She knew that in his eyes she was nothing more than a piece of ass to be tapped when he had time to fit her in. And no matter how hard she'd tried to turn the tables, she could not get Hilton to play by her rules.

"I'll pick you up at the salon at five. After I make a few runs, I'll swing by your spot around nine. You all right with that?"

"Sounds perfect," she chirped, attempting to hide her bruised feelings when she felt like shouting, "No, I'm not all right with it!" Milan had hoped that tonight she'd be able to draw out his true emotions and reveal hers, but it looked like they'd continue to hide behind sex.

Her stomach tightened into a knot. Rejection hurt. Hilton thought of her as a money-grubbing, heartless, insatiable slut, someone to fuck when it was convenient for him. The thought depressed her, sapping her anger and self-righteous indignation and leaving her worn out and resigned. How foolish of her to think that the smoke and mirrors of a romantic dinner with candlelight would alter his perception of her. She'd acquired his chauffeuring services by bullying Maxwell, so Hilton knew firsthand how greedy and ruthless she could be.

CHAPTER 21

Nine o'clock sharp, Milan was dressed casually in a pair of skinny jeans and a stretchy gold cowlneck sweater. She'd chosen to forgo her pricey jewelry and high-fashion couture in an attempt to score points with the former jock by appearing more down to earth and more attainable. Though she appeared laid back and relaxed, she'd actually spent an enormous amount of time achieving the unfussy look. Her barely there makeup took almost an hour to apply and she'd arranged her hair in an upswept 'do that required forty-five minutes of concentration as she created an off-center part, gathered her hair tightly into place, and then strategically released strands of hair, allowing the tresses to dangle, successfully pulling off the impression of whimsical "undoneness" that was both capricious and exceedingly sexy.

It had taken a lot of hard work. The next time she wanted to enchant Hilton with a carefree, girl-next-door persona, she'd make sure to use the services of a group of stylists and a makeup artist.

Hilton liked beer, and for his pleasure she had a dozen bottles of Heineken chilling inside the fridge. Milan preferred wine and though her collection was worth a fortune, she'd never acquired a taste for the dry, bitter, expensive stuff that she kept on hand merely for show. Sipping a modestly priced fruity wine, she was working on her second glass when the doorbell rang.

Showtime!

She opened the door. He was wearing workout wear—baggy sweats and sneakers—but he was still looking as hot as ever.

"Hi, sexy and handsome," she greeted, feeling overly amorous and a bit playful. No doubt her animated teasing was a result of the effects of the wine.

Smiling appreciatively, Hilton's eyes traveled from her new 'do down to her bare feet and then his gaze lifted and rested on her face. "Hey there, cutie," he said, returning the compliment. "You're looking rather sporty."

He raised a flirty brow, which she found both endearing and sexy. Hell, everything about Hilton was sexy, from his silky brows to his hard-muscled ass, which she would have cupped in a hot second if she was behaving in her typically brazen style. But tonight she was trying a new tactic, subtly introducing Hilton to her sensitive side.

But he wasn't playing fair. Being called "cutie" was a curve ball; it wasn't the type of compliment she was accustomed to hearing. She blushed, showing vulnerability. Not good. Men took advantage of needy women. Cutie! Okay, she had to get herself together and regroup because cutie she was definitely not! Cutie was synonymous with adorable and petite and Milan had grown up being told she too tall, too gangly, and unattractive, with horribly big feet. In her adult life, she'd worked hard on being stylish and glamorous. When she heard people refer to her as beautiful, she smiled, proud that she'd managed to pull the wool over their eyes. Her so-called beauty was a façade.

Hilton was slick. He had to know that giving her such an unexpected compliment would throw her off balance. *Not fair!* She'd planned on controlling the tone of the evening and he'd hit her with a curve ball that was akin to surprising her with a bouquet of demure daffodils or tulips or some other romantic gesture.

Frazzled, Milan took another swig from the delicate crystal glass.

"Would you like a beer?"

"Sure," he replied.

"Follow me," she said, inviting him to join her in her kitchen, one of the many rooms in her lavish home that they rarely spent time in together. Hell, she alone rarely spent time in her kitchen. It was a breathtaking and opulent showplace with recessed overhead lighting that displayed shiny chrome fixtures, granite countertops, stainless steel appliances, and a custom-built island that resembled modern art. Milan's kitchen was stocked with every gadget imaginable but it was a room designed to be admired, not made messy with cooking and dining.

Her bedroom had always been the focal point of their no-strings-attached affair.

Hilton, enjoying the change of scenery, made himself comfortable on a leather stool. She could feel his eyes perusing her from behind as she opened the fridge, bent down, and grabbed a beer.

She handed him the bottle.

"Thanks." He flashed an appreciative smile that made her want to kiss him, but she restrained herself and tapped her crystal wineglass against the bottle he gripped.

"To us," she blurted, unintentionally divulging her desire for a more meaningful connection between them.

Hilton cocked his head to the side. "Yeah, uh, here's to lots more good times together."

He laughed, but the sound was strained. She was instantly embarrassed and told herself to sip slowly. The wine was obviously going to her head and making her say things that she'd later regret.

Collecting herself, Milan joined him and sat on the stool next to him. "How was your day?" she asked, making uncharacteristic chit-chat as she nervously twirled a tendril of hair between her fingers.

"Not bad," he said, looking perplexed at her show of interest.

"Tell me about it," she ventured, knowing full well that she was throwing him off with her sudden penchant for small talk.

"Tell you about what? What are you getting at?" Annoyance lined the area between his silky brows.

"I had a rough day and was hoping yours went better than mine," she said, her eyes wide with innocence.

Hilton relaxed visibly. "My day went pretty good. In fact, it couldn't have been better." He bestowed her with a gleaming smile, prompting her to want to cease with the chatter and march him upstairs to her boudoir. "My knee is almost as good as new," he went on. "A couple more months of therapy and who knows...I might be back in the game." His dark eyes sparkled with hope, melting her heart.

She set down the wineglass and squeezed his arm, a gesture meant to convey encouragement.

"That's good news," she said, nodding and reassuringly tightening her grip.

"I bumped into the Eagles coach at the Sports Center today. We've never been friendly, you know. When I was playing for the NFL, no one could catch me and a game against the Eagles was like child's play for me. I've made some of his players look like straight wimps and then gloated whenever I scored against them." Hilton looked off in thought. "That's strange," he said in a whisper.

"What?"

The coach asked about my knee and after I told him it was healing nicely, he said exactly what you just said, 'That's good news, Hilton." Hilton beamed. "It must be an omen, baby. I can feel it."

Baby! No one had ever called her that. She wasn't sure if he'd ever get back in the game, but she sure liked the way he called her baby. A second later, Hilton pulled Milan in his arms, hugging her tight, as if thankful that she believed in his dream.

She didn't actually believe that a player could make a comeback after a two-year absence, but she could pretend, if that's what it took to get inside his arms. And hopefully in his heart.

"I love the way you smell," he said, sniffing her neck. "That fragrance you wear is uniquely you. I don't think I've ever smelled it on anyone else."

She buried her face in his chest, hiding her flattered smile. Then she recovered and slipped from his embrace and eased her hands beneath his sweatshirt, brushed the hair on his chest, and delighted at the feel of his stiffening nipples. He jerked against her touch. Emboldened by his response, her hand drifted downward, and questing fingers reaching and stretching. She located the prize, at first cupping the swell of his manhood and then giving it a firm squeeze. The throbbing of his hardening heat sent a tremor that shook his body, inciting both him and Milan to greater heights of desire.

"Milan," he whispered her name and held her face between his palms, staring at her questioningly, but seeming too entranced to speak.

Milan, desperately needing the hardened steel of his arousal, quickly undid her jeans. The sound of unsnapping metal seemed to jolt Hilton out of his spell. In an instant, he began assisting, tugging and pulling down her skin-tight jeans.

He led her over to the granite island, the closest available space. He hoisted her up and then gently laid her down. Standing over her, he took in the mocha-colored perfection of her long slender body. Bending down, he kissed her lips. His skilled fingers quickly unclasped the front of her bra. He dipped his head and licked her bared nipples and then hungrily took in mouthfuls of her small oval mounds.

She sucked in a deep breath. Was she drunk from lust or was it the wine that had her head spinning? At any rate, the room seemed to rotate, and Milan had to grasp the sides of the island to steady herself. Hilton's strong hands kneaded her thighs, his thumbs pressing deeply as they worked upward to the soft texture of her thong. Pulling the elastic, he slid the fabric to the side, exposing her most intimate body part, the part of her that needed him most. She shuddered as the cool air chilled her womanhood. Instantly, he warmed her slick passageway with the heat of his tongue. Trembling, Milan released a long sigh of delight. She dug her fingernails into his deltoids and drew up her legs, knocking over salt and pepper shakers as she kicked out. With her knees widely spread, she urged him to probe deeper.

He lathed her soft flesh with his tongue, moaning in enjoyment at the tart taste of her womanhood. Heat swept over her skin and concentrated on her distended clit. He sought and captured her straining bud between his lips, tugging and pulling at the sensitive knot of nerve endings until she cried out, pleading for him to stop.

He repositioned Milan, turning her body horizontally, pulling her forward until her long limbs dangled off the sides of the granite and her pussy faced him. Milan lifted up halfway, talking a long lustful look at the brawny dick he pulled out of the slit of his sweatpants. The tip of the huge knob glistened with pre-cum. She would have gladly placed it close to her lips and licked it clean if it weren't already being fitted against her silken opening, making her vibrate with wanton need.

Surrendering, she eased down on the cool granite. Standing, Hilton pushed himself inside her. She wrapped her legs around his waist as he explored her tunnel with deep, driving thrusts. Groins locked, their bodies writhed together in a primitive dance, she felt a fever burning inside her, quickly convulsing a chain of spasms. Biting down on his lip, Hilton fought to hold back, but persuaded by her rapid cunt-clenches, Hilton let go, flooding her with his white-hot explosion.

Later, in bed, her head resting upon his chest, he tenderly stroked her hair, which was unpinned and had come completely undone. She reached up and caressed his stroking hand until their fingers affectionately entwined.

His pattern of breathing changed, telling her that he had lapsed into a sound sleep. Milan propped up on an elbow and stared down at his beautiful face, marveling at his dark lashes that were even longer than she'd realized. Unable to resist, she brushed his heavy lashes with her fingertip. His lashes fluttered, but his eyes remained closed in sleep. She studied his sleeping face a little longer and then touched his cheek.

"Guess what, Hilton Dorsey?" She paused. "I think I'm in love with you," she whispered, knowing he was somewhere in dreamland, unable to hear her confession. She gave him a quick kiss and then snuggled close, draping an arm across his waist and molding herself into him. Then she contentedly drifted off to sleep.

He lifted her hand, pressed his lips against her long finger, before placing her open palm next to his beating heart and whispering, "I love you, too."

Milan awakened with a start as if the soft-spoken words had been shouted and echoed inside the bedroom. Was she in the midst of a sweet dream? Or had she actually heard Hilton say, "I love you, too?" She forced her heavy eyelids to stay open, sat up, and peeked at him. He was so deep in slumber; his snoring was a loud and rumbling vibrato of sound.

Yup, she'd been dreaming, all right. Disappointed, she eased closer to Hilton, running her hand against the expanse of his back, and pressing her cheek against his skin. She threw a leg over his, cozying up even closer, seeking comfort from his body heat.

CHAPTER 22

The next day, Milan sat at her desk daydreaming about Hilton. The buzz of her phone brought her out of the sweet reverie.

"Royce was late for work," Milan's secretary said briskly.

"So? What makes you think I care?" How annoying to be disturbed with such trivial information.

"He's downstairs at his post, but he wanted me to extend his apologies for being fifteen minutes late."

"Okay, thanks," Milan said without interest.

"He's on the other line," her secretary persisted, "waiting to find out if you want him to come to your office to discuss his tardiness."

Briefly perplexed, Milan frowned. "Why would I want him to—" Mid-sentence, she had an "aha" moment. She hadn't spanked Royce in weeks and it had been ages since she'd utilized his abnormal tongue. She'd assumed that he appreciated the respite from her mistreatment, but apparently he'd developed a proclivity for the harsh treatment, crude name-calling, bondage play, the long and rigorous tongue strokes she required of him, and of course, the sting of her paddle.

"All right," Milan said dryly. "I guess I should discuss disciplinary measures with him. Send him to my office."

Shame-faced, Royce entered her office minutes later, his cap respectfully in his hand, his hair showing premature streaks of gray. He closed the door discreetly and in the next instant, he began unhooking his handcuffs, head lowered, repentant.

"What can I do for you, Royce?" she asked coolly.

"Didn't your secretary tell you—I was fifteen minutes late."

"I've made a note of it and, of course, I'll have to dock your pay."

He grimaced and then wiped his hand over his face as if he'd just been informed that she planned on garnishing all his future earnings.

"Is there a problem?"

"No." He shifted his feet and started to perspire. "Well, I thought we had an understanding, Ms. Walden."

"And what would that be?" she asked, feigning innocence.

"You said you wouldn't dock my pay if I did those things for you that you like me to do."

She leaned forward. "Royce, I have good news for you. You're off the hook. You don't have to worry about being physically reprimanded anymore."

He didn't take the good news very well. He flinched and actually looked as if he were about to tear up. Milan went on. "If it makes you feel better, I won't dock you. But I won't be so generous the next time you're late."

Royce brightened. "Whatchu gon' do to me next time, Ms. Walden?"

She sighed. She'd created a monster. "What would you like me to do?"

"I can take all your punishments."

"Which do you prefer?" she asked out of curiosity.

Scratching his head, he looked up at the ceiling thoughtfully. "It's a toss-up. But since you're making me choose. I think I'll go for the paddle."

"Why?" She really wanted to get a better understanding of male submission.

He shrugged uncomfortably. "I can't explain it."

"Try," she persisted.

He took the liberty of lowering his large frame in the seat across from her.

"At first I was mad. I didn't like the way you ordered me around and had me doing all those unnatural things. Then you stopped sending for me and I was relieved, at first. But I found myself trying to get my wife to treat me like you do. But she never really liked oral sex. She's holy and sanctified, considers it a sin. I joked around with her to see if she might have some interest in paddling, but she screwed her face up like it might be time to get me some type of counseling, so I just left the subject alone."

"You haven't answered my question."

"What?"

"Why do you like getting paddled?"

Royce wiped his face with his roughened hand as if trying to remove the embarrassment. "I'd be lying if I said I like getting paddled. That thing hurts. For me, the pleasure is all mental. I like the idea that a member of the weaker sex can command me to drop my pants and order me to do all sorts of nasty things. Just thinking about you taking control of me gets me in a heated state that makes my nature rise." Royce shook his head in bewilderment. "I would have never guessed I was capable of having such a freaky nature."

His admission wasn't in depth and she hadn't unraveled any deep-seated, psychological mystery. She surmised that like her—like most people—Royce had a tendency toward sexual deviance. He just needed the right person to unleash his inner freak.

Until Milan introduced him to his submissive side, he hadn't realized that being docile, a sexual doormat, was such a powerful aphrodisiac. Milan knew. She'd already been down that path. But never again. Or at least she hoped not. *Never say never*, she reminded herself again.

She smiled, wondering if Hilton had a secret kinky side. And if so, where was the chink in his armor? She had strong feelings for her driver and if he wanted to, he could most likely bring out her dormant submissive side. She'd kiss Hilton's feet in a heartbeat, but would prefer doing it because she wanted to, rather than being directed to do so.

She pulled herself away from her thoughts and refocused her attention on Royce, who was turning puppy dog eyes on her, quietly waiting for her to command him to pant and drop his tongue out like a begging dog.

"Royce," she said softly. "As you've noticed, Pure Paradise's clientele is expanding. To be honest, I don't have time to dole out discipline—"

Royce sagged in his seat. "I won't be in your way, Ms. Walden. I can crawl under your desk and lick you while you're taking care of your business."

"I'd be distracted."

Judging by Royce's woebegone expression, one would have thought that Milan had handed him a pink slip.

"I'm going to recommend someone."

"I'm hooked on you—"

"You don't have a choice," she said sternly. She lifted the phone and pushed a button. "Royce is in my office," she said into the mouthpiece. "I'm going to have him fill out a new disciplinary form and then I'm sending him to your office to be reprimanded." Milan scowled in thought. Sumi was in a terrible mood and she might take her frustrations out on Royce, harming him to the point of hospitalization or maybe death. Milan gulped. "Better yet, why don't you come down to my office; I need to observe and make sure that things don't get out of hand. Royce only requires mild disciplining; nothing harsh."

"I want it harsh," Royce whispered in the background.

Milan rolled her eyes at him, gave him a hand flip, and continued talking on the phone.

"Do you understand what I'm saying? I want you to go easy on him; I don't want to see a repeat of last night." She hung up the phone and tapped her finger on the desk in thought.

"Who'd you send for, Ms. Walden?"

"My assistant will be handling you from now on."

Royce exhaled hard. Disappointment crumpled his face. "I appreciate what you're trying to do and everything, but seriously, Ms. Walden, I need somebody who knows what she's doing. A strong black woman like you. That tiny little Sumi couldn't hurt a flea."

Milan gave him a smirking smile. "Don't underestimate Sumi. I think you're going to be pleasantly surprised."

CHAPTER 23

Sumi was so harried, her once perfectly formed bun now drooped as she suffered under the oppression of an unrelenting taskmaster. Tension lined the features of her beautiful face. It wasn't easy, trying to placate a boss who never lifted a finger to help out, who seldom left her office to conduct business but preferred to view a monitor for enjoyment and adult entertainment, and often summoned members of her working staff to put out the fires of her insatiable sexual desires.

Sumi's eyes flared with anger at Milan.

"Where's your paddle?" Milan asked.

Royce was a perfect target for her aggression and misplaced anger.

"You should be better prepared, Sumi," Milan said, goading her. "There are plenty of extra paddles in the spanking room, as you well know."

"At your insistence, that room is being occupied," she spat vehemently. She tilted her head. "Ms. Warminster paid for an extended treatment, remember?"

"Oh, yeah," Milan mumbled. Sighing, as if Sumi had asked to borrow a pair of her underwear, Milan grudgingly opened a desk drawer and retrieved her personal paddle. It had only been used on Royce, so it wasn't as if his behind would contaminate the weapon.

But it was the principle. "This is my personal paddle and I'm not comfortable loaning it out. In the future, I expect you to be better prepared. Is that clear?" She knew she sounded unreasonable, but it was important to keep Sumi in line.

She was so irritated by Sumi's lack of preparedness, Milan didn't notice Royce slinking backward toward the door.

But Sumi noticed. The instant she had the handle of Milan's personal paddle within her grasp, Sumi sprang across the room and stood on her toes as she seized Royce by the collar. "Where the hell do you think you're going?"

"I, uh, have to get back to my station," he sputtered.

Sumi hooked him in the jaw. Stunned, the security guard's hand flew up defensively. She tossed the paddle over to the settee and then, with a slight bend at her knees, Sumi moved into a fighting stance position, hands held up to guard her face.

"What the fuck is wrong with her?" Royce asked Milan, cowering as he moved out of Sumi's range.

Next, she brought her knee up, her ankle flexed downward in a chamber, a technique where her foot was positioned to generate power and to control of the speed of the kick.

Seeing her foot quickly snap out aiming for his groin, Royce dropped down. Sumi's small but powerful kick landed in his chest. Coughing and heaving, he rolled away from further harm. Crawling as fast as he could, he scurried to the other side of Milan's desk.

"I can't deal with all that jujitsu and karate and whatnot," he said, sniveling as he squeezed past Milan's long legs and wriggled until he had squeezed himself under the cover and safety of her enormous desk. "I don't like the way she operates," he complained, face frowned up, voice raised in indignation.

"I told you not to underestimate her," Milan said, leaning downward, speaking in an amused tone.

"Get over here!" Sumi snarled.

Royce would not leave the safe haven beneath the desk. Curled in a ball, he shook his head adamantly. His widened eyes beseeched Milan to save him from the petite tyrant who threatened to do him bodily harm.

"Scared?" Milan taunted.

He nodded. "Make her go," he said in a whisper. "If you let me stay right where I am, I promise I'll take care of you, real good."

"I'm sorry, Royce. You were late. And Sumi has taken over that aspect of the business—"

"And I have zero tolerance with sorry bastards who can't show up for work on time."

Sumi crossed the room, breathing fire. Milan scooted back, allowing her access to Royce. She dragged him from his hiding place and pulled the large man up.

"All right, all right," he yelled, holding up his hands in surrender as if Sumi had a gun pointed at his head. "Beat me with the paddle. I was late; I admit it. I deserve to be punished," he said, as he unbuckled his belt and pulled his pants down.

Sumi retrieved the paddle from the settee. "You better get your ass to work on time! Do you understand?" she yelled as she smacked his ass with the leather paddle.

Royce flinched, his body thrust forward with each forceful smack of leather against his skin.

Milan watched with mild interest. Her na-na wasn't in an

uproar; she wasn't even moist. In fact, she was bored and was about to suggest Sumi continue lighting a fire to his backside in the privacy of her own office, when Royce suddenly shot a load against the side of her precious desk.

"I'm sorry," he whimpered.

"Lick it up!" Sumi shouted, looking deranged and haggard. Her hair was now completely undone and she'd ripped the seam under the armpit of her jacket.

"I don't think that's a very good idea, Sumi," Milan intervened.

"Why not? He needs to learn the rules. I didn't tell this moron to ejaculate."

"I understand," Milan said patiently as if talking to a mental patient. "However, as skilled a tongue as Royce possesses, I don't think he can manage cleaning my desk in a way that would suit me. I'm very particular about my desk, Sumi."

Coming to her senses, Sumi nodded in understanding, then she shot a menacing look at Royce. "Are you deaf or something? Get out of here and get back to your post."

Royce hurried out of Milan's office.

"I hope you've relieved of some of your frustrations. Do you feel better?"

"Yes, much better."

"Okay, get my desk cleaned. I'm going downstairs to get a pedicure."

"From Shin?" Sumi asked curiously.

"No, I'm going to have Ellen give me a regular, old-fashioned French pedicure."

Sumi cocked her head to the side curiously as Milan rose from her chair.

"Make yourself presentable before anyone sees you," Milan

suggested, giving Sumi an up-and-down, disapproving glance before she whisked out of her office.

꧁꧂

As her feet soaked in the whirlpool jet tub filled with a mixture of essential aromatherapy oils, Milan relaxed and allowed her thoughts to wander back to Hilton. Smiling, she recalled the sweet dream where he'd mumbled that he loved her. Suppose it hadn't been a dream, she asked herself, enjoying the warm feeling that coursed through her. Supposed she'd actually heard his confession of love? *Yeah, and then what? What would I do about it? What could I do about it? S*he gave a helpless mental shrug. Love wasn't in the cards for her and even if it were—even if by some remote chance, Hilton actually loved her—what did she know about giving love in return? Absolutely nothing!

Ellen nudged her away from her nagging thoughts with an almond loofah scrub that was ticklish in a wonderful way. By the time Ellen had dipped her feet in warm paraffin, Milan had the brilliant idea of giving Hilton an at-home pedicure and foot massage. *Tonight!*

"Skip the white tips, just apply a base coat and the peach-colored top coat. I have to get back to my office," Milan told Ellen excitedly.

After applying the final layer of top coat, Ellen slid foam slippers on Milan's soft and smooth feet. "By the way, Ms. Walden?"

"Yes?"

"Are you expecting another shipment of that Japanese fragrance? The customers love it. It sold like hot cakes, and now we're completely out."

Normally, Milan would have flipped over such a glaring over-sight. She should have been notified the moment the fragrance was down to the last case, but recalling Hilton's words that Kimochi was her very own unique scent, she had no intention of ever again sharing her signature scent with her clients or any other woman here in the States. If they wanted Kimochi, Milan suggested they plan a trip to the Far East. Good luck on getting it past Customs. She smirked, grateful she'd had enough foresight to stash away a case of the fragrance, lotion, and bath gel safely in her home.

"Kimochi's no longer for sale."

"What!" Ellen gawked as if Milan had informed her that Pure Paradise was going out of business and would soon be selling all the equipment and merchandise at a garage sale.

"I lost my connection." Milan gave Ellen a pitying smile.

"But we have…like, a trillion orders." Ellen stared at Milan, her mouth open, her hand resting on her hip, as if waiting for Milan to admit that her statement had been a prank.

Realizing Milan wasn't kidding, Ellen smacked the counter-top in frustration. "I kept meaning to buy a couple bottles for myself…"

Ellen scowled so deeply, the lines in face seemed pronounced and several rows of wrinkles instantly developed on her fore-head. *Poor thing.* Instead of worrying about Kimochi, she should have been investing in Botox or Juvéderm injections. Why go around looking haggard when there were a ton of youth-restoring remedies available to stave off the signs of aging? Ellen's lined face was not a good representation for Pure Paradise. Milan would have to speak to her about her appear-ance, Not today. The woman was bereft over the Japanese fragrance. But she'd definitely have to discuss her fine lines and wrinkles in the near future.

Milan wondered briefly how she'd react to getting old. How would she stave it off? At twenty-eight years old, aging was unthinkable, a misfortunate reversal of beauty and youth that happened to others. Not her. Not ever!

"I'm sorry you didn't get hold of a bottle or two." Milan patted the top of Ellen's hand, which was traversed with thick blue veins. Ugh! She pursed her lips in repulsion. The poor woman was totally falling apart and she was really starting to feel sorry for her, but not enough to part with even one box of her signature scent. She wondered if Maxwell could persuade the manufacturers to take it off the market. It wouldn't hurt to ask. With all his influence, he should be able to scare the company into producing the product exclusively for Milan. Hell, there were plenty of other fragrances that Japanese women could wear.

"We're going to have a lot of disappointed customers," Ellen said with a sigh.

"I know. It's a pity. But good things don't last forever. Pass the word on, okay?" With that, Milan sashayed back to her office. Heads would roll if she detected even a smidgeon of dried cum on her desk.

CHAPTER 24

A faint smile appeared on her lips at the sight of Hilton waiting outside the Rolls, looking sexy in his spiffy uniform which, despite its cut, couldn't conceal his muscles. When he noticed her approaching, he scrunched his marvelous lips together and nodded, a signal that he liked the way she looked. She turned her head slightly as she felt her smile widening into a big grin. Oh, fuck it! She was delighted to see him. She waved and hastened her steps. Her thumping heart prompted her to run to him, to fly if she could, but common sense and her bad experience with Gerard cautioned her to calm down and slow her stride.

While most girls were chasing boys and getting their hearts broken—learning through trial and error all the complicated rules that were required when dealing with boys—Milan's head was buried in books, worrying about her grades and summer learning camps, all the necessary activities that would lead to a successful future. Well, she'd achieved success and now she had to make up for lost time, read a book or find a DVD that taught the rules of dealing with the opposite sex.

"Greetings, Ms. Walden," he said courteously.

Though she felt slightly stung by his formal tone, she couldn't complain. After all, she'd set the regulations. Feeling slightly off kilter, she slid into the backseat of the Rolls. As Hilton strolled around to the driver's side of the car, Milan quickly spritzed her wrists with Kimochi and then waved her wrists around, filling the luxury vehicle with her wonderful signature scent, which would hopefully be a reminder to cut out the dutiful chauffeur routine.

Once situated in his seat, he turned around. "Hey, baby. How was your day?"

Her heart did a quick flip. A couple squirts of Kimochi and he had switched from referring to her as Ms. Walden to calling her baby!

"My day was typical," she lied. "I'm just doing my best to keep the women in Philly women looking and feeling as if they've been pampered at one of the top salons in Paris," she answered with a chuckle.

"The way they flock to Pure Paradise, I'd say you're handling your business; you got the pamper business on lock," he assured her and then turned around and started the ignition.

Hilton had no idea about the Specialty menu or the Couples Fantasy rooms on the lower level and he never would. She didn't know very much about the inner workings of a man's mind, but she had more than just a hunch that her unconventional involvement with Maxwell stood in the way of furthering her relationship with Hilton: Why give him even more information that questioned her sanity, her ability to participate in a normal relationship, and most important, her capacity to love?

As they cruised in silence, Milan wondered how she'd let Hilton know that she really wanted to take their "thing" to the next level. Last night, she'd tried to show him that she had sincere feelings but it seemed he was comfortable keeping things as they were.

Milan frowned. She wanted more. What did she have to do to get him to commit? Her thoughts traveled back to her childhood when she used to routinely hand-deliver love notes from her sister, Sweetie, to the current boy of her dreams. Sweetie's notes were always the same: *I go with you. Do you go with me? Circle yes or no.* The penciled notes were written in block print, followed by her poorly scrawled signature. The boys always circled *yes!* Sweetie had a body; she'd developed early. Thick legs, fat tits, and a plump ass were important assets, and her pretty face was an extra bonus. Milan, however, was a long, tall, lanky mess, with no redeeming qualities as far as boys were concerned.

Well, it was a new day and she was now the bright star of the family. She rolled her eyes in remembrance of Sweetie's successful love notes. She'd come up with something more adult, more clever and sophisticated.

"Baby?" Hilton said when he stopped at a red light, craning his neck to make eye contact.

She absolutely and unequivocally loved the way he called her baby. "Yes?" she purred the word.

The grim set of his jaw, gave him a look that bespoke the coming of bad news. "I had a meeting today with some of the hot shots in the Eagles camp. I'm, uh, I have to go out of town for a week."

Milan felt kicked in the stomach. No, worse. His words jammed into her abdomen with the brutality of a dagger, leaving her breathless and feeling completely gutted.

"Why?" The word came out in a much higher pitch than

she'd intended, but what the hell, she couldn't stuff it back in her mouth so she went for broke. "Why do you have to leave at a time like this?"

"Training camp."

"Your knee isn't completely healed. Why would you risk further injury to chase after a dream? Your football playing days are over, Hilton. When are you going to face that fact?"

Hilton winced, visibly taken aback by the blast of insults that erupted from her mouth like a violent explosion.

She covered her mouth, shocked as well by the hurtful words she'd hurled.

They drove to her estate in silence. The tension inside the car was thick enough to cut with a knife. *Oh, Jesus.* Any hope of a romantic relationship between her and Hilton had been ruined by her big mouth. Her mind raced. She needed to remedy the situation, send him off with well wishes.

She leaned forward, rested her arm on the back of the driver's seat. Then she gently touched his neck. "I'm sorry for that—"

"Sit back, Ms. Walden," he cut her off. "You should have your seatbelt fastened," he said, using a formal tone that altered their relationship and reduced the dynamics back to employer and employee.

As they entered the gate and coasted down the long driveway that led to her estate, Milan was in a panic. Other than falling on her knees and begging his forgiveness, Milan didn't know what else she could do to express her apology.

He came to a stop at her front door. "I'm going to arrange for Mr. Torrance's chauffeur to drive you until you can find a replacement."

"Are you quitting? You can't be serious. Isn't this Eagles

thing…like a tryout or something?" She spoke in a voice that was deliberately hushed. Raising the volume might release the hysteria that pushed at the edge of her throat.

"No, it's not a tryout," he said, his voice icy. His coldness effectively put chills down her spine. Unhappiness furrowed her brow, revealing her deep discomfort.

Her obvious distress put a glint of tenderness in his eye, but that look was quickly replaced with a gaze that was cold and unreadable.

"Yes, Milan. I'm quitting," he said firmly. "I was going to tell you tonight, over champagne. I thought it was a reason to celebrate."

"It is. I was just shocked that you—"

He held up a stiff hand, silencing her. "You're good, you know that? Really had me fooled last night, made me believe that inside that mixed-up, scattered brain, maybe there was hope for you." He swallowed. "Hope for you and me—together."

"Hilton, there is. I'm really sorry."

"Me, too. But I have to admit, I'm glad your anger allowed you to be honest and express your true feelings. Dealing with you was going to require a lot of work. You're into some stuff that I don't agree with and as long as we kept our relationship strictly sex, I could close my eyes and not think about your weird, BDSM lifestyle." His lips turned down in repugnance. "But you started changing the script, acting like you needed me to give you something real." He gave a sardonic laugh. "Guess I was wrong. But a word to the wise, that shit you're into is not healthy for your mind. Be careful. All right?"

"No, it's not all right." This was her final opportunity to turn things around. "I have true feelings for you. It's just…" She looked down, her face flushed.

"It's just what?"

"The way you have your heart set on football. I thought you were reaching for something that was out of your reach. I can help you…" She fiddled with her fingers, nervously twisted a newly acquired diamond and pearl ring around. "I can help you rebuild your life."

"Football is my life! Beside, how could someone as screwed up in the head as you help me? Huh? You enjoy controlling people. All you do is play head games." He gave a harsh snort that made Milan squirm and gnaw on her bottom lip. "I wanted to help *you*. I thought I saw something soft, a confused young woman who had flipped love around to something that resembled hate. I thought you were misguided. A simple statement, just asking me about my day, had my heart doing cartwheels for you, baby. I thought we had finally made a connection and I was ready to call what I was feeling love." He gave a head shake at his own stupidity.

"I…" she stammered.

"You were messing with my head, that's what you were doing." He gave a little shrug. "I played myself. I've been around you long enough to realize that the only person you care about is *you!* But it's cool, though. Go ahead. Keep on doing you. I'm about to get back into my favorite sport." He beamed a sincere wide grin that explicitly told her he had already moved on with his life. Then his expression dimmed a little. "It's not the way I planned to get my game on—but like I said, football is my life."

Not the way he planned? Milan had no idea what he meant by that. She was near tears and her breaking heart was so painful, she was not in a position to try to decipher the meaning behind his words. Hilton was hitting below the belt, slamming her with one low blow after another. She needed to get her thoughts together quickly and change the discussion back to mending their relationship.

"Give me another chance?" she pleaded, her remorse thickly coating every word.

"You're high maintenance. You have issues. You're selfish. I don't want, and I damn sure don't need, a woman like you." He let out a harsh breath. "Milan, would you get out of the car so I can park. I have to go home and start packing."

Taking one last look, her eyes, teary and forlorn, raked over him. But the finality in his tone forced her out of the Rolls. She walked away from him and did not allow her shoulders to slump from the weight of defeat. But once inside, her knees gave out. Curled in a knot on the floor, she allowed her tears to spill. How could she have been so incredibly dimwitted to allow some thoughtless words to throw her life into a complete upheaval? Carelessly, she'd tossed away her only chance of obtaining that mysterious and extremely hard to acquire thing called love. Now, she was left with a hole in her heart.

CHAPTER 25

She was dressed and ready for work as usual, but the sight of Maxwell's limo and his driver put a newly formed lump in her throat. Hilton! She missed him already. Where was he? What was he doing? Had he moved seamlessly into his new life and forgotten her already? The ache in her heart was unrelenting. She doubted that she could keep it together at the salon. Undoubtedly, in her current state, she'd either fire someone undeservedly or whip the shit out of Royce—whether he'd been late for work or not.

The driver held her hand and helped her inside the limousine. His professional courtesy didn't help; it made her yearn for Hilton even more. No, she couldn't bear going to the salon today. At times like this, she really needed a hug.

"Take me to Willow Grove," she said and then gave the driver her sister's address.

Milan called Sweetie. "Wanna do lunch?" She glanced at her watch. "I mean breakfast?" She chuckled, trying to sound bubbly.

"This must be a crank call or somebody has a wrong number," Sweetie retorted. "I know this can't be my sister—the sister who promised to get back to me three days ago."

Milan forced another tinkling sound that mimicked laughter.

"I know, I should have called, but you wouldn't believe how busy I've been. I'm sorry. Okay?" Her voice suddenly became low and heavy with the unhappiness that she could no longer conceal.

"Oh, Lawd," Sweetie said, sighing, after hearing Milan's sorrowful tone. "What has happened now? Is your world caving in again? Because you only call or come visit when you're going through a personal disaster."

"That's not true. I call and talk to the boys every now and then."

"Um-hmm," Sweetie said skeptically. "You only call Dominic and Diamante on their birthdays and holidays."

"But I always send them nice gifts."

"They'd like to see you sometimes, Milan. Spend a little time with you. You're not a very good aunt."

Milan sighed. She'd put her sister and family in a wonderful neighborhood, set her stupid husband up in a stupid business—a crappy take-out restaurant—and Sweetie still wanted more. She wanted Milan to pick up her brats and take them on outings—to the zoo or Hershey Park or wherever people took kids. Milan was supposed to spend quality time with them but it would never happen. She loved her nephews but she refused to devote precious time to breaking up fights and squabbles between the two little hellions. Ugh! If she wanted that kind of a headache, she'd be married with kids.

Ouch! The thought brought back the pain. It suddenly occurred to her that she'd marry Hilton without reservation and have at least one kid. Wow! Where was all this coming from? She needed Sweetie's advice quickly before she lost all her good sense.

"How come you didn't get back to me when I told you Mommy needs some help with that house?" Sweetie asked and Milan could imagine her sister's lips poked out.

Milan shrugged as if her sister could see her.

"So what's wrong? Did something bad happen? Oh my goodness…" Sweetie said in a complaining tone as if Milan had already told her something disastrous that would affect the cushy life she lived in Willow Grove. "I'm sweating over here, Milan. What's going on? Please don't tell me you're losing your business. Mommy is depending on you to start giving her a bigger monthly allowance."

Fuck her! Milan wanted to say, but Sweetie and their mother were very close, and Sweetie would have felt personally offended had Milan spoken of their mother with such blatant disrespect. So Milan kept her sentiments to herself.

"Actually I have an appointment with my accountant. I'll get back to you in a couple of days regarding a bigger allowance for the upkeep of Mommy's house," she said, lying through her teeth. She had no intention of giving her greedy, ungrateful mother another red cent. She didn't give a shit if her mother's yard started looking like a damn forest. It would serve her right for treating Milan like a stepchild her entire life.

"I don't feel like putting on any clothes, Milan. I'm comfortable in my sweats and I like chillin' in my own home. So if you want to talk over breakfast, we're going to eat right here. I'm not in the mood for dining in any of those high-class places you like to go to."

"Not a problem." Milan was eager to accommodate her sister.

Thirty minutes later, Sweetie swung her front door open and spread her arms to embrace her sister, but dropped her arms when she noticed the limo. "Why'd you come in a damn stretch limo? Always puttin' on airs. It's bad enough when you come through in your Rolls. This is a regular, middle-class neighborhood, Milan. Damn! Now the whole neighborhood gon' be gawking over here, swearing Beyonce or somebody done come through." She eyed Milan up and down critically, taking in her exquisite teal-colored caped suit. "On second thought, you're not blond and you don't have enough bootie for anyone to mistake you for Bey." She ushered Milan inside. "You look more like that model—the one who's always cussing out cops at the airport and knocking her assistants upside the head with her cell phone." Sweetie fell out laughing. Milan didn't join in. "I guarantee you, the word is gonna spread quick. Whoever saw you stepping out that limo is gon' be calling up folks, talkin' 'bout Sweetie hangin' with that British supermodel, uh-huh, that's her limo outside the crib."

Sweetie was funny enough to do a stand-up routine. She was known to have her friends doubled over in laughter when she got started with her biting wit. Milan, however, was too sad to even force her lips into a sliver of a smile.

Milan made an impatient sound, which prompted Sweetie to cut out the comedy act and head for the kitchen. "Whatchu wanna eat? Eggs and bacon?"

"I'm not hungry. Just coffee."

"Just coffee?"

Milan nodded, her expression miserable.

"All right. Suit yourself, but I need a real breakfast. I only had instant oatmeal after I got the kids off to school."

Milan was relieved to hear that it was a school day and that Sweetie's two little hellions wouldn't be racing around from room to room. While Sweetie took her time measuring coffee and gathering up ingredients for a breakfast large enough to feed an army, Milan paced the kitchen, fretting and wringing her hands. Her troubled expression pleaded for attention.

"Milan, please sit yourself down. You're making me nervous. We're gon' talk about your problem—give me a minute. Please," she added irritably as she cracked open an egg.

A short time later Milan sipped Sweetie's horribly bitter coffee while her sister dug into a pile of fluffy scrambled eggs.

"Okay, whassup?" Sweetie asked, chomping down on a piece of bacon while already chewing eggs. Only Sweetie, with her girlish face, could pull off such gluttonous behavior.

"Oh, Sweetie…" Milan began weeping and covered her face with her hands, muffling her words, and making them inaudible.

"Pull yourself together, Milan. I can't understand what you're saying." Shaking her head and frowning, Sweetie chewed her food more intensely, preparing herself for whatever crisis Milan was about to unburden on her.

"My driver quit," Milan sobbed.

Sweetie scowled and set down a forkful of hashed brown potatoes. "You're kidding me, right?"

Sniffling, Milan shook her head.

"You hired a limo to bring you all the way over here to cry on my shoulder because your driver quit? Milan, you are not in Beverly Hills somewhere, so stop acting like you're so fragile that every little thing that happens to you is a reason to fall apart. So what if your damn driver quit. You got bank; hire another one."

"Sweetie, you don't understand."

"I truly don't. I could be relaxing and watching *Maury* right about now. Why did you come over here, bothering me with some bullshit?"

"We were in a relationship."

"You were in a relationship with your driver?" Stunned, Sweetie held a half-bitten slice of bacon in mid-air.

"You never met him, Sweetie. He's not your average driver. Big, muscular, and gorgeous. He's a former NFL player and—"

"Oh, yeah? What's his name?"

"Hilton Dorsey."

"Sounds familiar. What team did he play for?"

"I don't know. I never asked. What difference does that make?"

"Quantez is a football fanatic. He would love to meet—"

"Why do all conversations lead to Quantez? This is not about your husband. I'm in the midst of a crisis."

"Okay, calm down. Let me guess—you and your driver were twisting up the sheets and he started hitting you up for a bigger salary?"

"No…I mean, yes, we were involved, but he wasn't after my money."

"Yeah, right."

"Sweetie, is it so hard to believe that a man couldn't just love me for me?"

"So, why'd he quit? What excuse did he give you?"

"He's trying to get a contract with the Eagles and I think he's at their training camp, trying out or whatever football players do."

"So, why are you crying over that? He's playing with our home team, so he'll be close by. Girl, see if you can get Quantez and the boys some free tickets to the games…and some good seats. My husband and kids are not tryna be up in the nose bleed section." Sweetie grinned and then excitedly rubbed her hands together. "Quantez is gonna be so shocked when I tell him my baby sister is hooked up with a member of the Eagles."

"That's the problem, Sweetie. We're not hooked up. We were on the verge of getting closer, maybe committing to a long-term relationship, but I ruined it." Milan's voice cracked.

Sweetie slammed her glass of orange juice down. "What did you do to ruin it? Damn, Milan, why you fuck up everybody's free seats? Quantez probably could have gotten some of the players to stop by his restaurant. It would be real good publicity for the restaurant if he could post up some autographed photos of the team." Sweetie narrowed her eyes, clearly annoyed at Milan for robbing Quantez of free publicity.

Quantez's take-out joint didn't even have a place for customers to sit, yet Sweetie was envisioning framed and autographed photos of the Eagles' top players on the walls. Milan ignored the fact that Sweetie didn't seem concerned about her heartache. She was hopeful that she'd get some good advice now that Sweetie had a vested interest in helping her get Hilton back.

"I said something insensitive...something really stupid..."

Sweetie screwed up her lips. "What did you say?"

"Uh...he's been working out for quite a while, trying to get his busted knee back in shape and I told him that his football days were probably over."

"Well, are they?" Sweetie glared at Milan.

"I don't know. He didn't say what he was going to do at the training camp."

"Whatchu think he's gonna do at camp—*train*, dumb ass!" Sweetie blurted.

Only Sweetie could get away with calling Milan derogatory names. Milan took the insult without a flinch.

"He could be trying out—trying to get on the team. And with the bad injury he incurred, he's probably not going to make the cut."

"Sounds like you don't want him to make the cut."

"I don't. I can support both of us. Why should he be running around with a football team, warming the bench while others play, when he could be home with me?"

"You are about as selfish as they come," Sweetie said, shaking her head. "Milan, if you ever plan on finding the kind of true love like me and Quantez have, you're going to have to stop putting yourself first. Now, I don't know who Hilton Dorsey is. Quantez is the football expert, he knows all the players and their stats from high school, college, and in the NFL, so I know he'll be able to give up some info on this dude. But in the meantime, I need to tell you something for your own good." Sweetie took a deep breath.

Milan put her mug of nasty coffee down and met her sister's eyes.

"You can't be stepping on a man's dreams. Athletes live and breathe their sport. They don't ever want to get out of the game. If you were trying to take that relationship to the next level, you sure fucked that shit up. You, of all people, should be holding him up, keeping him motivated. Even if you truly believe that his career is over, you needed to co-sign with him every step of the way. Milan, that's the kind of thing women do for their men. It doesn't hurt to co-sign on his dream. If his dream falls apart, he'll come back to you for comfort. But you done went and practically told the man that he wasn't nothing but a bum."

"I did not!"

"Might as well have."

Milan's shoulders sagged. "So, what can I do?"

"I don't know. I'm gon' ask Quantez to do some digging and find out if this Hilton Dorsey is training with the Eagles. If he is, I don't think it would be a good time to bring the man any more drama. You're gon' have to give him some space and let him focus on training."

"I can't. I want to talk to him; tell him that I'm sorry—"

"If you bother him right now, all you're going to do is mess up any chance you might have had to get him back." Sweetie looked off in thought. "Look, go back to the salon—"

"I can't. I don't feel like looking at the clients or my staff. I'm in a foul mood, Sweetie."

Sweetie shrugged. "Well take your ass shopping in Paris. Isn't that the type of shit you're into?"

Normally, a trip to Paris and a private showing of the Chanel collection would put her in a wonderful state of mind. But not today. She was frustrated, angry with herself, and furious with Hilton for not understanding that she was ill-equipped to show love.

Milan left Sweetie's with a wicked plan in mind. She needed to lash out at someone. Why not Maxwell? He claimed to enjoy pain. Pain that she was only too happy to assign to someone else. As usual, her role would be to direct, prompt, and make sure the punishment was executed to her exact specifications.

Back in the limo, she called BodySlam and set up a very special appointment for Maxwell. It didn't take much convincing. She made him a monetary offer that only a fool would refuse. Besides, she knew BodySlam held bitter resentment against Maxwell for putting his girlfriend, the ex-mistress Veronique, out of business.

CHAPTER 26

Milan tracked BodySlam's every move on Maxwell Torrance's high-tech security monitors.

Seemingly jolted by the dizzyingly vast and brilliant skyline, BodySlam unconsciously grasped the edge of the opened elevator to steady himself when the doors slid open on the forty-seventh floor. The unobstructed, sparkling blue sky and puffy white clouds displayed through a clear, massive window were beautiful. Like heaven.

Complementing the magnificent view, a pretty receptionist sat poised behind an elaborate desk with all of heaven serving as a glorious, ethereal backdrop. The receptionist greeted him with a welcoming smile, which gave no hint that she was disturbed by his peculiar attire, his size, or by his bare chest.

"Good afternoon, sir. Mr. Torrance is expecting you. Come with me." She maintained her perfect smile and led the heavily muscled man down a short corridor lined with plush carpet. With each cushioned step, BodySlam looked increasingly uncomfortable, which greatly pleased Milan.

Totally unaware of the purpose of the strange man's visit but knowing better than to pry, the young woman tapped politely on an imposing-looking mahogany door and then opened it.

"Mr. Torrance, your visitor is here, sir."

"Thank you, Karen. Good to see you again, young man. Come in, come in," Maxwell Torrance offered jovially, as if receiving a visit from an oddly dressed man with bloated biceps was business as usual. Though courteous, Maxwell's voice rang with the confidence and clarity of a man accustomed to wielding power.

Milan watched from an adjacent room as BodySlam's eyes panned Maxwell's office suite. From Maxwell's desk, there was yet another view of the sweeping skyline. The posh interior, elegant furnishings, and of course, the skyline, created a monument to the man's success. BodySlam appeared both awed and disturbed. And bitter. Milan could tell that he resented Maxwell's privileged circumstances. Hopefully, he wouldn't hold back. She wanted him to dispense unmerciful punishment on her unruly slave.

Maxwell sat behind a colossal corporate desk. Neat piles of work were stacked on one side. Glimmering picture frames, pens, and snazzy gadgets were strategically arranged on top of the desk.

The receptionist left, closing the door behind her. With an impatient hand wave, Maxwell Torrance motioned for Body-Slam to take the seat opposite him.

BodySlam approached, slowly, hesitantly. He was obviously out of his depth. Noting his discomfort, Maxwell Torrance's eyes twinkled with amused interest, as if he were a benevolent king granting a commoner a bit of his time.

Milan had seen enough. She felt personally insulted by Maxwell's smug attitude. She stormed out of the adjacent room. "Cut the crap, Maxwell."

Thinking he and the mogul were alone, BodySlam whipped around, surprised by Milan's presence. She wore a black corset, a lacey black thong, and thigh-high boots with stiletto heels, and she wielded a whip as she stalked across the room.

"Get up!" Milan barked at Maxwell. "How dare you sit behind that desk, pretending as though you have balls," she said scornfully. "Do you have balls, Maxwell?" she demanded.

Fear replaced the arrogant twinkle in the business tycoon's eyes. He sprang up from his seat and scuttled around the desk. Maxwell had on a shirt, tie, and suit jacket, but he was nude from the waist down. BodySlam's eyes widened slightly in surprise. Maxwell's appendage, shrunken with fear, was barely visible. "No, mistress. I don't have any balls," he admitted.

Dropping to his knees, head lowered in shame, his pale exposed buttocks poking upward, he crawled to Milan and kissed the toe of her shiny black boot.

She cut a glance at BodySlam, her former adversary, and gave him a triumphant smile. Then she swept her gaze toward Maxwell's genitals and down his bare legs. "As you can see, I had my property prepare himself for your special brand of punishment." She emphasized the words *my property*, hoping to raise BodySlam's ire. He had, after all, co-owned Maxwell briefly, and she felt certain that he deeply regretted losing the masochistic billionaire.

"Get over here," she hissed, looking down at her boots. Maxwell scrambled over and kneeled. His naked ass was several shades lighter than his face. She glared disdainfully down at her chattel who now kneeled at her feet. "He's my property," she repeated tauntingly. "Worthless property, I might add. But I own him, nevertheless."

BodySlam shifted his eyes menacingly from Milan and down to the groveling executive, looking as if he'd like nothing better than to wring both their necks.

She watched BodySlam process the situation and then set his hateful eyes on Maxwell. *Wise choice.*

"Tell BodySlam why his presence is requested today," Milan ordered.

"Mr. BodySlam," Maxwell Torrance said, his tone now soft and meek. "Sadly, I can no longer satisfy my cherished mistress."

"Because…" she prodded.

His face went red and he dropped his head in shame. "Because I'm ill-equipped to satisfy my dear mistress."

"Ill-equipped?" Milan scoffed. "Explain your problem in simple words."

"My penis is inadequate," he uttered, his voice filled with angst.

BodySlam grunted in disgust and scowled at the shuddering billionaire.

Milan shared BodySlam's revulsion and sucked her teeth. "There's another thing—"

"Yes, Mistress?"

"I expect you to refer to our visitor as *sir*. Got that!" She gave Maxwell's head a disdainful smack. "Now, be more specific about your pathetic penis problem."

"Yes, of course, Mistress." The CEO crouched down in a position of worship at Milan's feet, lifted his head, and shifted his gaze upward toward BodySlam. "Mr. BodySlam, sir…my cock is very short and thin, sir. It's miniscule, sir, and it's too small to satisfy my mistress."

"My clit is bigger than his dick," Milan mocked.

BodySlam laughed but the sound held no joy. Then his face

hardened. He seemed to growl as he incredulously bared his teeth, exhibiting frothy anger and deep loathing toward the despicable billionaire.

BodySlam's ferocious anger had Maxwell shaking and he was beginning to scare Milan as well. Maybe she should get out of the way and let the sadist take out his disdain on Maxwell, who wanted and deserved the highest form of punishment.

But she stood in position, refusing to show fear. Focusing on Maxwell, she spat, "You're a pathetic excuse for a human being. Our visitor is repulsed and it's your fault." She swatted his pale rump. Then she raised the whip. She would have preferred disciplining Maxwell with a paddle, but being that he was prone to run away, she was given no choice but to toughen up and give him the excruciating pain he yearned for. Grimacing, she delivered a disgusting succession of whip lashes. She involuntarily flinched with the landing of each hot whip lash. Maxwell's closed mouth muffled his moans of erotic distress. Eew!

As she whipped Maxwell, she noticed a protrusion in the front of BodySlam's tight leather pants. Who would have thought that such a posh domain would contain such depravity in such a lofty office in the midst of the workday? Red marks appeared on Maxwell's backside, but Milan was quickly growing tired. She'd worked herself into a sweat, and BodySlam's hand worked itself down to his groin. His fingers brushed his stiffening manhood that pushed against his leather crotch. He began rubbing circularly. His dick, bulging against the zipper of his pants, demanded freedom from the leather confines.

Finally exhausted, Milan dropped the whip and kicked Maxwell as hard as she could. "Prepare our guest!"

Maxwell crawled over to BodySlam, and then rose to his knees. He unsnapped and unzipped the tented area of Body-Slam's pants.

Approvingly, BodySlam petted Maxwell's narrow shoulders as the CEO devoured the Haitian's impossibly long phallus. Maxwell's body shivered at BodySlam's touch. Seeking more approval, he sucked and slurped loudly, striving to give good head.

A feeling of warmth seeped through Milan as she witnessed Maxwell sucking a man's dick. She thought it a disgusting freak show, but her wet pussy apparently didn't agree with her. Maxwell gave surprisingly good fellatio, pulling the huge dick in and out of his mouth with ease.

Suddenly dissatisfied with Maxwell's performance, or perhaps annoyed that Maxwell was enjoying himself too much, BodySlam grabbed the back of Maxwell's head and plunged his engorged manhood deeply, gagging and choking Maxwell with his iron-hard erection.

It appeared to Milan that BodySlam was seeking a quick release, but she had another idea.

She popped Maxwell upside his head. "That's enough, cock-sucker."

Obeying his mistress, Maxwell gleefully pulled back, releasing BodySlam's throbbing penis, allowing it to pop out of his warm mouth. BodySlam winced in discomfort as his cock was abandoned and exposed to the chilled, air-conditioned air.

Milan smiled at BodySlam. "He's all yours. Do with him as you please." She crossed the room and sat behind Maxwell's desk. She observed the walls, which were adorned with plaques and other framed tributes to Maxwell Torrance's accomplishment and let out a burst of mocking laughter.

Maxwell's neck drooped, causing his head to hang so low, he

seemed to burrow his forehead into the thick carpet. With his eyes closed tightly, he braced himself for the kind of flogging that could possibly leave him maimed. BodySlam was a ferocious master, and had been jilted by Maxwell. His anger was thick and palpable. It filled the air. Maxwell trembled in fear and excitement.

BodySlam paced menacingly, muttering in an island patois that was sensual but also invoked fear. He glowered at the tycoon with every rambling word.

Milan sat on the edge of her seat, excitedly watching the scene unfold. Soon, Maxwell would be emasculated and she planned to savor every second of her sex slave's agony and extreme distress. She took such pleasure in being a voyeur rather than a participant in this type of sex play.

As if weary, BodySlam plopped down on a very expensive Edwardian settee made of fine French silk. With his chained vest, leather pants, and worn boots, BodySlam looked completely out of place. The delicate piece of antique furniture was no doubt intended as decoration and not to be sat upon.

Relaxing further, BodySlam propped his boots heavily upon Maxwell's rear end, deliberately inflicting more pain on an area that was bruised and quite sore from Milan's flogging. Maxwell made the dreadful mistake of letting out a pitiful sound. In one swift movement, BodySlam lifted Maxwell up and cruelly threw him over his lap. Scolding Maxwell in a rush of words that were issued in a heated Haitian dialect, Body-Slam raised his large hand and gave Maxwell a sound spanking. Maxwell's whimpering lament incensed BodySlam, provoking him to greater heights of fury. He flayed Maxwell's buttocks until they bore a tapestry of red-shaded handprints. Maxwell writhed and groaned painfully.

CHAPTER 27

BodySlam examined the pattern of handprints on Maxwell's naked ass. He stared with intensity as if looking for an unblemished area to brand with his trademark. Maxwell wriggled uncomfortably. Infuriated by the twisting, moaning captive, Bodyslam sadistically brought his hand down firmly and began to apply harder, thunderous slaps. He furtively slipped his arm beneath the tycoon and viciously imprisoned Maxwell's tiny cock and scrotum inside his monstrously large, ball-crushing bare hand.

Maxwell howled. BodySlam knocked him off his lap and worked the unzipped leather pants off his hips. He pulled Maxwell by his hair and pressed his face against his groin. He smiled with wicked satisfaction as his organ lengthened and hardened. He used his big dick as a smacking device against Maxwell's miserable face. Finally, he brushed the swollen tip alongside the CEO's quivering lips.

He silenced Maxwell's whimpering with his sturdy cock, switching its usage from a face smacker to an extra-large and extremely hard pacifier. Maxwell wrapped his thin lips around BodySlam's girth and sucked, bobbing his head up and down, obviously preferring dick sucking to having his ass whipped.

"Harder!" Milan shouted from across the room. "Shove it down his throat." She didn't like the idea of Maxwell enjoying his assignment.

Refusing to take orders, BodySlam ignored Milan. Swiftly, he unbuckled his boots, kicked them off, and removed his leather pants. His hard-muscled ass and soaring appendage made Milan's mouth water. BodySlam was ripped like an ebony god. With the skill of a trained wrestler, he flipped Maxwell across the room. While Maxwell lay on his back panting, BodySlam stalked over and pounced. He lifted Maxwell's legs up and held them open, the way a man would prepare to fuck a woman. Though his cock was moist from Maxwell's mouth, he spit in his hand and slathered his dick with saliva then rubbed his glans against Maxwell's puckered asshole. He slowly penetrated his anus, hurting Maxwell with his bulging sex organ.

It was a fascinating sight. Milan's mouth fell open. She'd never seen anything like this. Maxwell moaned and she couldn't tell if it was a sound of pain or passion. Her eyes were glued to BodySlam's high, well-formed ass as it undulated in the act of giving Maxwell a tender and sensual fuck.

Then he quickened his pace, behaving sadistically, plunging now instead of gently gliding. The sound of pounding flesh echoed inside the room as he shoved his dick in to the hilt.

BodySlam bit down on his lip. Perspiring, he appeared to struggle to control the pressure rushing through his veins. He began to make sounds...words. "You got good pussy, my man. It's hot like an oven. You're nice and tight. But you already know that, eh?"

Maxwell murmured affirmatively. He seemed to enjoy having his ass penetrated much more than getting it smacked.

Milan was shocked! The tangle of hairs at the mouth of her own pussy moistened. Astonishingly, she was aroused by the sight of two men fucking.

"Ah, yes." BodySlam groaned as he worked his hips, perspiring profusely, totally into it. "Do you like me? Eh? Do I fuck you good?"

Maxwell cleared his throat and murmured softly.

Milan felt her vagina tense. Watching BodySlam's dick and balls bounce while he rammed Maxwell up the ass was another unexpected and powerful turn-on.

"Talk dirty to me, man. Tell me how good I'm fucking your tight cunt."

Maxwell wrapped his arms and legs around BodySlam and clung to him as he got served, murmuring sweet words in his ears.

Her patience was near to breaking. It was time to end the party. She made an impatient sound and then clapped her hands, making a scolding gesture that indicated she wanted them to stop copulating. But BodySlam and Maxell ignored her and kept at it. The sound of men moaning in sexual rapture was disturbing and titillating.

BodySlam was no wimp and she doubted she could control his wanton behavior. Milan sighed. She caressed her wet sex. *If you can't beat 'em, join 'em.* She pulled Maxwell's arms from around BodySlam and pushed his head to the floor.

"Suck my pussy, you cheating bastard," she hissed, straddling his head and squatting down. Her parted pussy hovered over his face, and then she lowered herself until her buttocks rested on his cheeks.

Maxwell didn't disappoint. He stretched his tongue to capacity and lapped inside Milan's cunt. Skillful at serving two masters, Maxwell's exploring tongue had Milan's body rocking.

"Give me that good pussy," BodySlam commanded Maxwell. Maxwell obeyed, thrusting his ass as quickly as he stroked Milan's cunt with his tongue. Maxwell's mouth became an aggressive sex provider. His lips sucked urgently, his tongue licking roughly as it sought to provide Milan with pleasure.

Feeling competitive, BodySlam yanked Maxwell closer, pushing his cock more deeply into Maxwell's ass as if to nourish him. "My man," he whispered. "You'd make a good woman for a wild man like me. Do you like the way I fuck you?"

Maxwell licked Milan's pussy with desperation while his lower body undulated, silently screaming a reply.

"Ah. So, you like the idea of giving yourself to me. That sounds good, man." BodySlam pumped dick as he spoke, his tone soft and mesmerizing.

Milan didn't hear Maxwell say anything. So why was Body-Slam claiming victory? Had she known this sadistic bastard would once again try to steal her chattel, she never would have hired him to help her give Maxwell the severe punishment she was unable to dispense. She moisturized Maxwell's lips with her juices, claiming her property and marking her territory.

"I've lost my woman, Veronique. You know that already, eh?"

Maxwell muttered something. BodySlam was taking it to another level and Milan didn't like it. She stopped moving, ready to physically fight the muscled sadist if she had to.

"That's it. Get out," Milan ordered BodySlam. He paid her no mind.

Working Maxwell to a crescendo, he asked, "Would you like to be my girlfriend? I can slap you, beat you, and fuck you all night long?" BodySlam spoke in a low, lilting tone, hypnotizing Maxwell with the erotic sound of his voice.

Maxwell responded with a harsh moan. His rush of excited breath, though disturbing, aroused Milan, who was still perched on his face.

Unable to control herself, she rocked against his tongue. Her fingernails scraped at the wall as she tried to give his tongue as rough a ride as BodySlam was giving his ass.

But she couldn't compete. Nothing could have prepared her for the way Maxwell was eating her pussy. He sent a shocking sensation through her when his tongue journeyed to her clit and slathered it, causing her to shudder and hasten her rhythm. Holding back her orgasm was torture. It was a worse sexual agony than she'd ever experienced. Milan felt a spasm in her stomach. She moaned loudly and squirted a premature shot of sticky cum. Maxwell's open mouth received it, slurping, sucking, trying to drain her.

At that moment of Milan's paralyzing orgasm, BodySlam asked again in a voice that was as soft as a caress, "Maxwell, my good man...my pretty woman, do you want to be with me?"

She couldn't believe it when she felt Maxwell's lips moving and his voice vibrating into her quivering pussy, speaking words of agreement. "Yes! Oh, yes. I do!"

Fucking faggot-ass bastard!

CHAPTER 28

Milan finished off her second glass of wine. Wine usually made her feel good—happy and amorous. But the euphoria she'd been counting on was brief at best. Her thoughts drifted to Maxwell. A couple hours after his encounter with BodySlam, Maxwell had to leave for Japan to finish up an acquisition. Though his anus was no doubt on fire, she was sure he'd board his private jet wearing a satisfied smile. What a sick puppy he'd turned out to be! Of course, she'd known he was weird when she first met him online, but at that time, she'd considered him no freakier than she was.

But now, his new lust for corporal punishment was taking her beyond her capabilities. It was just a matter of time before she was going to have to give Maxwell the boot. Of course, she'd have to get her hands on a lot more of his money before she bailed.

Maxwell and BodySlam may have been satiated by today's depraved interlude but Milan was left bereft. Getting involved in that S&M scene had not helped her mood at all. In fact, she felt soiled. Watching Maxwell getting knocked around and reamed by another man was gross and she regretted having participated in the increasingly dark activities that were taking over Maxwell's life.

Being bossy, giving orders, and having emotional control was sexually stimulating, but indulging Maxwell's dark urges was taking a toll. His quiet demand for pain and punishment put her in the awkward position of taking orders. In his own twisted way, Maxwell Torrance was calling the shots and in reality it was he and not she who was actually in control. After all, his needs were being met and he had virtually turned her into a prostitute. She was getting a hefty financial benefit and a bad case of nausea from exchanging deviant sex for pay.

To get her hands on even more of Maxwell's fortune, she'd have to devote more time and energy into thinking and implementing creative ways to keep him happily submissive. She frowned. It had been so much easier when all he required was humiliation.

Thankfully, his trip to Japan would give her some alone time to figure out a way to get Hilton back. She got an instant visual of Hilton's heavy dark lashes, the smoothness of his honey-colored skin. And then she recalled the softness of his kiss. Stricken by an intense pang of regret, she poured herself more wine, hoping for a little relief. Maybe the third glass would be the charm. It wasn't.

She missed what she and Hilton were beginning to build— the flirty interactions, the cuddling, the underlying feeling that their sex-based relationship could possibly develop into something long lasting and real. But she'd ruined it. The romantic liaison they'd been on the verge of assembling was over before it had even begun.

After downing the third glass of wine, she felt lonelier than before. Hilton had escaped to some field of dreams, football heaven, and with a football tucked beneath his arm, he was probably running and leaping like a happy gazelle while she was sitting home alone. Milan felt so forlorn, so abandoned. She was as grief-stricken as if someone she loved had died. She set down her wineglass and dabbed at the stinging tears that began to fill her eyes.

She'd promised herself after her trainer had broken her heart that she'd never again give another person permission to hurt her. She could feel herself sinking, succumbing to new depths of depression. So what could she do to ease the pain? *Make money!* Creating new avenues for cash flow was the perfect remedy for heartache. She'd take her mind off Hilton by throwing herself back into running her salon as efficiently as she once had. Lately, she'd been allowing Sumi to oversee Pure Paradise and quite frankly, Sumi was mishandling the business to such a degree that Milan shuddered to think how much money she had lost while her head was in the clouds dreaming about Hilton. Everything was out of balance. Employees were showing up for work late, if at all. Foot fetishists were filling in for spanking masters. Milan shook her head. It was time to get back to business and personally oversee every aspect of the salon, from the sordid lower level to the classy upper levels. Clearly, she had to get her staff whipped back into shape.

Planning on getting completely inebriated, Milan took a gulp of her fourth glass of wine. Thinking about her out-of-control staff, she abruptly stood. Teetering slightly, she steadied herself and, with a wineglass in one hand and a chilled bottle of cheap wine in the other, she walked determinedly toward the stairs and headed up to her home office.

She clicked open her laptop and guzzled more of the fruity elixir while she waited. The monitor finally sprang to life. She tapped the keyboard with one hand and turned the wineglass up to her lips with the other as she accessed the Pure Paradise files. Squinting, she reviewed a series of spreadsheets. Amazingly, despite Sumi's lackadaisical management style, earnings were up. Way up. The large figures on the spreadsheets made her beam. After getting dumped and replaced by a damn football, Milan was surprised that her lips remembered how to smile. Chuckling with drunken laughter, she viewed the images of dollar signs. Her bad case of the doldrums quickly changed to giddy excitement.

Determined to use a more hands-on approach to her business, Milan arrived at the salon earlier than usual the next morning. She sent Sumi to the lower level to manage things downstairs.

First on Milan's hit list was Asian Spice. Something had to be done about the backed-up-traffic, the clogged entryway. Clients were lined up to get Shin's special foot softening treatment, and there was standing room only. Not a pretty sight for a posh salon. Stroking her chin, she considered several options as she whisked behind the reception desk and peered over the harried receptionist's shoulder at the computer monitor. Someone—probably Sumi—had overbooked the manicurist, who, of course, was just a guise for customers who really wanted some Asian Spice.

Milan couldn't redirect everyone down to see BodySlam. To expect everyone to be easily converted into masochistic submissives was a totally unrealistic notion, so she decided to take another tack. At Milan's urging, the receptionist called the next name on the list. "Ms. Landers, the manicurist will see you now," the receptionist announced in as cordial a tone as she could manage with Milan breathing down her neck.

Acknowledging her name, a poised and perfectly groomed woman gave the receptionist a tight smile. Wearing a well-tailored suit with a smart-looking gray-streaked bob haircut, she set down a copy of *Vogue* and rose to her feet. Ms. Landers, Milan noticed, appeared to have a fresh French manicure and Milan suspected that her top-designer pumps were hiding a fresh pedicure. This pampered matron, obviously dissatisfied with her life, wanted to add some extra zest to her life by adding a little Asian Spice. *Tough!* She wasn't in dire need of a manicure; she was not an emergency case. It was Milan's responsibility to get things in proper order.

Milan looked at the appointments on the monitor and quietly directed the receptionist to call the next person on the list.

"Uh, Ms. Marlton?" the befuddled receptionist said.

A frumpy woman sprang from her seat and happily pushed past the gray-streaked, bobbed client and then rushed over to the receptionist's desk and uttered a breathless, "Yes?"

Milan cut an eye at the woman's nails and was satisfied that she was indeed badly in need of a manicure.

In a hushed tone, Milan instructed the receptionist to redirect Ms. Landers to the miniscule cubby that was Shin's workspace, the place where he gabbed on the phone, sent texts to his friends, or played games on his computer—bullshitting around until Ellen called him to execute the specialty he was paid to perform.

"Is something wrong?" Ms. Landers inquired sharply as she approached the counter. "My appointment is for ten-fifteen." She glanced at her watch and then looked up at the clock on the wall for confirmation.

Unaware that Milan had switched appointments, Ellen, the manicurist, came out at precisely ten-fifteen and greeted Ms.

Landers with a solicitous smile. "Good morning. Come with me, Ms. Landers."

"No, no," Milan interjected crossly. "There's been a mix-up. Follow her, Ms. Marlton." Milan gestured for the frumpy client to follow the manicurist.

"This is preposterous," Ms. Landers exclaimed in a voice strengthened by indignation. The idea that someone else could get bumped in front of her was absolutely incomprehensible.

"Ms. Landers," Milan said softly, while giving the woman a telling look. "Shin can take care of you right now." Milan ushered the woman back to Shin's meager quarters, where the Asian hottie was caught off guard, shirtless and wearing headphones while practicing new dance moves.

Milan cleared her throat. Startled, Shin jumped. Ms. Landers pursed her lips in disgust at Shin's paltry workspace, but cast an approving gaze at his marvelously defined chest.

"I'll leave you two alone," Milan said and, with a knowing smile, she stepped out of the small room and closed the door, assuring Shin and his client privacy.

Back at the reception desk, Milan motioned for the reception-ist to get up. Milan took the woman's seat.

"Look at this! Who scheduled all these back-to-back clients?" Milan shot the receptionist a look of disapproval. Sulking, the receptionist hovered over Milan's shoulder as if she hadn't already seen the long list of names on the computer screen.

"I didn't overbook," the receptionist mumbled.

"Then who did?"

Tight-lipped, the receptionist shrugged.

"Pure Paradise is supposed to run smoothly. I'm horrified that I nearly allowed an incompetent screw-up such as you to ruin my business and damage my impeccable reputation."

The receptionist flinched. Her face flushed and a deep scarlet shade stained her cheeks. "I'm not the person responsible," she mumbled beneath her breath as she dragged a shaky hand through her hair.

Milan propped a hand on her hip, so angry she feared she would spit and sputter if she tried to speak. She took a deep breath and managed to keep her voice at a low and professional register that reached only the receptionist's ears. "If you didn't do it, then who did?" Milan spoke slowly and with a deadly tone that threatened that heads might possibly roll.

Wanting to keep hers, the receptionist suddenly became chatty. In fact, she sang like a bird. "It was Sumi! Sumi booked all those clients. I really tried to stop her, honestly, Ms. Walden, I really did. But Sumi was adamant. She said it was imperative that we squeeze in as many clients as possible. She said we had to increase the volume to keep up with our competitors. She said she only cared about the bottom line."

Milan was taken aback. Yes, Sumi was a hard worker—under Milan's prodding and direction. Since when did her assistant start caring about increasing volume and the financial bottom line? Milan had assumed Sumi was more interested in spending time with her new female lover than running Pure Paradise.

Still, she wasn't running it efficiently. Sure, Sumi was bringing in additional revenue with her creative ideas, but how long would that last if Milan allowed Sumi to antagonize the clients by making them wait endlessly?

The Pure Paradise clientele were mainly a bunch of spoiled, pampered matrons and being made to wait was an indignity that most would not be willing to suffer much longer. So before they took their business elsewhere Milan was hell-bent on getting things rolling smoothly once again.

Perhaps the pretty little thing hoped to get back into Milan's good graces and into her bed if she more than quadrupled Milan's income. Flattered, Milan grinned to herself. Still, Sumi shouldn't hold her breath if she expected her latest performance to grant her a pass back into Milan's bed.

After being with Hilton, after sharing such tender moments, Milan was feeling less and less inclined to engage in sordid, meaningless sex. There was no room in Milan's life for Sumi. She hadn't given up on Hilton. Throwing herself into her business was just a distraction until she could figure out a way to regain her place in his heart.

CHAPTER 29

A few moments after Milan had sufficiently brought order to the chaotic appointment list, separating traditional manicures, pedicures, therapeutic massages, and body wraps from those waiting for a selection from the specialty menu, Ms. Landers cleared the waiting area. She let out a piercing scream that sent the waiting patrons scurrying toward the exit sign.

Royce came running, huffing and puffing with his long tongue hanging and his hand pressed against his weapon, ready to draw. Grimacing, Milan imagined clients who were in the midst of enjoy a soothing massage, scrambling off the towel-covered padding and finding a safe haven beneath the sturdy wooden table while the massage therapists took refuge behind potted plants or wedged themselves into corners, hiding from whatever horror awaited them outside their cloistered confines.

"Oh my God!" Milan whirled on her heel and, with Royce at her side, she hurried into Shin's cubicle. Ms. Landers was standing, still screaming as she gawked down at her cum-covered bare feet.

With his sizeable dick still in hand, Shin gave a one-shoulder shrug. "I squirted her feet with the deluxe softener and she started yelling her head off before I could massage it in," he explained.

"What kind of sordid, sick, disgusting hellhole are you running?" Ms. Landers shouted at Milan.

Milan was bewildered that Ms. Landers was making such a big fuss. Shin had squirted a copious amount of semen on her perfectly pedicured feet. She couldn't imagine why the woman was screaming like a banshee.

"What's wrong?" Milan asked, sincerely perplexed. "Aren't you pleased with Shin's work?"

Ms. Landers fluttered her lashes in shock and then dropped her gaze down to her semen-soaked feet. "Are you out of your mind? This maniac—this perverted sex fiend— pretended that he was going to apply a top coat to my pedicure and then out of the clear blue sky, he extracted his penis and sexually assaulted me."

"No, no. It was a misunderstanding," Milan interjected, holding her head at the horror of making such a monumental blunder. "I must have accidentally switched your appointment with someone who wanted The Spicy Asian pedicure. Please accept my apology."

"I will not." Ms. Landers stole a look at her feet and grimaced. "I'm calling my attorney." She pulled a cell phone from her purse.

Milan glared at Shin. "Hurry, clean her up!" she demanded shrilly.

Shin rushed to get a warm, moist towel.

"No!" Ms. Landers shouted. "I need evidence." Using her phone, she started snapping pictures of her creamy feet. "I'm filing assault charges—"

"Against whom?" Shin questioned, his voice trembling with fear. "I didn't commit a crime; I was doing my job." He shot a glance at Milan, expecting her to corroborate his claim. Milan rolled her eyes at Shin.

"Your job!" Ms. Landers squawked. "That's ludicrous! Young man, you are a sick pervert and I'm having you both arrested. I want you both brought to trial, and I'm going to make sure that this bordello is shut down!" Ms. Landers declared and snapped a couple more pictures before dropping into a chair and allowing Shin to clean his gook off her feet.

"Ms. Landers," Milan said, in the calmest voice she could muster after hearing such terrifying words as *arrested, trial*, and *shut-down*. Oh dear Lord, she doubted she could endure any of the threats. The possibility of doing hard time was like freakin' déjà vu. Her heart was pounding like a sledgehammer, seemingly loud enough to be heard echoing throughout the corridors of her prized salon. "I'd like to offer you manicures, pedicures…any service of your choice…free of charge, of course. For a year," she threw in and then forced her lips to stretch into a hopeful smile.

Ms. Landers replied with a snort, "I wouldn't cross this threshold again if you gave me ten years of free services. My attorney is going to file sexual assault charges and we're having you both arrested. The doors to this vulgar sex den are going to be permanently closed."

The woman's threats had Milan so dizzy with fear, she staggered out of Shin's cubicle. Pushing buttons on her cell, trying to get a hold of Sumi, Milan stumbled past gawking staff and the remaining die-hard patrons who were still hoping to keep their appointment with Shin.

After entering the sanctuary of her own office, she finally got Sumi on the phone. "Where are you?" Milan hissed, wondering why Sumi hadn't come running at the sound of Ms.

Landers' high-pitched scream. Then it dawned on her that the lower level was soundproofed to keep down the hollering, yelling, and pleading that erupted when BodySlam throttled his clientele.

"I'm holding down the fort downstairs as you instructed, remember?" Sumi said snippily.

Like Milan, Sumi preferred her own spacious office to the meager office housed in the lower level. Her sarcasm didn't escape Milan and it would be dealt with later. At the moment, Milan's focus was on getting the hell out of Pure Paradise before the police arrived.

"There's a minor problem upstairs. I need you to multi-task—"

"Isn't that what I've been doing for the past year?" Sumi snapped.

More sarcasm. Oooh, Milan couldn't wait to put Sumi in her place, but her punishment would have to wait.

"Tell BodySlam to get his client out of here, now. Tell him to leave also. Have Harper padlock the spanking room and then lock off the entry to the lower level. I want you to get upstairs and discreetly send all of the specialty staff home. Then get Harper to shut down the specialty website. Don't leave a trace. Make it appear that it never existed."

"Why would you want her to do that? Milan, what's going on?"

"You overbooked and there's such a clog of traffic, the neighboring businesses are complaining. They claim that our clients are parking in their designated spots," Milan lied. "Some of the business owners are actually threatening to call the law." Milan heaved a great sigh. "Sumi, I can't believe you placed me in such a terrible position. You created a hell of a disaster," Milan accused as she snatched files and quickly stuffed them inside her briefcase.

"Is that so," Sumi shouted. "Nothing I do pleases you—"

"There's no time for a tantrum. This is a place of business," Milan said coolly. "Listen, I'm distraught and I'm going home for the day. Call me when you've managed to sort things out." Milan snapped her cell shut, grabbed her purse, and darted down the stairs that led to a back exit. Outside, she took a sweeping glance of the area and walked briskly away from Pure Paradise. She didn't call her driver to pick her up until she had walked three blocks away. She ordered him to bring the limo two blocks over, where she walked to ensure that she was nowhere near Pure Paradise and safe from being entangled in a raid.

Safe inside the limo, Milan tried to settle her nerves, but gruesome images of police badges and handcuffs flashed through her mind. Suddenly, her cell jangled, the sound causing her to practically jump out of her skin. She flipped the phone open and squinted at Sumi's name but was afraid to answer. A part of her wanted to know what was going on, but another part thought it best to wait until she spoke with Maxwell.

She looked at her watch. Shit, she really needed to remember to keep a watch on hand that kept track of the time in Japan. *Damn you, Maxwell!* Why'd he have to be on another continent when she needed him most?

She truly needed to talk to Maxwell and bring him up to speed so he could assemble his legal team to repair the damage. She called his cell and it went straight to voicemail. Milan rubbed her tummy. She could feel a horrible case of nausea coming. When the phone rang again, she hit the ignore button and shut off the annoying jangle.

But Sumi wouldn't be deterred. She called repeatedly. Obviously she hadn't been arrested or she wouldn't be able to make so many back-to-back calls. And Milan hadn't heard sirens or any signs of police involvement, so she assumed Sumi was just calling to brief her on the spectacle Ms. Landers was creating. Milan wasn't in the mood to hear any more bad news. If Sumi hadn't created the specialty menu, none of this would have happened. So, until she spoke to Maxwell and had access to his highly paid counsel, Milan would not be taking any of Sumi's calls.

Good luck, Sumi; hope you don't end up in the clink. But then again… Sumi could use a reality check. A night or two behind bars might be just the attitude adjustment the self-important assistant needed.

But Sumi rang Milan's cell incessantly. Though annoying, each ring assured Milan that Pure Paradise had not been raided and shut down.

CHAPTER 30

Around ten o'clock that evening, and after hours of trying to hunt down Maxwell to no avail, Milan finally took a call from Sumi.

"Why the hell didn't you return my calls?" Sumi sputtered into the phone.

"I'm sorry, Sumi, I've been resting," Milan said softly, rubbing her temple and hoping Sumi would imitate her calm tone.

No luck. "Do you realize that I had to handle an irate client who was threatening to sue and have Shin arrested because he mistakenly ejaculated on her feet?"

"How'd that happen?" Milan feigned innocence.

"Don't pretend like you don't know what happened. Shin told me you were there. How can you be so deceitful? According to the receptionist, you switched appointments. You screwed up and left me to clean up the mess. That woman, Ms. Landers, was incensed, making all sorts of threats. You knew she intended to get the police involved, and what did you do? You fled the scene and threw me under the bus. How could you do that to me, Milan? After all we've meant to each other, I can't believe you'd actually try to set me up for something I didn't do."

"Listen, you little twit, that specialty menu was your idea and I'm not taking a fall for you or that stupid Shin!"

"I noticed you enjoyed raking in all that money the specialty menu brought in."

"All good things have to end." Milan gave a solemn sigh. "So, what happened with Ms. Landers? Is she going to take legal action?"

"It was a very close call. She wanted her attorney to call the media and have Pure Paradise exposed as a whorehouse. The clients could hear her loud complaints. She was very disruptive, so I remembered how you redirected the last dissatisfied client down to BodySlam."

Milan gasped. "Oh, God. Please tell me you didn't take that prissy woman downstairs! Sumi, you have to use judgment when you introduce someone to corporal punishment, and I seriously doubt if Ms. Landers would be the right candidate for a session with BodySlam."

"Don't worry, Ms. Landers didn't get the spanking she deserved. BodySlam had gone. Remember? You told me to send him home for the day."

"Oh, yeah. Right." Milan breathed a sigh of relief. "So, how did you appease her? Did she accept free manicures? Everything is okay now, right?"

"Right!"

"Thank goodness!" Milan wiped perspiration from her forehead. "That heifer's panties were twisted in a really tight knot," she joked, laughing as she spoke. Now that everything was all right and the smoke had cleared, she was able to show a sense of humor.

"I managed to untwist her panties," Sumi said smugly.

"Meaning?" Milan arched a brow.

"I gave her what I used to give you."

She gasped again. "You introduced her to your pussy snaps?" Milan said in a screechy voice she hadn't intended.

"I sure did. Licked her snatch, too. She went crazy, pulling my hair while she came all over my face. She wants to see me again."

"But...but you're not on the menu."

"You left me in the lurch, so I had no choice but to offer myself as the day's special," Sumi said snidely. "Ms. Landers left me a very generous tip. You can thank me for sparing Pure Paradise all that unwanted publicity. I also had to promise to see her again tomorrow. Turns out her husband has been neglecting coochie. Gives her some cock every now and then but he's not taking Viagra and he doesn't last very long. She says he never bothers with foreplay, so you can imagine how very grateful she is for my special technique. She says she only wants to have sex with women now and she also said, starting today, she officially hates men. I think she's in love," Sumi bragged. "The woman's loaded. She's good looking for her age, but she's really not my type. What do you think I should do? String her along in the manner that you treat me?"

Milan winced at the jab and then went though a swift range of emotions: shock, jealousy, anger, and finally acceptance. "Do whatever it takes to keep her mouth shut. Thanks, Sumi. You're a true friend."

"Friend? I thought I was your lover."

Milan heard Sumi swallow as she nervously waited for Milan to respond. Milan switched subjects. "I've been thinking... I want Pure Paradise back the way it used to be. After this scare,

I'm through with all the smut and sordid sex. I want my salon to run smoothly, like a normal, upscale salon. Seriously, Sumi. I'm bored with all that decadent sex."

"Are you bored with me?"

Sumi had her on the spot and Milan was squirming. "Uh… not really," she stuttered.

"You have an odd way of showing it." There was an edge to her voice.

"Aren't you involved with what'shername?"

"Harper." Sumi supplied her assistant's name.

"Yeah, her."

"No, we're just friends. *Cohorts* would best describe us, especially when you use us to do your dirty work to Maxwell."

"I see," Milan said uncomfortably. Sumi was really laying it on thick; trying to make her feel guilty for the things she was paid to do. True, the way she had rescued the day by pussy snapping Ms. Landers was above and beyond, but that was the dynamic of their relationship. It wasn't based on anything remotely resembling equality.

"I was involved with Lily…on the rebound," Sumi went on. "Anyway, with Lily, it was just about sex. Nothing like the way I feel about you. What happened to us, Milan? Why'd you cut me out of your life?"

Milan felt a terrible twinge of guilt. She'd never felt anything except lust for Sumi and it was time to allow her to get on with her life. Find true love with Ms. Landers, Harper, or someone who wanted a lesbian affair. It was time to tell Sumi the truth.

"Sumi, I'm going through something right now. I can't be in a relationship with you…or anyone else, for that matter." Milan relayed the news as gently as she could.

Sumi was briefly silent. Then, as expected, she erupted into a violent, profanity-laced tirade, a searing mixture of Korean and English curse words, hurled like knives.

Milan quietly disconnected the call, truly grateful that she wasn't within the range of one of Sumi's chamber kicks.

Who knew what vengeful tactics Sumi would come up with? Pure Paradise still wasn't out of the woods yet. Milan still wanted to talk to Maxwell and hear his take on the subject. Whatever he thought best, she'd still demand that he send a team of top-notch attorneys to counsel her on the right course of action.

₰₰

Though the single beep from her cell was barely audible, Milan was jolted awake. She sprang upright, disgusted that she'd slept through the ringing phone and had missed Maxwell's call. Urgently, she reached over to the nightstand for the cell, expecting to see the voicemail message icon lit. But, surprisingly, Maxwell had left a text. He never did that.

Curious, she clicked on the text icon, and was startled to see a one-word message: *Baby…*

Her eyes shot upward and spotted Hilton's number. She flattened her hand against her heart to control the excited pounding. He hadn't said anything really conclusive, didn't ask how she was doing, didn't state that he missed her or was sorry for the way things had ended.

But that one word, *baby*, said it all.

The breakup wasn't irreversible. There was hope for their relationship. Hilton still cared!

And Milan had enough sense to know that Hilton wasn't ready

to discuss their problems. He just wanted her to know that she was on his mind.

In her darkened bedroom, she imagined that she saw sparks of multi-colored lights shaped like miniature valentines, igniting like an array of fireworks.

She peeked at the one-word message again and then snapped the phone shut. With a smile on her lips, she tugged the duvet over her head, snuggled into a cushy pillow, and fell into a dreamy sleep.

CHAPTER 31

Milan sneered at the monitor in her office. Sumi was such a slimeball! There she was in living color, climbing up on the massage table and working her tight pussy muscles on Ms. Landers' clit. Ms. Landers, or Jill, as Sumi had taken to calling her, was too prudish to get naked. She was still wearing her designer clothes and pumps. Her dress was hitched up around her waist, her spindly legs gapped open. Sumi was putting it on her so good; Ms. Landers' cosmetically tightened face was contorted in a horrible sexual grimace.

And Sumi, behaving like the slutty ho from hell, was pussy snapping hard and fast like she was possessed, while talking dirty in Korean. Ms. Landers arched upward, clutching Sumi's small waist as she pulled her closer, on the verge of cumming.

Sumi pulled away and hopped off the table.

"What's wrong? Don't stop. Please. It was right there. My orgasm was right there." Ms. Landers looked distraught, reaching out for Sumi, her arms flailing like a woman drowning.

"Shh," Sumi comforted. "Lie down. Relax," she urged. "I have a big surprise in store."

Though furious that Sumi had disregarded her orders and continued to run Pure Paradise like a whorehouse, Milan leaned forward, eyeing the monitor, eager to know what other deviant sex act Sumi had in store for the horny, rich matron.

"I want us to come together, Jill," Sumi said softly, as she stroked Ms. Landers' salt-and-pepper hair. "Have you ever made love to a woman with your mouth?"

Ms. Landers grimaced and shook her head adamantly.

"Don't care about me, Jill?" Sumi purred.

"Yes, but I don't know how."

Sumi was already climbing back on the massage table. "It'll come naturally," she assured her new lover. Turned in the sixty-nine position, Sumi aligned her vagina with Ms. Landers' pursed and unwilling lips. Stretching her neck, she aimed for the woman's clit, and then applied light, teasing tongue strokes until Ms. Landers became so excited, she parted her own lips and drove her tongue deeply inside Sumi's tight walls.

Milan watched furiously as the two sluts gave each other pleasure. Sumi had a hell of a nerve, conducting her illicit affair right in Milan's face and in her place of business. Sumi was deliberately continuing to desecrate the business that Milan was trying to clean up and put back on track. She and that rich ho could have conducted the co-mingling of their cunts in a hotel or at Sumi's place. It was disrespect of the highest degree and Sumi would be dealt with eventually.

The moaning and sighing coming from the speakers was so loud and annoying, Milan wanted to slap the shit out of both boisterous bitches. And just when she thought they were finally ready to bust a couple of nuts, the door to the massage room eased open.

Milan's jaw dropped when she saw Deputy Dawg enter the room, his chest poked out in self-importance, badge gleaming, one hand on his nightstick and the other on his gun as if Milan had personally called him to handle some shit.

Then to Milan's utter amazement, Royce instantly lowered himself down to his knees and began to stealthily crawl toward the massage table. It was both stunning and sickening to watch him crawling across any floor other than the one inside her office, but she thought she'd pass the hell out when he started sniffing the air like a dog in heat, his long bumpy tongue lolling outside his mouth, his eyes glazed over with lust, and even more unsightly were the streams of drool that spilled down the sides of his hanging jowls.

Ms. Landers, preoccupied with her first venture into the intricacies of pussy sucking, had no idea that Royce had entered the room. While Sumi licked Ms. Landers' clit, Royce lifted up to the table and braced himself with the heels of his hands; his fingers hung limp, positioned to resemble a dog's begging paws. With his bump-roughened tongue, he licked the length of Ms. Landers' parted labia, lapping up her pouring juices while Sumi sucked the old broad's clit.

Milan clenched her teeth and clamped her hands over her ears in preparation for Ms. Landers' big orgasm and the accompanying explosion of deafening sound that the loud woman was bound to emit. Milan had heard her scream yesterday and knew Ms. Landers was capable of hitting notes high enough for a dog to hear.

She was not, however, prepared for the violent tremors and body-shaking that sent both Ms. Landers and Sumi crashing to the floor. Certain she heard skulls cracking and bones breaking, Milan shut off the monitor, unable to bear the sight of their broken bodies lying in a crumpled heap.

Having a client injured on the premises was really bad news. This latest fiasco was again beyond her scope. Unwilling to hang around and get threatened with another lawsuit, she picked up her purse and called her driver. She didn't have time to fire Royce, but she'd hand him his pink slip tomorrow. How dare he crawl around, sniffing, panting, and drooling for another woman's pussy flavor. Admittedly, she hadn't been using his long and gifted tongue, but before she'd trained him and brought out the canine in him, he hadn't bothered to use his tongue to its fullest potential.

Right now, Milan was trembling, hyperventilating, and perspiring so badly, the armpits of her charcoal bouclé, collarless, classic Chanel jacket were completely sodden. She needed to get the hell out of Pure Paradise. She knew she wouldn't stop shaking until she was locked inside the safety of her home.

Sumi was probably injured from the fall, but she had work to do. Milan didn't know and didn't care how Sumi would manage it…she could limp, hobble around on a makeshift set of crutches, whatever it took. One thing was for sure, that slutty little twit had better get herself together and slip into damage control mode.

※ ⁂

She required the services of Maxwell's team of high-powered attorneys more than ever. So, where the hell was that rat bastard? He hadn't responded to any of her calls. Distressed, Milan pressed the back of her hand against her forehead. Oh, the hell with it! She was sick of Maxwell's ass. He'd given her the impression that Veronique was sent packing to some place akin to Siberia. But she had a sneaking suspicion that Veronique was somewhere in the shadows and had a hand in Maxwell's unwillingness to return her calls. If Veronique was back in the picture, Milan might as well throw in the towel.

As ugly and haggard as she was, the woman was a trained dominatrix. Milan was a master at emotional torture but she was no match for a trained dominatrix. Even with the help of Sumi and Harper, Milan couldn't compete. Sumi and Harper were mean-spirited and kinky; they didn't know crap about any of the equipment that was installed in Milan's basement. Milan thought about the mummifying kit that came with instructions she hadn't bothered to read. She'd bet Veronique knew how to mummify a submissive without an instruction manual.

Milan was really weary of her kinky lifestyle. She wanted something meaningful. She was at the verge of opening her phone and gazing at Hilton's one-word message, when her better judgment told her to keep her head on straight and to postpone going all gaga until she got some more money out of Maxwell. He owed her for all the services she'd rendered. And if she planned on keeping her business running, she'd have to have counsel from his superior legal team. Sure, she had originally planned to go after all his billions, but Maxwell was becoming more and more of an unbearable headache. Veronique could have him—after he settled his account with Milan.

She wanted to move on with her life and was willing to settle for…hmm. Twenty-five million or so. Yes, twenty-five million seemed appropriate, it was a fair price for the year and a half of dominatrix devotion she'd extended, not to mention how she'd catered to his sick desires by turning the basement of her home into a freak show of a dungeon. Damn! It was going to cost a bundle to disassemble all that creepy equipment—the cell, cages, bondage tables, and other crap, many of which were bolted to the floor. Milan shook her head, thinking about the cost and inconvenience of having her basement remodeled. But it had to be done. Soon! She couldn't bear to look at any of those torture devices much longer.

⚜

Later that night, the ringing telephone brought her out of a fitful sleep. Her silent cell lay on the pillow next to her. Both Maxwell and Hilton usually called her on her cell. It had to be Sweetie. What now?

"Hello!" Her voice was hoarse with irritation.

"Milan Walden?" an official male voice asked.

Aw, shit. Milan sensed trouble. Adrenaline started pumping. She was instantly wide awake. Fully alert. That fucking bitch, Ms. Landers, had called the law on her. And that fucking Maxwell and his team of high-paid and highly intimidating attorneys were nowhere to be found to get her out of this trouble.

"Ms. Walden, this is Agent Whitaker. I'm with the Federal Bureau of Investigation."

Her mouth fell open. Surely, her ears were deceiving her. She did not hear the person on the other end of the phone identify himself as the motherfucking FBI? A call from a regular Philadelphia officer of the law would have been earth shattering enough, but the FBI! *Oh, Lord! What kind of clout did Ms. Landers have?*

"I apologize for the late hour," the voice continued, "but my partner, Agent Pulliam, and I would like to come by and have a talk. Shouldn't take very long. Just want to verify a few facts."

A few facts, my ass! She knew exactly why they wanted to talk. They wanted to involve her in a sex scandal and accuse her of using Pure Paradise as a front for hooker-related activities. Her thoughts racing, she thought about that governor who was ensnarled in an FBI probe. Milan gulped in fear, praying that none of the sex providers on her payroll had crossed any state lines. God, she hoped they were all from Pennsylvania. She didn't need to be slapped with an additional charge of conspiracy to sex-traffic across state lines. What else could they pin on her? She wondered. Ms. Landers had most likely sustained some pretty bad injuries from that fall. *Oh, Christ! They're going to hit me up with assault and battery charges, as well!*

What was going to happen to her? Would she be thrown in one of those country-club, white-collar-crime-type prisons, or would she be treated like an average Joe and sent to a women's penitentiary? Oh, Jesus. Where was Maxwell? She wouldn't make it very long behind bars. She fully intended to take Sumi down with her—Harper, too. This was their fault for putting up that website for the specialty menu and bringing unnecessary attention and chaos to Milan's well-run salon. Her place of business was her own private piece of paradise. Now it would be splashed in the headlines. Tarnished and disgraced, forever. Pure Paradise would now be a place for that gaudy double-decker sightseeing bus to make a pit stop so the polyester tourist crowd could point, gawk, and snap pictures to include in their Philadelphia slideshow.

"I don't understand. Uh…what is this about?" Milan feigned innocence, trying to buy herself time to string together a bunch of lies—some sort of alibi.

"We prefer to speak in person, if you don't mind," the agent said.

There was an explosion inside her head—the thunderous detonation of her world collapsing around her.

CHAPTER 32

Where was Sweetie when she needed her? Fast asleep with her phone unplugged, most likely. *Lazy heifer!*

Milan quickly threw several items in an overnight bag—a small tote on wheels. She packed underwear, a pair of jeans, a couple T-shirts. Ballet flats. Casual and comfortable travel wear.

She had no intention of sharing a few facts with the feds. That was out of the question, at least tonight! She had to flee—seek refuge somewhere, get her head together while she got her story straight.

She could kill that fucking Sumi for getting her in this position. She could easily strangle that hussy with her bare hands for creating that scandalous menu. All this drama, including Ms. Landers' concussion, or whatever had happened to the ol' bag, was Sumi's fault.

Milan should have known better than to give an unqualified person so much power. But because she had tried to uplift another person, she'd been destroyed. It was outlandish that an ex-secretary—a virtual nobody—had driven her business into the ground. And now Milan had to scurry out into the cruel world, back on the lam, again. *Fuck!*

She zipped her luggage closed and then remembered she hadn't packed any toiletries. Inside her elaborate bathroom, she scooped up her essential beauty products, the notions and potions she absolutely could not live without.

Then the doorbell rang. "No, no, no!" Milan stamped her foot in time with each word. With her getaway plans foiled, she slid the packed tote on wheels under her massive bed. She checked her appearance and then quickly spritzed her neck with Kimochi. Perhaps the unusual fragrance could entice the agents, woo them senseless with her seductive scent, persuading them to look down another path for the real criminal—some lowlife type who wore stinky, cheap cologne. It was worth a try.

The doorbell rang again. The sound seemed louder, more persistent, and extremely intimidating. She doused her wrists with the fragrance and went downstairs to open her door to two very unwelcome guests.

Milan wore a welcoming smile that was so wide and so fake, her eyes slanted and her face hurt. But this was not a social call. The agents didn't smile back. Their faces were stern and offered not even a semblance of friendliness. They were on official business and made it clear by not cracking a smile or uttering a sound that remotely resembled a greeting.

Both agents flashed gleaming badges encased in leather. Very impressive. But under the circumstances, it was hard to appreciate the badges' high-polished shine. Royce would no doubt have given a canine tooth to sport such an elaborate badge, displaying an eagle on top and the words *Federal Bureau of Investigation*, along with other initials that warned that the bearer of the badge was not to be fucked with.

In Milan's mind, Deputy Dawg and Sumi should be the people the agents wanted to question. It was they, and not Milan, who were responsible for Ms. Landers' injuries. In fact, Milan had personally witnessed Sumi working the woman into a frenzy as she sucked her clit and then Deputy Dawg used his bump-ridden, long-licking tongue to literally throw Ms. Landers over the edge.

I will not take the rap for Sumi and Royce, she vowed inwardly. But her rational mind knew that by being the owner of Pure Paradise, she was going to take a hard fall. She swallowed the knot of fear that had formed in her throat.

"Good evening," she said pleasantly, her insides quivering as she willed her knees to stay still and stop knocking together.

"Good evening, Ms. Walden," said a ruddy-complexioned agent with intense brown eyes. The other agent merely nodded.

Milan gestured for them to enter. They crossed the threshold, wearing somber expressions.

Inside the foyer, the ruddy-faced guy said, "I'm Agent Whitaker." His intense eyes seemed to be in motion, darting about and already searching for clues. He made Milan nervous.

"This is agent Pulliam," Agent Whitaker introduced in his official no-nonsense tone, and nodded toward his partner, a tall man with hazel eyes and a receding hairline. Agent Pulliam gave Milan a quick smile. Her eyes moved from Pulliam to Whitaker. *Good cop, bad cop*, Milan decided.

"Why don't we sit in the great room," she suggested with a pleasing smile, and motioned them to follow her. She allowed a little suggestive sway to her hips, just in case the two agents could be bought off with sexual favors of the kinky kind. She'd do anything to save her neck and there was nothing beneath her at this point. Her basement was a few feet away, fully equipped with freaky furniture and loads of gadgets.

The agents took in her opulent surroundings: the plush furnishings, the marble floors, the artwork, the floor-to-ceiling Palladian windows, and the magnificent fireplace. Instead of looking impressed, both men appeared offended. Their eyes moved suspiciously from one item to the next inside the vast room, as if all her possessions were the result of ill-gotten gain. Their eyes were appraising and calculating as if they were ready to start the bidding to auction off furniture, personal effects, any and every one of her undeserved goods.

Trying to appear calm, she offered the agents a seat as she eased down and reclined on a long, beige couch.

Whitaker pulled his resentful dark eyes away from the oil paintings. "We prefer to stand. This won't take long."

Great! She was antsy as hell but managed to look poised while she waited for the quickie inquisition to begin. Her teeth chattered and then it occurred to her that a drink might calm her down. She hopped off the sofa and headed toward the liquor cart on the other side of the room.

"Can I offer you gentlemen something to drink?" she asked sweetly.

"No, thank you," both agents answered in unison. The impatience in their tones was evident.

Well, she sure needed a drink. Hopefully, a couple sips would steady her nerves. She picked up a crystal bottle that contained the hard stuff—scotch. She poured and drank it straight, draining the glass quickly and then reaching for the bottle for a refill. Scotch whiskey did not suit her palate, but the nasty, bitter-tasting liquor would calm her nerves much quicker than her preferred libation.

"Ms. Walden, when is the last time you spoke to Maxwell Torrance?" Agent Whitaker asked.

In the midst of swallowing, she choked on the scotch. Giving the agent a quizzical look, Milan shrugged and continued hacking and coughing. Finally, the hacking subsided. "Maxwell?" she asked, totally bewildered as to how Maxwell fit into the scheme of things.

"Yes, his cell phone records indicate that he speaks to you often. However, we want to know if he's been recently—"

"Is he here now?" Agent Pulliam piped in.

"No, he's not here. He hasn't been here in three or four days. He's on a business trip in Japan." Milan looked at both agents questioningly. "What's this about?"

The FBI agents exchanged glances. Pulliam cleared his throat. "His private jet crashed and—"

Milan placed her glass on the liquor cart. She felt woozy. "Oh my God," she murmured, though she felt not a trace of grief. With Maxwell's money on her mind, Milan threw the back of her hand against her forehead. She felt nauseous and faint. "Maxwell's dead?" She shook her head in disbelief. She wouldn't be getting that twenty-five million dollars she was counting on. *Stupid, stupid, stupid!* She should have pushed for marriage. If she were his wife, she'd be rolling in billions and dancing a happy jig right now. There'd be no shame in her game. If she were legally married to Maxwell, her hands would be planted on her small hips while she launched into a convincing imitation of *Riverdance*, clicking her heels and skipping about right in these agents' stern faces. Is it a crime to celebrate the death of an irritating spouse? She thought not.

But she wasn't his wife. *Damn, damn, damn!* She picked up her drink and took a swig.

Tears rolled from her eyes, blurring her vision as she staggered to the closest seat, a regal, pale-gold silk wing chair, which she flopped upon in an undignified manner, scotch splashing out on the arm of the elegant chair. "I can't believe Maxwell's dead," she murmured in shock, body slumped, legs stretched and splayed over the loss of all that money.

"Well, ma'am. We suspect he's still alive," Agent Whitaker said.

Hope straightened her shoulders. "What do you mean?"

"We found the wreckage of his private jet, his ID, but not a trace of Mr. Torrance," Agent Whitaker spoke without emotion.

"That's good news, right?" Milan asked, looking from one agent to the other, waiting for confirmation.

"At this point, we're not sure, Ms. Walden." He squinted as if struck by a sudden thought. "By the way, what is your relationship with Mr. Torrance?"

"He's my, uh…we…er…we're involved."

"Romantically?"

"I guess you could say that."

"You guess?" Pulliam wondered dubiously.

"We had an uncommitted, uh, relationship."

"Sexual?"

"Yes, but what does that have to do with anything?"

"Did you receive monetary benefits for these sex acts?"

Milan took a gulp from the glass and then sat upright in a proper position. Enough was enough, dammit. No way was she going to allow them to label her as a hooker. "I'm not a prostitute," she said, lips pursed.

"I didn't say that, ma'am. Just trying to get to the facts."

She wanted to start cussing in indignation, but these FBI guys had a lot of power. It wouldn't benefit her to get loud and self-righteous with them the way she was itching to. So Milan collected herself and forced herself to speak in a cordial manner. "Yes, Maxwell was a generous man. He gave me monetary gifts from time to time. I want you to understand that all his generosity was strictly out of the kindness of his heart."

"How'd he pay...cash, checks?" Pulliam said abruptly.

"Uh..." Milan knew the answer but paused to think, wondering if her response would get her into trouble.

"Ms. Walden?"

"Wire transfer. He, uh, usually transferred money into my business account. But why do you want to know that?"

Both agents shared a significant glance.

Whitaker's eyes darkened even more. "It has been discovered that Mr. Torrance has been involved in insider trading, embezzlement, and misappropriation of several employee pension funds. As you know, Mr. Torrance is the CEO and sits on the board of a number of corporations both here in the States and overseas. Until we unravel this mess, there will be a freeze on all of your business accounts and personal bank accounts, Ms. Walden."

A freeze! Not again! Oh, how she hated that word, especially when it was associated with her money. Why, why, why didn't she learn a lesson from the last time she'd gotten in financial trouble? She should have put at least a million inside a hidden safe. She'd been so blinded by her social status, she didn't see this coming and, therefore, didn't even have the foresight to have some cash tucked away—sewn inside her mattress, or hidden in secret places behind the gilded frames that adorned her walls.

"You can't take my money," she blurted. "I have my own business. A legitimate business. I need access to my funds. I have employees who expect to be paid their wages on time...this is so un-American," she cried.

Whitaker looked grim. "Are you speaking of Pure Paradise?"

"Yes, that's *my* salon."

Pulliam cleared his throat. "Actually, it isn't."

Milan scowled. "You're misinformed. I am the sole proprietor of Pure Paradise."

The agents' expressions hardened. Uncomprehending, her eyes wide with dread, Milan looked back and forth, searching their faces for enlightenment. But no light shone from their eyes. Sensing doom, Milan rose from the chair and moved toward the liquor cart where she poured more scotch, filling her glass to the brim. Squeezing her eyes shut, she guzzled down the awful-tasting whiskey.

CHAPTER 33

"**M**axwell Torrance was the sole proprietor," Agent Pulliam revealed. "You were just a front he used for tax purposes. According to our records, Pure Paradise was gifted to Sumi Cranston over a week ago. She may possibly be involved in—"

Milan didn't hear the rest of the sentence. Her brain shut down right after they announced that Sumi owned Pure Paradise. In a state of shock, she slumped in the beautiful wing chair.

"Ms. Walden," Whitaker said coldly, "don't leave town. We have to ask you to stay in the immediate area while this investigation is being conducted." She nodded dumbly, still stunned that Maxwell had pulled a fast one that caused her to lose access to her money.

She checked her Pure Paradise accounts online and thanks to the heads up from the agents, she didn't have a heart attack when she discovered most of the money had been withdrawn from those accounts two days ago. *Damn you, Maxwell!*

Then she checked her personal funds. Her palms became damp,

her heart rate accelerated, as she spied all the zeros that indicated her millions were still safe inside her account. For now. It was money she'd acquired when she ended her engagement to the so-called wealthy Noah Brockington. That relationship had really been a trip. Milan shook her head. Her life was like a soap opera. Perhaps one day, when she was settled and could think straight, she'd write a book about her disastrous dealings with wealthy men. She'd call it *A Bona Fide Gold Digger*. Now, that was a hot title, if she said so herself. She'd write it explicit, with graphic sex scenes scorching the pages. She'd provide complete details of her sexcapades, starting with the anonymous sex she used to have at the private sex club Tryst. With all the kinky sex she'd indulged in, her book was bound to be a red-hot, page-turner.

Milan laughed at herself. A couple of years ago, she'd entertained the idea of writing a how-to book: *Weekend Escape: Your Spa at Home*, which she'd never written. Now she was toying with the idea of writing erotica. She really had a decadent, steamy, spicy story to tell. *Someday*, she promised herself and returned her thoughts to the dire matters at hand.

The feds said they were going to freeze all of her accounts. Should she try to beat them to it by switching the money to an off-shore account? She needed Maxwell for that kind of wheeling and dealing and Maxwell was no longer on her side. Milan felt like crying. No matter how hard she tried to scheme and maneuver, someone else always ended up on top. And this time it was Sumi! Someone she'd never expected to have a hidden agenda. Sumi had played her, pretending to be lovesick, whipping Maxwell's ass just to endear herself. Dishonest people were absolutely sickening.

Fuming, she called Sumi repeatedly, determined to curse her out and let her know that she was aware of her treachery, but Sumi ignored her calls. The sneaky little bitch! Milan seriously hoped that the FBI was hounding the tycoon-thieving, salon-stealing, no-good, cunt-clenching slut as badly as they were hounding her.

In a rotten frame of mind, Milan picked up the phone and started poking buttons, trying to get a hold of Royce. That Deputy Dawg-looking, dirty, deceitful dreg of the earth deserved to be cursed out, ghetto-style. And fired! She'd pretend that she still owned the place and give him his walking papers over the phone. But to her great disappointment, her call went straight to Royce's voicemail. *Bastard!*

Grief-stricken over losing her business and intoxicated from too much alcohol, she climbed into bed and turned on CNN. Maybe there was some news relating to the plane crash. *Please don't let his body turn up*, she prayed. If he were still alive, per-haps he'd get in touch with her. If that happened, Milan was sure she could use her powers of persuasion to convince him to give her a couple million—strictly cash, of course. But what leverage did she have? Nothing. He'd stolen her business and given it to Sumi, no doubt as payment for giving him such a sound thrashing in Milan's dungeon. No wonder Sumi was arriv-ing for work late, taking long lunch breaks, and always acting distracted. She probably had Maxwell tied up in her apartment where she beat his ass numerous times a day just to keep him addicted. Harper had provided him with strap-on dick, but on Sumi's orders. It was simply unbelievable that Sumi had stolen Milan's very own billionaire slave.

She wondered if Maxwell was using the sexual services of

Royce as well? Milan should have known that Royce and Sumi were too close for comfort when he slithered into the massage room and licked Ms. Landers' pussy with his abnormal tongue.

Milan hoped Ms. Landers sued Sumi for all she was worth. Hell, she'd go to court with the woman and testify on her behalf. Oooh, she'd like to wrap her hands around Sumi's slender neck. Given a chance, she'd choke the shit out of the slimy little twit.

Angrily, Milan threw back another mouthful of scotch. Her blurred gaze traveled to the TV. She caught the tail end of a newsflash scrolling across the bottom of the screen. Had she seen Maxwell's name? The words went by so fast, it was hard to tell.

If she wanted to know whether Maxwell had been found dead or alive, she'd have to stay alert and wait for the anchorman to announce it while simultaneously keeping her eyes focused at the bottom of the screen to catch the scrolling text.

Without meaning to, she'd become emotionally attached to Hilton. She'd turned soft and had given Sumi too much power. Now she was in a terrible predicament. Lost in her thoughts, she missed the scrolling text at the bottom again. She caught the word *plane* at the end of the newsreport. *Shit!* She'd have to wait until tomorrow. She'd be better equipped to deal with Maxwell's plane crash and her frozen assets when she was nice and sober.

But at the moment, she was happy to dull her pain. Milan tilted the glass to her lips, only a few drops left. Irritated, she made the trek downstairs, stumbling and bumping into furniture on her path to the liquor cart. She grabbed the crystal container and held it to her chest as she carefully made her way back upstairs.

Feeling morose and alone, she crawled into bed with the bottle of scotch. Tears, seemingly from nowhere, filled her eyes as she drank straight from the container. *What the hell am I going to do now?* Her money would be frozen for weeks, months, maybe years to come, leaving her destitute once again. She'd gone full circle. Over a year ago, she'd been booted out of Pure Paradise by the board of directors, accused of falsifying her credentials (which she had but that really shouldn't have been such a big deal) and accused of stealing money (which technically she had, but that too was minor as far as Milan was concerned). Those bastards had threatened her with jail time and sent her running, had her out on the lam. Then she came back, with Maxwell as her henchman, fired the board, and took over Pure Paradise. Now, that was justice. So, why, oh why was she back in the same position—ass out with frozen bank accounts?

She put the bottle down, curled up, and draped a cover around herself, wishing she were wrapped in Hilton's protective arms. She wanted to call him so badly it hurt, but she balled her fist, restraining herself from picking up the phone. Hearing his deep voice would be a comfort. But who knew what drunken outpouring of love would spill from her lips? Yes, she was intoxicated but still cognizant enough to know that calling Hilton was a bad idea. His one-word text message conveyed that he wasn't ready to talk...he still needed some time and some space between them to come to terms about how he really felt about her.

If he didn't make the cut, which she was certain he wouldn't, she was willing to start out fresh with him. They could start a business—work together. Even with her money on hold, she could sell some of her assets. Hell, she could sell her home. She'd buy a smaller one. It sucked the way the housing crisis might force her to sell her chateau for less than its value. But she'd take the loss. For Hilton. For their future together.

She laughed at herself for having the audacity to envision a fairy-tale, happily-ever-after ending. Her track record didn't bode well for true love or any kind of long-lasting happiness. It was quite comical that she hoped Hilton would come to her rescue and infuse her with the love she'd needed her entire life.

But she could dream, couldn't she?

CHAPTER 34

The pounding in her head was unbearable. It was one of the worst hangovers of her life. But then last night had been one of the worst nights of her life.

She limped to her bathroom, looking for aspirin or something to ease the pain. She stopped moving and stood thoughtfully in the door frame of the luxurious marble and chrome paradise that was her personal bathroom. Something was wrong. What? Aside from the throbbing headache, she felt edgy. Bad dreams, perhaps. No, something really horrible must have gone down for her to get sloshed to the point of forgetfulness.

The phone rang. She picked up the extension in the bathroom without identifying the caller. "Hello?"

"Hey, Milan." It was Sweetie. Her tone was somber, like she was depressed. Milan was not in the mood for another lecture about what she should be doing for their mother. "Bad news, girl."

Milan braced herself for what felt like something worse than their mother's gardening problems. She still hadn't made it to the medicine cabinet to find some relief for her pounding head.

"What's wrong?" Milan flinched. The vibration of her own voice worsened the pain.

"Ya boy Hilton Dorsey ain't in the lineup with the Eagles," Sweetie announced with hostility. "Quantez checked it out."

"I said he was trying out," Milan defended meekly.

"Rookies and selected veterans already reported to training camp. They had their first practice. The remaining team members are reporting tomorrow; they're about to prepare for the first pre-season game. Quantez said that Hilton Dorsey is not in the lineup."

Milan was silent; she didn't know what to say.

"Ya boy's been talking a bunch of crap; blowing your head up with lies. He's still living in the past. Trippin'! He gotta be crazy if he thinks he's ever gonna play for the NFL again. Quantez said the boy blew out his knee something terrible. Irreparable damage! He says everyone knows Dorsey's knee injury ended his career. He might have a chance with some corny overseas league, but he told you that he was picked up by the Eagles and that's a damn lie!" Sweetie sounded furious. And her anger wasn't over her sister being misled. Milan realized that Sweetie was fuming over the Eagles game tickets that she wanted for Quantez. "Dorsey had to hang up his spikes for good and he knows it. I don't know why the man is faking like he's in some big negotiations for a deal."

Milan sighed. She had no idea why Hilton had concocted the story. In fact, if memory served correctly, it was Hilton himself who told her about his failed career. Back when he first started driving for her, over a year ago, he'd felt the need to explain his humbled position in life and told her that he was a former NFL player and had sustained a knee injury that ended his career.

Yup, those were his exact words, she recalled. So, why was

he so hell bent on getting in playing shape and why was he so upset that Milan had expressed doubt about him getting back in the game? *Beats me!* Football players must be like boxers—won't believe it's over until they're too punch drunk to know right from left. Milan crept up to the marble vanity and slowly slid open the mirrored medicine cabinet, afraid that quick movements would exacerbate her headache.

There were troublesome thoughts flitting at the back of her mind—something far worse than Hilton's lie. She squinted as she shook out two pain killers into her palm and returned to her bedroom for bottled water that she kept on hand. She spotted the nearly empty crystal bottle next to the bed, evidence that something was really, really wrong. Milan enjoyed wine—only the best when she was out in public, but behind closed doors she preferred the cheap, sweet stuff. So, why had she drunk herself into oblivion with scotch when she abhorred its bitter taste?

"You still there?" Sweetie yelled.

"Yes. Stop hollering, Sweetie. I have a hangover. A bad one."

"So, whatchu think your lying boyfriend is up to? Umph, pretending to play for the Eagles...that's pitiful. Quantez was all hyped, thinking we were gonna be getting season tickets and shit until I told him ya man's name. But he still went online and checked it out, just in case there was a grain of truth to ya boy's story."

Under different circumstances, Milan and her sister would have mulled over Hilton's lie together. They would have tried to make some sense of things, but at that moment, Milan had a sudden flash of memory—and the images that blazed across her mind were downright awful. The FBI had paid her a visit.

She couldn't remember all the details, but she saw vividly the alarming flash of their badges. What had they wanted? Whatever it was had her still quivering inside. Something about Maxwell! she suddenly recalled. Then it hit her: The dirt bag pervert had faked a plane crash and had absconded with millions as if he needed more money than he already had. Greedy! He was, plain and simple, purely greedy.

And Sumi, the slut, had assisted Maxwell in ripping Milan's precious salon from under her. It was unfathomable that the little twit was that shrewd, but sadly, it was true. Milan should have seen it coming. Hell hath no fury like a woman scorned. She'd played with Sumi's emotions, and Sumi hit her where it hurt. Her bank account.

The feds said she was not and had never been the true owner of Pure Paradise and now her precious salon belonged to Sumi. Sumi! A lowly, fuckin' assistant had outmaneuvered Milan.

"Milan! Why do you keep zoning out on me? When you gon' call your lying boyfriend and ask if he's at least in touch with some of the real players? Quantez had his heart set on those free tickets."

Milan didn't know how to respond. Her mind was on something else entirely. "I have to go, Sweetie. I'll call you back," she said abruptly and hung up.

She'd lost Pure Paradise. She eased herself down and sat on the side of her bed, trying to come to grips with the uncovered information. *I lost Pure Paradise. My precious business.* Like last night, the pain was felt at a visceral level. Milan could imagine the horror of having Alzheimer's; she felt like a victim of the disease as she recalled the horror of last night all over again. She continued to sit, without a clue about what she should do.

Check on your money, she told herself and called her bank.

The representative who took her call was extremely courteous and told her in the cheeriest, most friendly tone that the bank had been ordered to put a hold on her accounts.

"For how long?" Milan said in a weak voice

"I'm sorry, ma'am. We don't have that information. Normally, we'd tell you to get in touch with your creditors and try to make arrangements on the late payments."

"I don't make late payments."

"I'm aware of that, ma'am. Your case is a federal matter. The government has put a seizure on your bank accounts. All I can suggest is that you be patient and wait."

I don't have any money! I don't have any money! she thought repeatedly. It was preposterous. *Don't panic*, she told herself. *Everything is going to turn out all right.* She bit down on her bottom lip. *How?* She didn't know. *When?* Real soon, she hoped. *Change your focus*, she suggested to herself and had an instant image of Pure Paradise, desolate and padlocked. It was a sad sight, even in her mind.

Milan had to see her business shut down with her own eyes. She showered and dressed and called her driver. To her utter dismay, his phone was disconnected. Damn, the driver was on Maxwell's payroll. Milan shook her head. She'd have to get used to wheeling herself around from now on or at least until Maxwell was smoked out of this hiding place. After she was granted access to her money, she'd hire another driver. Outside her front door, she released a huge sigh when she saw her Rolls sparkling in the sunshine, untouched by the feds. It was a miracle! Then she remembered they probably hadn't taken it because it was gift from Maxwell and the title was in her name as was the deed to her home. Thank God!

But her jubilation was short-lived. When she rolled up in the parking lot of Pure Paradise, she couldn't believe her eyes. No padlocks, no warning signs that the business had been shut down. The parking lot was filled with luxury cars. And even worse, she could see Royce, his jowls swinging as he smiled, nodded, and greeted the high-society lunch crowd. He was acting as if it was business as usual, meeting and greeting the clients in the manner in which he was trained—by Milan, who sometimes rewarded him by letting him take his twenty-minute break under her lavish desk where he gave her one of his famous lick-downs.

My desk! Milan pictured Sumi sitting behind her custom desk and felt on the verge of a nervous breakdown.

If Milan didn't love her vehicle so much and if she still had money to burn, she would have stepped on the gas pedal and driven her Rolls straight through the plate glass window and plowed Deputy Dawg down, and then driven up the escalator straight to her former office, taking down whomever and whatever was in her path.

Sumi could pull out every martial arts trick in the book, it wouldn't do her a bit of good. Once Milan got ghetto on her ass, that slimy thief wouldn't be able to do anything but plead for mercy and beg for her life.

Her delicious reverie was interrupted by the ring of her cell phone, which she had trouble locating in her stunning and rare, oversized Chanel hobo bag. By the time she retrieved the phone, it had stopped ringing. A few moments later, she was shocked to discover a message—left by Hilton.

Nervous and jittery, she could barely remember her passcode. She pushed a series of wrong numbers until she finally got it right. "I'll catch up with you a little later," he said in his deep, silky voice. Hilton paused and released a sigh. "Miss you, baby," he admitted, his voice dropping even deeper.

I miss you, too! Hearing his voice was healing. It made her feel tingly and warm all over. She could feel her anger toward Sumi, Royce, and Maxwell dissipating as she pulled out of the lot and cruised into traffic. They no longer mattered. Fuck 'em; her mind was on her man.

CHAPTER 35

When it came to vanilla relationships, Milan didn't know zip. All of her liaisons had been kinky, adventurous explorations without emotional commitment. Her encounters could be described as sexual skydiving—risky, exciting, and dangerous. She'd had countless fuckfests with both genders. In her world of decadent sex, no promises of true love were ever made.

She could really use some sisterly advice. Despite Sweetie's numerous flaws, she knew all about love and relationships. Sweetie had a good husband who loved her and their two bad brats. Sweetie and Quantez had been in love since high school. They were so into each other, it was sickening, but Milan was ready to take the plunge and commit to the same type of nauseating devotion—if Hilton would have her. She didn't care if he had a football contract or not. He could have the position of the team's water boy and her love would not diminish. Wow! She really loved her some Hilton. *Love.* The word sounded good, made her heart feel good, and distracted her from her problems.

She would have loved to consult with her sister to find out the rules in the vanilla world, but Sweetie would most likely give her the brush-off or berate her for falling for a NFL has-been. Quantez took his sports seriously and if Hilton couldn't help him get Eagles tickets, Milan doubted that Sweetie would offer anything other than criticism.

She was so anxious to talk to him; to tell him she was sorry for hurting his feelings. Hmm. Maybe she shouldn't reopen that can of worms. Should she return Hilton's call? Or wait until he felt the urge to hear her voice again? She was so green in the rules of love. The last time she'd fallen hard for a man, it was her strict trainer, Gerard. She'd played herself and blown up his phone. He didn't like being pestered and had warned her in advance to never call unless she was instructed to do so. She'd disobeyed and hounded him mercilessly. Gerard had no qualms about expressing his disapproval. He punished her severely for exhibiting such obstinate behavior. Recalling the hot candle wax that her trainer had dripped on her shaven pussy made Milan cringe.

But that was a lifetime ago. That Milan was a different person, lovesick and submissive. This Milan was in love. She wanted a healthy relationship.

She stopped for a red light and mindlessly watched a couple crossing the street, holding hands. How sweet. She'd never done that with anyone. Public displays of affection were as unfamiliar to her as discount shopping. In fact, anything other than fucking for the sake of getting off was completely foreign to her. She and Hilton had flirted with the idea of being a romantic couple, but she'd blown it before their affair was even off the ground.

She imagined holding hands with Hilton and became instantly flushed and goosebumpy. The light changed and honking horns snapped Milan to attention. Okay, what did she have to do to be a part of regular society? Get honest. With herself. And with Hilton.

Inside her chateau, Milan dropped her bag and immediately returned Hilton's call, holding her breath as she listened to his phone ring.

"Hey, baby," he answered, making Milan feel so welcome and wanted.

"Hi," she said shyly.

"I want to apologize—"

"You do?"

"Yeah, for acting like a jerk. I acted real immature at your crib the last time I saw you."'

Really? She thought she owed him an apology. "That's okay. I hit a touchy subject. It was real insensitive of me, but as you surely must know, sensitivity is not one of my strong points." She inhaled. "But I'm working on it, Hilton. I really am."

"You were keeping it real. Don't even worry about it, baby."

Baby! Oh, how she loved the way he called her *baby*.

"Look, I called because I got some good news, a reason to celebrate."

Was he celebrating being a water boy? Okay, she'd stick to her promise and support him in whatever he did. Water boy, team mascot, whatever. She knew for a fact he wasn't on the team. *Do water boys get free tickets?* she wondered on her brother-in-law's behalf.

"Management is making the big announcement tomorrow, but I'd like to have a private celebration with you tonight. Wanna clink champagne glasses with me, baby?" he asked, his voice low and deadly sexy.

Of course, she wanted to celebrate with him. Whatever he was celebrating was inconsequential.

"Think you could make a trip to…" He paused and then laughed. "Feel like making a trip to Bethlehem, Pennsylvania? I know it's the sticks…can't compare to Paris, but that's where I am and I'd love it if you were here with me. If just for one night."

"Who needs Paris?" she said sincerely. "I'm there!" She'd be unafraid to show the burning desire, as well as the love that was stored up in her heart. Milan was going to whip it on him. She and Na-Na missed Hilton and Big Hammer real bad. Love and lust were a powerful combination. She'd have to try to control herself because she was liable to kill Hilton, fuck him to death with her overzealous way of showing him love.

Bethlehem, PA—the Eagles training camp was only about an hour-and-a-half drive from Philly's Main Line, where Milan lived. She did a quick happy dance and mentally started packing. Then her heart sank as she remembered the tote under her bed. With that imagery came the warning from the feds: *"Don't leave town."*

Oh, shit! Would the feds consider a sixty-mile trip as leaving town? She didn't know and seriously didn't care. She had to be with her man. Fuck the feds. They'd already disrupted her life as bad as anyone could by stopping her cash flow. Could they lock her up for spending the night in Bethlehem? She doubted it. And if they could, so be it. Being with the love of her life was worth a day or two behind bars. And she meant that shit with all her heart.

"What time does the party start?" she asked, her tone playfully flip.

"Are you really coming?"

"I wouldn't dream of blowing a chance to make amends with you."

"You don't have to—"

"Shhh. I want to make it up to you. I should have been more supportive of your dreams. And I'm sorry," she said softly. "Now, tell me...when and where?"

After Hilton filled her in with the pertinent details, Milan hung up. She ran to her bedroom and yanked the tote from under the bed. She replaced the casual wear she'd planned to escape with for slinky and sexy. She tossed out the ballet flats and tucked in a pair of fuck-me-all-night stilettos.

The drive to Bethlehem, Pennsylvania was surprisingly pleasant. She used the time to fantasize about her private celebration with Hilton. Along with the triple X-rated scenarios that flitted through her mind, her heart was filled with love. Sex combined with love would be a strange and exhilarating experience and Milan could hardly wait.

When she finally arrived and strolled inside the hotel lobby, she took a deep breath and touched her heart and then called Hilton's room. "I'm here," she said softly, her tone deliberately nonchalant. She wanted to jump and shout with joy, but Milan maintained her composure.

"You're in the lobby?" Hilton sounded excited.

"Uh-huh."

"I'll be right down."

Nervous jitters didn't come close to describing the quivering and quaking that shook her insides as she watched the bank of elevators like a hawk.

She saw him the moment the elevator doors slid open. Hilton exited the elevator, looking elegant and as well put together as a Sean John model coming down the runway. Her heart skipped, her pulse became erratic. He was gut wrenchingly-handsome. Sure, Milan knew the man was fine but she'd never seen him dressed up and looking so debonair! *Whew!* Her coochie caught a quick fit—it got so hot, she was sure that sparks flared up. Milan wanted to bend down and fan between her legs but keeping up a ladylike appearance, she cautiously squeezed her thighs together and extinguished the imaginary flames.

In a dark gray tailored suit, cream-colored dress shirt, a colorful silk tie, and matching pocket square, he was totally GQ. From his low-cut fade down to the high-shine leather shoes, Hilton looked extra fly.

Hilton scanned the lobby, his handsome face set in a serious expression. When he spotted her, he broke into a thousand-watt smile and hurried toward her.

Milan pressed her lips together to keep from giggling like a girl. *Oh, the hell with it; appearances be damned*, she decided and let out a shriek of delight. She was happier than she could ever remember being and could no longer contain her joy. Rejecting any semblance of keeping her cool, she threw caution to the wind and ran briskly to meet her man.

Right there in a public area, they smothered each other in kisses. "You look beautiful. Ooo, I missed you, girl," Hilton murmured, running a hand over the swell of her derriere.

No Chanel showing, nor the best seats in her favorite restaurant, not even receiving the VIP treatment aboard Maxwell's private jet—nothing she'd ever experienced had made her as blissfully happy as she felt at this moment.

Hilton beckoned a bellhop. "Take her bag to room 1907," he said and handed the young man a tip. Then he told Milan, "We have dinner reservations." He shook his sleeve to check the time; his sparkling cufflinks twinkled in the light. With an arm around her waist, he steered Milan out of the lobby and out to a waiting car. "I tried to get in touch with your driver to tell him to—"

"I don't have a driver. He quit," she said and then faked a laugh, trying to make light of the subject.

"He quit?" Hilton scowled, looking peeved enough to punch out her driver. "He just left you hanging? Why'd he quit?"

"I'll explain later," she said as the driver of the Lincoln Town Car got out, smiled, and opened the door. Milan slid in and Hilton got in beside her, sitting close. He smelled good, she noticed, enjoying his closeness and somewhat awed that she and Hilton had never shared the backseat of a car before.

Hilton scrunched his lips together, concerned. "And how'd you get here?"

"I drove," she said matter-of-factly.

He looked surprised.

"Anything for you," she answered. The sincerity of her words shone in her eyes.

The restaurant was nice enough. It was most likely the best in the Lehigh Valley area. In the past year she'd enjoyed fine dining all over the world but had never felt so at ease and satisfied with her surroundings as she did right now.

Hilton pulled out her chair. This gentlemanly action that was previously part of his job description was now done from the heart. Milan was touched. "Thank you," she said, enjoying the chivalrous behavior.

"Would you like something from the bar?" the waiter asked.

Milan was no wine connoisseur, but she knew enough to speak the jargon and to choose the perfect wine to complement a meal. Her mind scrolled through her mental Rolodex of words associated with wine: *vintage, crisp, full-bodied viscosity.* Prepared to impress the waiter with her vast knowledge, she leaned forward and fixed her lips to describe her preferences, but Hilton patted her hand, hushing her before she could speak.

"She'll have a glass of white wine. Nothing dry," Hilton quickly added, speaking on Milan's behalf. "In fact, bring a bottle of White Zinfandel." He glanced at Milan, gauging her reaction, expecting her to protest. She didn't.

Surprisingly, she wasn't insulted by Hilton's take-charge manner, nor did she feel ashamed that he'd publicly exposed her preference for cheap wine. All was well in her world. Hilton could have ordered a bottle of Thunderbird, and she wouldn't have flinched if the waiter served it in a plastic cup. Milan sent the waiter an agreeable smile and then gazed at Hilton, the sparkle in her eyes telling him that she was happy to defer to him.

"And you, sir? What will you be having?" the waiter asked.

"I'll have what she's having." He winked at Milan. They both knew he preferred beer.

"Thank you; I'll be right back with your order." The waiter left.

"Thanks for ordering for me."

"I hope it didn't bother you." he said, unsure whether or not her remark was facetious. "I want you to enjoy yourself, baby. You're with me. No need to put on airs and to suffer through that dry, nasty stuff you drink when you're feeling the need to impress."

"I'll admit, having a man take charge is a different experience for me, but I liked it, I really did. I found it extremely gallant."

Pleased that he'd made the right move, he nodded and relaxed in his chair. The waiter returned and uncorked the wine and poured the pale liquid into the stemware.

Hilton held up his glass. "Let's make a toast."

Beaming, Milan sat up and uncrossed her legs. Eagerly, she lifted her glass.

Then a somber look crossed Hilton's face, changing his expression from animated to serious. "To no more bullshit," he said, his toast throwing Milan for a loop.

Milan's smile became tight and then faded. Disappointed, she lowered her arm. Stunned, she asked, "What? What are you talking about?" She'd been prepared to hear a romantic promise, forgiveness for her previous bad behavior and unsavory past, an oath of devotion—a long speech pertaining to true love.

"This is a new beginning. Let's make this pledge. I'm into you, baby, but if we expect to take this to the next level, you gotta cut the bullshit. You have to get honest and start being yourself."

She'd been fake and manipulative for so long, she wondered if she were capable of getting honest. She toyed with her drink, ran her fingertip around the rim of the glass. Shame whirled inside her. With her head held low, she battled to keep her emotions from appearing on her face.

"You're absolutely right and I've been given a couple of reality checks that have brought me down to earth—"

"Can we make the toast?" His expression was stern and his brash tone cut off her unnecessary rambling.

"Okay." She raised her glass. "To no more bullshit." There

was no hesitation this time. Her voice did not waver. What was the point? Her life kept falling apart. Money came and money went. Life was an unpredictable fight and she was bone tired of getting knocked down, clawing her way back up, only to get beat down again. She was weary of the fight, prepared to throw in the towel. She wanted to be enveloped inside Hilton's strong arms and protected from future harm. His position with the team, whatever it was, didn't matter. Nothing mattered except being in his life. Milan's freaky playing days with multiple partners was over. She'd always be a freak, but she wanted to share her freaky sex acts with Hilton, exclusively. She hoped Hilton felt the same.

Immediately after Milan and Hilton clinked their glasses together, the waiter reappeared with menus and began to rattle off specials. Milan didn't hear a word he said. Her thoughts were on her rapidly changing life. In the blink of an eye, she had agreed to put her own wishes aside. In order to get her relationship with Hilton off the ground and running, she'd kept her mouth shut and deferred to him.

And it didn't hurt her pride. Not in the least. A quick study, Milan realized that if she wanted to keep this man, she'd have to come to accept that being in a relationship would require a willingness to compromise, communicate, and at times—such as tonight—she'd have to concede.

Milan drifted back to their numerous, meaningless sexual encounters. In the beginning, she'd only wanted Hilton for a quick sex fix. She wanted to be in charge of his dick. Demand it whenever she wanted it. But Hilton would not give in, refused to allow her to put him on an invisible leash. He called the shots, doling out dick as he saw fit. And somewhere along the way, her heart...her emotions got caught up. Pretending that all she wanted from him was an occasional fuck became an impossible deception to keep up.

Lost in thought, she came back to the moment when she felt Hilton's eyes on her, studying her.

"What?"

"There are a couple of problems. This thing you have going on with Torrance—I know he keeps your finances tight, but I want you to end it."

"It's over."

He gave her an odd look. "Care to elaborate?"

"The FBI came to my house. They said Maxwell stole a bundle...billions of dollars from his corporations and then faked his death. They found his crashed private plane. No bodies were found, just Maxwell's ID."

Hilton reared back, shocked. "Damn! Dude was already stackin' billions—why'd he have to steal more?"

Milan shrugged. "Maybe he took a big hit when the stock market started declining. I really don't know. They froze my bank accounts." She took a deep sip of wine and swallowed. "Turns out Maxwell stole Pure Paradise right from under me and then turned around and gave it to my assistant as a gift. Sumi owns my salon," Milan said in a matter-of-fact tone.

Hilton touched her hand gently. "You okay?"

Milan nodded and forced a smile. "It's supposed to be a temporary freeze." She gave a small shrug. "They didn't put a lien on my house, so I can always sell it if things get really tough." She shrugged again and smiled bravely. "I doubt if I'd get as much as it's worth...you know...with the housing crisis and all." She took another sip of wine.

Driving to Bethlehem had taken her mind off her frozen bank accounts and her stolen business. She'd hoped her visit with Hilton would keep her thoughts from trailing back to her troublesome situation, but here she was, forced to face her crisis and all she could do was shrug and give a goofy, crooked smile. It was the wine, she figured. Yeah, the wine had her head spinning, had her thinking about a picket fence around a much smaller home and hearing the patter of tiny footsteps. How many glasses of wine had she downed? She had to be drunk as a skunk to be thinking about rugrats. She giggled out loud.

Hilton looked at her, arched a brow, waiting to be let in on her private joke. When she didn't fill him in, he said, "I'm glad you're taking your loss so well."

She brushed her fingers over his hand. "Like I said, it's supposed to be temporary. I refuse to worry about it. Right now, I'm focused on you." There was no mistaking the suggestive tone in her voice. They exchanged a glance. With their eyes, she and Hilton decided dinner could wait. Words were not necessary; it was time to get back to the hotel and fuck.

Hilton drained his glass, stood up, and beckoned the waiter over. "Check, please."

Milan stood, too.

In the backseat of the Town Car, Hilton wrapped an arm around Milan. "We can order room service later," he said and then kissed her deeply.

CHAPTER 36

Fully clothed, Hilton sat on the end of the bed. Still wearing her dress and her heels, Milan stood in front of him, on edge, her heart pumping unmercifully. His hands, so hot she could feel the heat through the fabric of her chiffon dress, cupped her hips and then moved down to the bubble hem. Desire pounded through her veins as he eased her dress up and moved the fabric past her thighs. A vibrating excitement, like a buzzing inside her body, caused her to shake.

He gazed at her lacy lilac thong. "Pretty," he murmured, his breath breezing through the sheer fabric and tickling the lips of her na-na. The sound of his voice was calming and electrifying at once. "So pretty," he repeated in a raspy whisper as he slipped his thumb beneath the fabric and pulled the thong to the side. Her mind was so clouded by lust, she was mystified as to whether his words, "So pretty," referred to her thong or her shaven pussy. Either way, she was flattered and muttered a sound of appreciation. Lil' Na-Na, on the other hand, was not confused. Accepting the compliment, Milan's pussy became instantly inflamed.

Milan's body quaked, her knees felt like they were about to give out, but she steadied herself enough to pitch in, taking over the task of holding up and gathering her dress around her waist while Hilton lowered his head and licked her petals open and then wriggled his tongue inside. It felt so amazing, her toes curled tightly inside her shoes.

He put a lip lock on her coochie, pushed his tongue in as far as it would go, moaning as he tasted her sweetness. *Ah! So good. Too damn good.* Her head lolled back, her arms relaxed and the soft fabric fell, curtaining Hilton's head as he sensually bathed her hot pussy with his honey-moistened tongue.

Her pussy ached with need, but she wasn't ready to cum. Not yet. Abruptly, she pulled her dress up, liberating a man who didn't seem to want his freedom. Ignoring Hilton's perplexed expression, she inched backward. He reached for her; she maneuvered away and sat on the bed next to him. "Hilton," she whispered with adoration and then wrapped her arms around his neck and licked the sheen from his honey-covered lips, distracting him as she unknotted and removed his tie.

Instantly intoxicated by his kiss, which tasted like a mixture of good pussy and sweet wine, Milan became wild and wanton and began groping between his legs. "Take your dick out for me, baby. I wanna see what I've been missing," she coaxed.

Hilton's groan assured her that he enjoyed her aggressiveness. Allowing her to take charge, he quickly unzipped and exposed his manhood, held the quivering shaft, keeping it steady in his grip as he presented it.

Milan got down on her knees and eased inside the space between his legs. At first she marveled at his big, beautiful, suckable dick, and then she covered it with tiny kisses. Her tongue darted out and swiped the cream that dripped from his large glans, and then she commenced to lick his shaft clean.

She pulled the head in and out of her warm mouth. After a few moments, she used her tongue and pushed his phallus out of the cocoon of her moist mouth.

Breathing hard and grabbing the sides of her face, Hilton desperately tried to push the large rounded head of his penis between her lips.

"Pull your pants down, Hilton. I want to show how much I miss Big Hammer." Hilton immediately pulled his pants down to his knees.

Taking charge, Milan pointed to his boxers. "Get rid of those, too. I want total access. No cotton barriers between me and the dick I love." She helped him tug down his boxers, which had a damp circle on the front. "Don't you want me to suck it right?" Milan cooed as she sank down to her knees.

"Oooh, yeah, baby," he groaned as he shoved his boxers down, his face twisted as if in pain.

She caressed Big Hammer and ran the pad on her finger over the branches of throbbing veins that bulged along his shaft. Too worked up to talk, Hilton responded with a grunt. That primal utterance motivated Milan to stroke him until he was hard as granite. Then she opened her mouth wide enough to accommodate his oversized glans. Tenderly, she wrapped her lips around his smooth, wide cap. She marveled at the smoothness, moaned as she welcomed the dick she loved inside her mouth. She never wanted him to leave her again. She'd give him head all night if he wanted her to. She commenced to work her lips, slurping hungrily as if sucking on a delicious, giant-sized, caramel-flavored lollipop. She paused and looked up at Hilton.

"What's wrong, baby?" he inquired.

"Nothing." She licked her lips. "The White Zinfandel was good, but not as good as what you've got. I need a cum shot," she explained and drew him back inside.

Just short of busting while enjoying the sweet warmth of Milan's mouth, Hilton managed to control his urges and pulled out. "I want some na-na, baby," he said as he wedged off his shoes. He stood, shook his pants and boxers off his feet.

Speeding up the process of seeing her man's hard, naked body, Milan worked on the buttons of his shirt.

Nude, Hilton was like chiseled bronze. All his rigorous work-outs had paid off. Her heart fluttered. He was magnificent. She touched her heart, awed that he was hers. At least she hoped so.

"Your turn, baby," he said in the darkened hotel room, which was illuminated only by the light emanating from the sound-less TV. Milan gave a shuddering sigh and then held her arms up as he slid her dress over her head. He eased her down on the bed and kissed her small nipples through the fabric of her bra. "I missed you, girl. Couldn't get you out of my head." He unsnapped her bra and gazed with adoration at her undersized breasts and then licked each nipple until it pearled. He ran his large hands up and down her arms, caressing them as he began to gently suck. He'd never touched her with such tenderness. Her eyes welled.

"Hilton," she said, her voice a whimper. "I'm sorry for the way I treated you. I didn't know how—"

He covered her mouth with his, kissed her as if devouring her. Kissed her with such yearning, tears sprang to her eyes and spilled. He wiped her tears and pulled her into his arms. "Don't cry, baby." She cried harder. "Milan, baby. You didn't do anything to me. You never hurt me. I knew it was just a matter of time before you figured it out."

"Figured out what?"

"That the power trip you were on was feeding your ego, but it wasn't feeding your soul." He lifted her chin and made her look into his eyes. "I dug you the first day I saw your stuck-up ass, but I'm a real man, baby. I wasn't about to put myself out there like that. The way you were treating my boss was scary, baby. I couldn't let myself go out like that. Seemed to me that all you wanted was to put a man on a leash, so I fought the feelings I had for you. It was hard, baby, I wanted you so bad. But it was like a struggle for my manhood every time we got together." He laughed. She laughed too, but the sound was weak, more embarrassed than cheerful.

"I'm different now. My needs are different." She continued swiping tears. "I'm going to take a huge risk and put all my cards on the table. Can I?"

"You can be real with me, Milan."

"My world is constantly collapsing, but I'm so driven...such a survivor, that I always manage to pull it together and rebuild better than before. This latest fiasco with the FBI...I'll get through it. I always manage to."

"I know, baby."

"But I'm tired, Hilton," she whimpered. "My priorities have been so fucked up. I need something real—something lasting."

"Whatchu need, baby?" he whispered.

"I need love. Your love," she admitted and her voice cracked. She could no longer fight the urge to cry. Milan gave in and broke down. Hilton tightened his arms around her, giving her a sample of what it felt like to be protected, to feel safe.

"You're not going to go through this legal bullshit by your-self. I gotchu, Milan. And don't worry about money. I got that, too."

She had yet to ask him about his position with the Eagles. He seemed pleased with whatever job he'd been given. He didn't seem to be worried about money. If he were, Milan was pre-pared to sell her house and hand over the profits to her man.

Shutting off her thoughts, Hilton repositioned Milan. One hand cupped her small buttocks and the other gripped her neck as he covered her body with his. Penetration was slow and excruciatingly blissful. Each inserted inch made her claw and cry out in pure ecstasy. Needing to do something, anything, she lifted her head and licked the sweat that glistened on his chest. "Oh damn, baby." Hilton drove himself in deeper. He couldn't help himself. She was sending him over the brink with her spontaneous act of sheer lust. With every tongue lash that lapped his sweat, Hilton fucked her harder. Milan held on tighter, writhing and moaning senselessly as she took the hard pounding. But she didn't still her tongue; she continued to lick perspiration from his chest and began to lathe the tiny beads of his male nipples, stroking them with the full width of her tongue.

He gave her deep dick strokes. Making her crazy. Making her body hot and damp. Making her pussy ache with the need to explode. She tried to hold back, she struggled to stave off an orgasm, but his hard thrusts sped her along, taking her much too quickly to the place she was destined to go. Desperately, she pushed his heavy body off her and scrambled down to the bot-tom of the bed. "I don't want to cum, not yet," she said. Before he could catch his breath to protest, Milan wiggled between his muscled thighs. She licked his taut scrotum with ardor, while stroking his dick that was wet and slick with her juices.

Hilton inhaled sharply and groaned. "I want some more pussy, baby. Let me back in it." Roughly now, he pulled her up on her hands and knees. "Why my baby been so bad?" he asked, his voice throaty with a hint of menace. Milan wasn't sure where this was going and didn't know how to respond.

He rose up on his haunches, bent over, and braced himself by slipping an arm beneath her tummy and held her in place by her waist.

Bam! He slapped her ass. "Why my baby so bad?" he asked again, his voice low and sensual. Milan gasped and tensed up from the shock of the slap. She shook her head, indicating that she didn't know why she was so bad. Hilton slapped her ass again.

"Ow!" she cried.

"How you gon' have your man dressing up like a chauffeur, huh?"

"I'm sorry."

"You weren't sorry when you were calling the shots." He smacked her ass again. Harder. Milan bit down on her lip, trying to stifle a scream. But she couldn't keep it in. With each sound smacking, she yelled louder.

"I'm so sorry." Her voice was hoarse from yelling.

"How sorry?"

"Real, real sorry."

He took a breather, rubbed the red spot that was beginning to appear on her brown skin. "I should have spanked that ass the first time you opened your mouth and started talking trash. You can be real disrespectful when you want to be."

"I know. I can be awful sometimes…a real bitch," she admitted. Clearly, an exchange of power had taken place. She was giving Hilton erotic control and had relinquished herself to sensual surrender.

He raised his hand and started again, slowly at first, and then he sped up the intensity of the blows, lighting her ass up, setting it on fire with a quick succession of fiery slaps. The sounds of his heavy hand landing on her tender flesh reverberated inside the quiet room.

Her pussy, hot and sticky, was twitching up a storm, needing some immediate attention. Milan gritted her teeth, trying to hold back words that were pushing at her throat. *Please, baby, please. Give me some dick!* On her hands and knees, she expressed her urgent need by rotating her hips and humping like a dog in heat.

Hilton penetrated her pussy with his long and sturdy middle finger. He slid it in and out, giving her a pleasurable finger fuck while he spanked the small mound of her burning ass.

The pain and pleasure were intense. She couldn't hold back any longer. She gave a shudder and then squeezed her eyes shut and clenched her walls around Hilton's bulky finger. "I'm cumming," she screeched. "Oh, God. Hilton!" Pleasure exploded inside of her and she released, showering his finger with her love.

CHAPTER 37

Milan stared at the headline: UNSCRUPULOUS EXEC-
UTIVE STILL MISSING.

*It is believed that Maxwell Torrance faked his death and absconded
with billions. Among the wreckage of his light aircraft was luggage,
his pilot's license, and three other forms of identification. His remains
have not been found.*

With a shrug, she closed the newspaper. Maxwell's disappearance no longer concerned her. The loss of Pure Paradise
and her frozen bank accounts were not at the forefront of her
thoughts anymore, either. She figured Maxwell had given in to
his fetishism and wanted to live in blissful bondage, twenty-
four-seven. However, his captors had to be paid and she imagined
that he'd taken the extra five hundred million to ensure that he
could afford to be flogged, flayed, and butt-fucked for the rest
of his life. Milan had done her own investigating—Mistress
Veronique and BodySlam were among the missing, but no one
was looking for the odd pair.

Milan's finances had been seized; those two co-conspirators
weren't even on the FBI's radar. *Oh, well!* As unbelievable as it
was, Milan felt no ill will toward anyone. Not Sumi, Royce,
Veronique, BodySlam, or even the deceitful scoundrel, Maxwell Torrance.

Due to her own personal happiness, it was rather easy to forgive and forget.

She turned her attention to her mother who was getting a makeover by an award-winning celebrity makeup artist flown in from Los Angeles. Milan's mother frowned at her image in the mirror.

"It's too heavy. This makeup job looks like something a mortician would put on a corpse," her mother complained. Grimacing, she swiped at her cheek. "And I don't like the shade of this blush. It's too bright." She turned down her lips. "Can't you find a color that looks more natural?"

Looking embarrassed by her mother's bad manners, Sweetie rushed to her mother's side. "I like it, Mommy. You look nice."

Forcing her eyes away from the hand-beaded Chanel gown, Milan crossed her bedroom and approached the vanity chair where her mother sat. She studied her mother's face closely. "You're absolutely right, Mommy," Milan agreed with her cross mother. She cast a glance at the makeup artist. "It's too thick; much too heavy. Tone it down," she instructed. "I don't want my mother being an embarrassment at my wedding." She shook her head. "Honestly, I'd be a laughingstock if my own mother were sitting in the front pew, looking like a bar-hopping floozy." Milan laughed. Her mother didn't. She flinched, not finding Milan's remark funny at all. So accustomed to disagreeing with Milan, her mother opened her mouth and then closed it again, unsure of what to say.

Milan waited patiently for her mother's comeback. After a few moments, Milan smirked. *Gotcha!* What could her mother say? "*Never mind, don't listen to Milan, Mr. Makeup Artist. Go right ahead and pile on the pancake makeup and don't forget to throw on some garish shades of blue and purple. Oh yeah, while you're at it, give me some ruby-red lips and matching cheekbones to make good and sure that I look exactly like the town whore!"*

Despite her perfectly coiffed hairdo and flawless makeup, Milan felt like rolling on the floor in hilarity. Her mother was unaccustomed to her disfavored daughter agreeing with her. She didn't like it, but there wasn't a thing she could say. Milan marveled at her newly acquired ability to outsmart her cranky mother.

The makeup artist slathered her mother's face with cold cream and used a tissue to undo her pinched, sour expression and to get rid of the foundation, blush, and eye shadow. Meanwhile, her mother twisted in her chair and groaned as if the removal of the makeup was causing her unbearable pain.

Her mother would never like her and, for the first time in Milan's life, she truly didn't care. It was a relief to no longer feel the sting of her mother's barbs, jabs, and complaints. Milan sighed blissfully. Hilton's love was like a coat of armor—a protective shield.

Was it really just a week ago that she had felt as if her world had crumbled when the FBI called and then shown up at her door?

On a day when most women would be a bundle of nerves, Milan possessed an uncanny, Zen-like calm. She and Hilton had agreed on a speedy marriage and, in less than an hour, she would follow the wedding party and walk down the aisle in a gorgeous Chanel wedding gown.

CHAPTER 38

Two Years Later

O ne of the NFL's biggest rivalries was in full swing as
the hosting team, the Dallas Cowboys, squared off
against the Philadelphia Eagles.

Milan still didn't understand the game, but she recognized a
touchdown when she saw one. Terrell Owens had just scored
one and was breaking into a celebratory dance, flapping his
arms like a bird, mocking the Eagles.

"T.O. better watch it," Quantez cautioned, jumping out of
his leather seat inside the lavish home theater.

"They gon' flag him, Daddy?" Dominic asked gleefully.

"Yup, Dallas gon' have to get a fifteen-yard penalty," Diamante
added.

"Nah, it's cool. He can dance as long as his teammates don't
join in and act the fool with him," Quantez advised his sons.

"Dang!" the boys said together, their faces scrunched in disappointment that T.O.'s shenanigans wouldn't cause his team
to lose some points.

Milan raised a brow. Her nephews seemed to understand all
the intricacies of football. *Must have something to do with that Y
chromosome*, she told herself. As hard as she tried, she couldn't get
a handle on the game. Football was too complicated. None of
the huddling, kicking, leaping, running, tackling, stumbling, or

fumbling made any sense. Hilton had tried to break it down, patiently trying to teach Milan the fundamentals of the sport, but her eyes would dim and her mind would shut down two minutes after he launched into a football tutorial, using expressions like *offensive and defensive sides of the ball*, *thirty-yard-line pass*, *seventy-six-yard return*, *kick returns*, and *punt returns*. Ugh! Football lessons made her temples throb. As far as Milan was concerned all the plays that preceded a touchdown were exercises in monotonous drudgery. The only exciting part of the game was watching a touchdown and viewing the scoreboard. Seeing the Eagles green helmet logo on top of the scoreboard signaled that the birds were winning.

In the midst of T.O. and the Cowboys giving each other high-fives, Hilton Dorsey appeared on the screen, handsome as ever and as physically fit and chiseled as the players. The NFL-issued sports attire looked good on Hilton.

"Hi, Uncle Hilton!" Diamante waved at the TV screen.

"He can't hear you." Dominic jabbed his younger brother with an elbow.

"Ow! Mommy, Dominic hit me!"

"All right, now. You two better watch it if you expect to get a slice of that gorgeous birthday cake," Sweetie warned. Meanwhile Quantez, absorbed by the game, turned deaf ears to his squabbling sons.

Hilton Dorsey, seemingly unperturbed by the opposing team's touchdown, kissed his index and middle fingers and then flashed a V.

"Can you believe that guy's confidence?" asked the voice of a sports commentator. "We're almost at the half; the Eagles are trailing badly; the coach has stopped the clock; he's yelling at the players, practically having a meltdown, and Dorsey's on the sidelines preening for the cameras as ostentatiously as T.O. Putting up a victory sign just doesn't seem appropriate. What do you make of that, Chuck? Is that wishful thinking or is Dorsey having a flashback of some kind? Seems like he's reverting back to his days of glory when he was the star running back for the Bears."

"I'm pretty baffled, Don. We know from his playing days that Hilton Dorsey is a confident—"

"You mean 'cocky,' don't'cha?" Don chuckled.

"Yeah, Dorsey was known to tauntingly put his touchdown ball right in the center of the field on the opposing team's logo," Chuck reminisced with laughter. "That guy has always oozed cockiness."

"Hold on, Chuck, Dorsey might have a good reason for his grandiose display. You know, he's only been an assistant coach with the Eagles for two seasons and already there's talk that he may be heading over to the New England Patriots—as head coach!" the other commentator stated, incredulous.

"If that happens, he'd be one of the youngest coaches in NFL history."

"I'd say, that's a darn good reason to start flashing a victory sign while your team is behind."

"I just got word that Dorsey wasn't flashing a victory sign."

"No? Then what was he doing? You wanna role that tape back, Chuck?" the other commentator said sarcastically.

"I was told that Dorsey was flashing a V for Vivianne, his year-old daughter. Little Vivianne Dorsey is celebrating her birthday today, back in Philadelphia with Dorsey's beautiful wife, Milan."

Beautiful! Milan hoped her mother was watching the game, and then gave her mom a mental brush-off. *Oh, who cares what she thinks?* she finally resolved.

Milan beamed down at her daughter, who was squirming on her lap, screaming for her father. Milan stood, hoisted Vivianne on her hip, and adjusted her daughter's birthday tiara as she hurried over to the mounted, extra-large TV screen. "Give Daddy a kiss!" Milan cooed.

A close-up of Hilton Dorsey's handsome face filled the screen. Held in her mother's embrace, Vivianne leaned forward, reaching out with both arms. She pressed her tiny palms of the screen and kissed her father's image. Abruptly, the shot cut to a commercial. Vivianne wailed.

Milan rocked her on her hip, showering her little girl with kisses. "It's okay, sweetheart. Daddy had to go talk to the players. He'll be right back," Milan explained. "Let's go un-wrap your presents, okay?"

"Marrying Hilton has made you more famous than when you were operating Pure Paradise. The local media covers you and Hilton like you're Philly's version of that couple from England—that Spice Girl and her soccer-playing husband."

"Posh…Victoria and David Beckman," Milan offered.

Sweetie nodded. "Yeah, those two. Now your name is starting to get mentioned on national television, too," Sweetie gushed, proud of her younger sister.

It was true. Milan and Hilton were media darlings and were treated like celebrities wherever they went.

"And Hilton is such a loving parent. You go, girl; you're soon to be the wife of the Patriot's coach."

"We haven't heard anything yet, but our fingers are crossed," Milan said modestly.

Frowning, Quantez shook his head as if the news caused him great distress. "I'm an Eagles fan. Philly all the way." He thumped a fist against his chest. "Will me and the boys be able to keep our seats at The Linc if Hilton goes with the Patriots?"

Milan didn't have a clue, but with Quantez, Sweetie, and their sons staring questioningly, she gave a reassuring smile. "I'm sure Hilton will be able to work something out."

"Yes!" Dominic gave his brother a knuckle bump and then offered his balled fist to little Vivianne.

Grinning, Vivianne squirmed out of her mother's arms. Standing on fat, wobbly legs, she reached out her tiny balled hand and touched her cousin's fist.

"Go, Vivianne." Sweetie clapped her hands. "Come on, Quantez, it's time to sing 'Happy Birthday' to the birthday girl."

Wasting no time, the boys sprinted out of the theater.

Vivianne tried to run behind her cousins. "You're gonna fall and hurt yourself, Vivianne." Milan caught her daughter's hand and slowed her down as they exited the room together.

Grudgingly, Quantez rose from the comfortable reclining seat. He froze as the Dallas cheerleading squad ran out on the field. With their tummies bare, rocking blue and white star-encrusted tops, white bootie shorts, and boots, the squad launched into a sultry routine.

"I don't know why you staring at those tiny little asses. Those half-naked heifers ain't got nothing on me—so let's go." Sweetie propped a hand on her well-padded hip.

"You know you got it going on. That's why we're still married. Don't nobody have nothing on you, baby." Quantez smiled sheepishly, craning his neck to get another glimpse of the cheerleaders' hot moves. "We're gonna have to get a media room installed if your sister moves," he mumbled, eyes glued to the screen.

"How we gon' pay for it?" Sweetie waited a few seconds for Quantez's response.

He shrugged.

"You can watch those sluts dance right on the plasma TV in our bedroom, where I can keep my eyes on you," Sweetie teased. "Come on now, Quantez." She reached for her husband's hand. "You can finish watching the game in the kitchen. You know Milan and Hilton have TVs all over this mini-mansion."

After Vivianne blew out her candle and opened her gifts, Quantez made a bee-line back to the home theater and Sweetie pulled Milan aside. "Girl, don't you worry about Hilton being out on the road with all those cheerleading sluts hanging all over him and throwing their pussies all up in his face?"

"Of course not!" Milan was appalled that Sweetie would even suggest such a thing.

"I'm just saying…"

"You don't worry about Quantez straying, do you?"

"No! But Quantez ain't traveling the country with a bunch of hoes coming at him from every direction. Seriously, you need to keep some type of tabs on your man. Hilton might not be playing football anymore, but he's still the finest thing out there on the field. And his pockets damn sure ain't hurting." Sweetie's eyes traveled over Milan's lavish surroundings to emphasize her point. "Plenty of bitches out there would love to be standing in your shoes. I read an article about how those money-hungry heifers be waiting for the teams in the hotel lobby, knowing that most men can't turn down freely offered pussy when their wife and kids are home and they got a big ol' empty bed up there in the hotel room."

Milan chuckled. "You read too many gossip columns."

"You can keep your head buried in the sand if you want to…

I'm just trying to school you, keep you on your toes."

"Thank you, big sis." Milan kissed Sweetie on the cheek and laughed.

"I don't know why you're not taking this seriously. There are some foul-ass bitches out there, just waiting to snatch up your man. Why do you think them girls break their necks to get on that cheerleading squad? Do you really think they believe that cheerleading is a career that could lead to something? Hell, no," Sweetie's voice rose. Though the children had all followed Quantez into the theater, Milan still looked around warily, making sure Vivianne wasn't in earshot of Sweetie's profanity.

"Them heifers are hitting the gym and keeping their bodies in shape so they can show off their half-naked selves in order to latch onto somebody else's man!" Sweetie poked out her lips and rolled her eyes as if a slew of cheerleaders were persistently propositioning Quantez.

"I hear you, Sweetie. But I can't help it if I'm content and unconcerned about cheerleaders or any other women stealing my man."

Sweetie shook her head, sympathetically. "All right, then. Don't come crying to me when the shit hits the fan. Like I said, you and Vivianne need to be right by Hilton's side at all times."

"Listen to the pot calling the kettle black."

Sweetie scowled, uncomprehending.

"You sit home and watch TV all day. I don't see you sticking by Quantez's side while he's toiling in his restaurant."

"That's different. Me and Quantez been together for so long, he ain't thinking about no other woman. Besides, his work doesn't require him to travel out of town accompanied by a pack of big-titty, flat-tummy, booty-shorts-wearing bimbos."

Milan fell out laughing. Sweetie did, too.

"Seriously, Milan. Let them bitches know that you ain't the one! It's not like you're still running your business. You have plenty of spare time. Mommy even said you being dumb to let Hilton spend so much time away from home unattended."

Milan bristled at the personal affront. The mention of her mother and the admission that she and Sweetie still found reason to talk about her behind her back was a stinging indictment that nothing she did would ever please either one of them.

But Milan let it go, let the anger melt away as she calmed herself with the memory of the first time she noticed a heifer flirting with Hilton. At that time, she was so offended, so outraged, she wanted to kick ass; to sue the bitch and the league. The bitch had tried to ride her husband's jock right in her face. Milan was so furious, she threatened to call a lawyer and bring a lawsuit against the entire NFL.

Hilton had tried to appease her, tried to reason with her. "Can't you see what they're trying to do? Don't let them win, Milan. I know you're bigger than that. How can you be jealous over a bunch of desperate women?"

Milan wasn't trying to hear it. That dick was hers and she didn't want another bitch to even think about sniffing, touching, or tasting it.

"Does your dick get hard when a half-naked bitch pushes her big titties in your face? Be honest."

"Sometimes," he had admitted, looking guilty.

And that was when Hilton and Milan made a decision that would keep their marriage safe and sound.

The recollection was sweet. Smiling, she took Sweetie's hand. "Let's go check the score. Lord, I hope the Eagles will get it together in the second half."

CHAPTER 39

Vivianne had an eventful day. The birthday girl was worn out. Trying to keep up with her older, rambunctious boy cousins had exhausted her. She didn't make a fuss as she usually did when her mother lowered her inside her crib. Milan stared at her sleeping daughter, shaking her head as if in disbelief. No one could have ever told her that she had so much love stored inside her, love that she so easily shared with the two people she lived and breathed for.

Though she doted on her daughter, she was careful to instill important values. She didn't want Vivianne to grow up like she had, feeling so misguided and unloved that she tried to out-maneuver and outshine everyone she encountered in order to feel a smidgen of self-worth.

She heard the beeping sound as Hilton pushed in the alarm code.

"Daddy's home," he greeted, his voice pitched loud enough to travel up the stairs. "Where are my girls?" he shouted.

Not wanting to awaken Vivianne, Milan didn't answer. She gave her daughter one more loving look and then her feet moved swiftly out of the nursery and down the corridor.

The Eagles had lost and though she didn't detect sadness in

Hilton's voice, she knew he didn't handle defeat well. Losing to the Cowboys was particularly painful, and she intended to soothe his soul with a warm bath and sensual body rub. And then she'd let Lil' Na-Na take over and put him to sleep.

Draped in a cream-colored, body-hugging negligee, Milan stood at the top of the stairs, smiling warmly at her husband.

Gripping the handles of an oversized duffle bag, Hilton took the stairs two at a time. His dark eyes emanated such passion, a fire instantly erupted inside her, burning a path down to her core, giving her tiny tremors before he'd even touched her. When he reached the landing, he dropped the bag and took Milan in his arms. She nestled inside his embrace, murmuring endearments to this man whose love had healed all her old wounds.

Clutching her chin, he raised her head until their eyes met. "I missed you, baby," he said, his voice hoarse with yearning,

The feeling of being cherished still felt as wondrous and new as the first time he'd said, "I love you." Back when he'd first confessed his love, his admission had taken her off guard, thrown her off kilter, and had rendered her speechless.

"Is Vivianne awake?" His voice brought her back to the moment. The devotion that shone in his eyes was a reminder that she'd made the right decision in taking a chance on love.

"No, she's asleep."

His handsome features crumpled; disappointment flickered in his eyes.

Milan didn't like seeing her husband's bright eyes go dim; it saddened her. "She played hard today, running around and trying to keep up with her cousins. You should have seen her trying to run and our little angel was actually trying to catch a football," she added, trying to cheer him up.

He cracked a big smile. "You're kidding."

"No, I'm not. She kept saying, 'Gimme Daddy football.'"

Hilton's grin widened and he pivoted toward the nursery. "Gotta give my little angel a good-night kiss."

With his arm around Milan's waist, he stared at his sleeping daughter and then at his wife. "She looks more and more like her beautiful mother every day."

"Do you think so? I don't see me at all; I just see you."

He stared at Vivianne. "Yeah, she's got my ears, my chin, but she gets her beauty from you."

Milan couldn't help blushing. "By the way, Vivianne totally enjoyed your special birthday signal."

"Oh, yeah? What did she do?"

"She kissed the TV screen and cried when I tried to pry her away from it."

A smile lit his face. "Does that mean that both my girls missed me?" he asked with a devilish grin.

Milan brought his hand up and brushed his knuckles with her lips. "Yes, we both missed you." Then she added in a breathy whisper, "Desperately."

The sportscasters had called Hilton cocky, but there was nothing cocky about the smile that spread across his face at Milan's heartfelt admission.

He kissed his sleeping daughter and then gave Milan a smooch on her cheek. "Baby," he said softly.

"Hmm?"

"I don't know how I lucked up on you, but I do know, it doesn't get any better than this."

Milan angled her head to the side and wore a slight suggestion of skepticism on her face. "Wanna bet?" She licked her lips suggestively. "Come with me to our boudoir and I'll show you how much better it can get."

⤙❧⤚

Inside their bedroom, Milan threw her arms around Hilton's neck. Hungrily, her mouth sought his. He kissed her back, gently at first, and then more deeply as his tongue mingled with hers, making the lump inside his pants press urgently, seeking release.

"I'm sorry about the game, sweetheart." She searched his face and caught the flicker of a wince. It pained her to know her man was hurting inside. "Why don't you undress so I can give you a hot bath and a rubdown—"

"Forget all that. I had a long, rough day. You know what I need," he said in a voice hoarse with yearning.

She nodded as her hand automatically traveled downward and caressed his bulge. "Yes, my darling, faithful husband, I know exactly what you need."

He uttered a low groan. Any other time, he would have enjoyed getting the VIP treatment from Milan. But not tonight. His stiffening dick was causing him immense discomfort, insisting that he pass up the hot bath and sensual massage. Though not totally erect, it was straining to be set free and catered to.

While Milan rummaged through drawers, he undressed hurriedly. Lying on the bed on his back with his arms and legs outspread, he closed his eyes and waited.

He didn't have to wait long. Moments later, he felt the love cuffs, soft and fluffy, being latched around his wrist. His facial muscles tensed, a low groan rumbled in his throat as she fastened his cuffed wrist to the bed post. Impatiently, he stretched out his other arm. Milan hurriedly climbed over his chest and secured his other wrist.

"Baby…" It was a deep, guttural cry of need. But Milan had more work to do.

She pressed her lips against his quickly. "I love you so much," she said, before she wriggled downward to shackle his feet.

Spread eagle and bound by love, Hilton lay waiting for the sweet pleasure of their sex game. Ripped from his shoulders down to his calves, Hilton's body was a work of exquisite art. She missed him so much. Needed him right now. But she had to restrain herself and take care of him from head to toe.

From the corner of her eye, she could see his dick bobbing demandingly, but she couldn't bear the sight of it. It was too tempting, and made her weak. She forced her eyes away from the dick she adored. Otherwise, she'd have to deprive Hilton of his well-deserved playtime and jump on him and ride his dick unmercifully, rocking on his body, her na-na trying to swallow up both dick and balls.

She'd get to that part soon enough. Right now, she had to give her man the kind of erotic sensations that drove him out of his mind.

With the tip of her tongue, she flicked at his knotted right nipple. Then she licked in circles, nipped at the tightened flesh with her teeth, and then pulled the tiny nugget between her lips and sucked while her fingers raked through the roughened hair on his broad chest and traveled to his ripened left nipple, which she twisted and pinched, making Hilton moan.

His handsome face was drawn into a grimace as desire shot from his chest and traveled straight to his thrusting groin. Her mouth closed around his other nipple. As she suckled, she reached up and ran her fingers through his wavy hair, massaging his scalp as her lips puckered and pulled on his stony bud.

"Milan!" he gasped.

"Baby," she moaned in response. Passion swiftly blazed through her, like a fast-moving brush fire. Unable to hold herself up, she briefly collapsed on his chest. Collecting herself, Milan lifted her head, kissed him, her mouth wide as she gave him tongue, sucking his as if trying to devour him.

She kissed his taut stomach, ran her hand appreciatively over his bulging muscles. Taking her head down lower, she inhaled the fragrantly masculine scent that emanated from the thick thatch of darkly coiled pubic hairs. Never had she wanted to suck a dick as badly as she wanted to suck his right now, but she restrained herself and softly bit his inner thighs.

Now standing at the bottom of the bed, she kneeled and kissed the sole of his foot, lathing it with her tongue before her lips puckered around his toes. Working on his other foot, Milan's tongue flitted in and out between his toes. His toes curled, trapping her darting tongue. Hilton groaned and shuddered violently, rocking the bed as if he were planted deeply inside Milan, giving her the dick she'd been waiting for.

It was time. They both knew it.

"You ready, baby?" Her voice came out raspy and pleading. She desperately needed to feel her man thrusting inside her. Her desire for Hilton consumed her.

"Yeah, baby. I'm ready," he said, the words a whispered, strangled choke.

Milan straightened and walked over to the nightstand. She drew in a deep breath and then picked up the key.

"Baby, baby, baby..." Hilton writhed, ready to be set free.

With nervous and trembling hands, she inserted the key inside the lock and turned it, liberating his straining penis from the chastity cage that confined it and had kept him faithful while out of town. Milan watched in awe as his endowed appendage bloomed into the full erection it had been denied.

Yes, Hilton Dorsey was a chastened man. He willingly allowed his wife to keep his dick on lockdown. He loved Milan with all his heart, but he didn't trust his dick. How could he rely on an appendage that could easily betray him and ruin his marriage by stiffening and throbbing and pulling him in the direction of the beckoning finger and moistened lips of the multitudes of scantily clad, money-chasing females he encountered while traveling on the road with his team? He loved Milan's sex so much, he even denied himself the pleasure of release from his own hand.

Milan straddled her virtuous husband and spread her pussy petals, welcoming him.

"Do you know how much I love you, Milan?"

Overwrought by the intensity of their shared love, she was unable to speak and could only murmur a husky assent.

His penis, hot and hard, pumped with juicy passion, poking and stabbing, in search of her sweet passageway.

Moaning as if in anguish, she pushed down on his swollen length.

Thrusting his shaft as if trying to impale her, Hilton felt his rigid member began to twitch in urgency. It writhed, throbbed, eager to spill its stored-up seed inside the warmth of the woman he vowed to love, cherish, and obey.

She'd get hers later. He needed to release his love. She pressed her mouth close to his ear and whispered, "Cum for me."

He grimaced, growled. His body bucked so fiercely, she had to hold on tightly to his massive shoulders. Widening her thighs, she prepared herself for the flood of his hot lust.

❦

Hours later, both spent and sweaty, their bodies entwined, Milan kissed her slumbering husband and cracked a smile. Her sister, Sweetie, and her mother loved to talk about her marriage, the way Hilton traveled and had much too much free time. They predicted a dire outcome for her marriage. But Milan knew better. Her man would never stray or disrespect their marriage. He couldn't—not with his dick on lockdown.

Contentedly, she snuggled closer. He wrapped a protective arm around her. Never in her life had she felt so safe. Hilton was right...it didn't get any better than this.

ABOUT THE AUTHOR

Allison Hobbs is the national bestselling author of ten novels and novellas: *Disciplined, One Taste, Big Juicy Lips, The Climax, A Bona Fide Gold Digger, The Enchantress, Double Dippin', Dangerously in Love, Insatiable* and *Pandora's Box.* She is one of the contributing writers of Cinemax's *Zane's Sex Chronicles.*

Her novel *The Climax* was nominated for the 2008 African American Literary Awards Show.

Allison received a bachelor of science degree from Temple University. She resides in Philadelphia, PA where she's working on her next novel.

Visit the author at: www.allisonhobbs.com, www.blackplanet. com/allisonhobbs or www.myspace.com/allisonhobbs

It had taken over a year for Milan to get accepted into the exclusive sex club, which she'd stumbled across on the internet. The club preferred couples membership. Single females were eligible to apply only once a year during open enrollment. Single males, however, were not permitted to join the club nor were single males permitted to enter the premises as a guest. Married men, Milan presumed, did not appreciate the competition.

Because of the rigid rule, Milan's prearranged sexual encounters were always with a couple. More often than not, the wife played the role of lesbo slut, commanded by her husband to tongue Milan's pussy until it was warm and slushy enough for him to slip his dick in with ease. Every so often, an occasional wife would select limited involvement and opt to watch, voyeur-like, through the glory hole—a circular opening in a wall that separated adjoining rooms.

Wives who liked to watch didn't bother Milan. Her only concern was getting hers. Getting, *not* giving, were the terms she'd agreed upon when she joined Tryst. She paid exorbitant monthly dues to be matched only with people willing to accept her conditions: she would not give a blowjob, or cunnilingus, or even lift a finger to give pleasure to another. Whenever she engaged in an erotic interlude at Tryst, the connection was made for the sole purpose of releasing stress—not to exhaust herself with the arduous task of sexual reciprocity.

Inside a dimly lit room, Milan waited. Apart from dark sunglasses and a golden blonde wig to disguise her identity, Milan lay naked on a large bed. Positioned on her side with her back to the door, her head resting on an outstretched arm, she felt her pulse race with anticipation when the door opened.

The anonymous married couple she'd selected from a database of dozens of potential sex partners had arrived. Although Milan had her head turned away from the door, she expected the pair to be naked, as she'd instructed on the sex club's request form.

"She's lovely," a female voice whispered.

"Quite," a husky male voice agreed.

She sensed the couple approaching the bed, and then felt the mattress sink on opposite sides as the man and woman knelt at the foot of the bed. The sudden sensation of two pairs of lips placed softly on the sole of each foot caused Milan to release a muffled gasp.

A warm tongue kissed and sucked each toe, and then licked the space between her toes. Her upper torso tensed, and she began to twist involuntarily at the waist. Her body seemed to make an unconscious attempt to thwart the shivers of pleasure that were shooting straight to her passion center.

While focused on the glorious dual stimulation occurring between her toes, Milan's attention was drawn to the tickly sensation of a mustache that grazed the bottom of her right foot, nuzzled her ankle, her leg, and quickly traveled upward, tickling the back of her thigh. A tongue, thick and warm, licked the flesh of her thigh while the mustache hairs teased her, sending a series of quivers up and down the length of her spine.

The triple sensation of two tongues and a teasing mustache was decadent pleasure. When the woman's mouth abandoned her foot, Milan, desiring more, moaned in desperation. Her anguished cry quickly turned to a breathy murmur of contentment when female hands began to lightly, tantalizingly fondle her buttocks. Next, the anonymous woman placed a flurry of soft kisses and light flicks of her tongue on Milan's smooth brown ass.

With her eyes tightly closed, she fought against the heat that was slowly building inside her pussy. Involuntarily, her hips moved in a circular motion. Needing to do something to take the edge off, she couldn't help rubbing her clitoris. Slowly at first, and then her finger started to circle the distended clit faster, creating a friction that was so stimulating, her pussy ached with desire.

The mustache pulled away. "Honey," the man said, sounding concerned. "I think our chocolate princess is ready for some cock now."

The wife withdrew her lips. Seconds later, she had made her way to the head of the bed. "We want to please you," the woman whispered seductively, her mouth pressed against Milan's ear. "I'm holding my husband's cock in my hand. Do you want me to stuff it inside your hot pussy?"

Stirred by the sexy low tone of the nameless woman's voice, aroused by the feel of large breasts brushing against her own, and tempted by the thick penis that rubbed against her flesh, Milan's pussy went into panic. It began pulsing rapidly, secreting syrupy fluids.

But fighting her carnal urges, Milan shook her head vigorously. "No, not yet," she murmured. She needed more foreplay—more titillating whispers, caressing hands, probing fingers, prodding tongues.

In an instant, strong male hands eased her body over and two sets of lips put suction holds on the nipples of her small, firm breasts. "Mmm," Milan murmured. The encounter enticed all her senses.

Female lips disengaged and were replaced by a moist tongue. Quick, wet, circular motions around her areola caused Milan to jump as if she'd been hit with electrical currents. The woman bit Milan's nipple lightly and then increased the intensity until Milan's head lolled from side to side in a curious combination of sexual pleasure and mild pain. Male lips sucked softly, yet intently, as if extracting nectar from a delicate flower.

Suddenly, the couple stopped sucking. Alarm coursed through Milan's system. Was she being abandoned by the twosome? She was immediately reassured when a strong, hairy arm lifted her upward and placed her back against the headboard. The man sat on the side of the bed. He cupped both her breasts with his large hands. Hungrily, his mouth went from one nipple to the other, while the woman's soft hands caressed her legs, gently encouraging Milan to spread them apart.

The anticipation of having someone whose face she'd never seen cater to her pussy while another person sucked her breasts was enough to make her cry out as if in pain.

Instead of performing cunnilingus, as Milan eagerly expected, the woman inserted the tips of two slender fingers inside Milan's well-lubricated vagina, twisting them in a spiraling motion as she delved deeper and deeper inside.

Hit with waves of almost unbearable pleasure, Milan arched her back. She clamped her thighs shut with such force, the woman reflexively removed her fingers. She examined her fingers, and after determining they were unharmed, she began to suck each finger, making a loud slurping sound.

She inhaled Milan's vagina. "Mmm. Smells as good as it tastes. Honey, come down here for a minute," the wife said to her husband. "You really have to eat some of this; she has the sweetest cunt I've ever tasted."

"No!" Milan raised her head from the pillow, but avoided making eye contact. "Just you," she told the woman, forcibly.

Promptly doing as she was told, the wife used a finger to delicately part Milan's wet spot and began giving the moist opening a superior tongue bath.

The husband stopped sucking to observe his wife's performance. Stroking his penis, he exclaimed, "My cock is getting so hard, I can't wait any longer; I gotta fuck." He sounded tortured and completely miserable.

Again, Milan shook her head. The husband returned his lips to her hardened nipples. His wife was giving such magnificent head, Milan couldn't help clamping her thighs around the woman's face. With her head trapped between Milan's thighs, the wife, a willing captive, drank from the overflowing fountain of lust, slurping, sucking, and swallowing as if she was in desperate need of hydration and dying of thirst.

Milan shuddered. Her nerve endings felt exposed and raw. She tightened her grip on the wife's head. At this heightened point of arousal, Milan was beyond caring if the woman smothered to death.

Finally, the warmth—the heat—started spreading up her thighs and swirled into the pit of her stomach. She parted her legs to free the wife from her pussy choke hold, but, declining her opportunity to escape to freedom, the woman remained in the confines of Milan's thighs and continued to suck and slurp.

A fire raged inside, weakening Milan's resolve, but she was determined to maintain control of the encounter. "Switch positions," she demanded in a forced authoritative voice.

The husband scrambled to the position his wife had held below. Milan felt him aiming for admittance. She relaxed her pussy muscles, rotated her pelvis, exhaled contentedly as she welcomed him inside.

Meanwhile, the wife crept upward. She cupped Milan's face and began tongue kissing her. The taste of her own juices on another female's tongue was an added stimulant, prompting her to thrust her twitching pussy forward and rub her clit against the base of the man's dick. "Tell your husband to fuck me harder," Milan implored.

"Give it to her harder, honey," the wife said urgently. She rushed to his side, cheering him on. "Give it to her hard, you fuckin' stud. Fuck that cunt; make her cum." Fueled by decadent passion, the wife gripped her husband's ass and pressed him into Milan, assisting him with each thrust.

Close to cumming, Milan stiffened. The woman slipped her hand between Milan's legs and stroked her husband's dick as well as Milan's engorged clit. Milan instantly exploded; her body shook from tiny quakes. A few moments later, the husband shot a load, groaned loudly, and then rolled onto his back.

"You're a great fuck, honey," the husband told Milan as he panted and gasped for breath.

Too exhausted to speak, all Milan could manage was a lazy smile.

The wife, still hungry with passion, took advantage of Milan's incapacitated state. She parted Milan's thighs and sipped her husband's semen until she had Milan's pussy revitalized, clenching and throbbing with desire. Finally, the woman straddled Milan and ground her clit against Milan's. Together, their bodies convulsed and jerked until they were both completely satisfied.

❧

Three weeks had passed since her dismissal—her unfair and improper dismissal, as far as Milan was concerned. She faxed ten to twenty resumes daily, but it seemed that every potential employer insisted upon having her college transcripts before even agreeing to grant her an interview.

The companies to which Milan sent her resume were all familiar with her. If they didn't know her personally, her reputation of being a dynamic leader should have preceded her. It was puzzling why she was being given such a hard time.

Undoubtedly, the board had put out the word. It was absurd that someone with Milan's experience and successful track record was being railroaded into returning to college. It made her nauseous to even imagine sitting in a classroom with a pack of pimply faced teens, being forced to listen intently while an asshole professor talked endlessly and expected her to take copious notes on the theory behind a profession about which she already knew everything there was to know. Hell, she could write a book about the business.

Write a book! Hmm. Now, that's a damn good idea! She'd write a how-to book. Women were so vain and gullible. They loved to be told how to enhance their beauty and improve their lives. She'd call her book, *Weekend Escape: Your Spa At Home.* Suddenly excited, Milan started jotting down notes. She'd use a pen name since she'd become such a pariah in the field. Her ego didn't require having her cocoa-colored face on the back cover, either. Concealing her identity—her African-American heritage—would ensure a mainstream readership. She'd keep her identity a secret until she appeared on the cover of *Fortune.* That would be a real shocker to the power mongers, who'd never intended for more than one black woman, Oprah, to reach the pinnacle of success.

Taking another gulp of wine, Milan happily envisioned herself making so much money she could not only buy out Pure Paradise, but also open an international chain of spas. Ah! It was such a delicious fantasy.

She felt so elated; she was ready to share the news with her mother and her sister. But no, she decided. She was feeling much too energetic and inspired to have them burst her bubble with negativity and warnings of disaster if she didn't return to school. She was battling for survival and couldn't afford to hear any unsupportive words. To hell with school; she'd never go back. She didn't need a formal education. She had skills and she'd make sure all those who opposed her, especially Dr. Kayla Pauley, would regret their harsh treatment of her.

Where should I start? Although she possessed a vast knowledge of beauty and lifestyle services offered by day as well as weekend spas, putting it all together in a book could be a daunting task. But she was up for it. She took a long swallow of wine and happily began to outline her future bestseller.

Her euphoria was short-lived, however. A phone call from the bank that had provided her favorite Visa platinum card—the corporate card from Pure Paradise with the unlimited balance that they had forgotten to repossess when they fired Milan—disturbed her peace.

"Is this Milan Walden?" asked the nasal voice of a bank representative.

"Yes, this is she," Milan said boldly. She'd known it was just a matter of time before the card was deactivated, but she hadn't expected it to be so soon. She'd thought the board had forgotten about the damn card. Her rent was due and she'd planned to use the credit card instead of dipping into her badly needed savings.

It seemed only fair to use the company credit card since the board claimed that the falsification of her credentials had rendered her ineligible for severance pay, or payment for her accrued vacation and sick time. She didn't get squat from Pure Paradise and felt a small measure of satisfaction every time she used the company card. As soon as she pulled herself together, found a new position, and got her bearings, Milan intended to sue Pure Paradise for discrimination and any other kind of lawsuit a good attorney could slap them with.

The woman rattled off the numbers of the credit card and then informed Milan of what she'd already presumed—the card was cancelled. What Milan wasn't prepared to hear was that practically all of the purchases she'd made with the card were considered fraudulent.

Intense fear clutched her insides. "Fraudulent?" she asked shakily.

"Yes, you'll be billed for numerous suspicious purchases made during and after your employment. A list of those purchases and the amount owed will be FedExed tonight."

Milan swallowed. *Could they really make her pay back the expenditures on a company card?*

"I have to inform you that if you don't pay the balance within ten days, you'll be prosecuted to the fullest extent of the law," the bank rep said, sounding as if she derived immense pleasure from scaring the hell out of Milan.

Milan hung up the phone with an unsteady hand. *Calm down and think!* How many purchases had she made since she'd left her job? *Car note, groceries, hair salon.* Okay, she had enough in her bank account to cover those. Then she remembered her wild online shopping spree at Bloomingdale's the very day she was fired. And the in-store shopping rampage at Neiman Marcus the day after her argument with her mother. She'd spent thousands in the store. Oh Lord! What else had she bought with the damned card? She searched her memory, terrified of the additional damning information her mind could possibly retrieve.

So far so good. She had some money in the bank and she'd pay off the purchases ASAP. But damn, she hadn't expected to spend her nest egg paying for things she already possessed.

⚜

The next day the bank sent a stack of papers that was so thick it filled a FedEx large box. The "suspicious" purchases went back nine months. Unwilling to pore over every item, Milan searched for the balance due. *Twenty-seven thousand dollars and eighty-one cents!* No way! They had to be out of their minds. Surely, their system was flawed. Now she had no choice but to scrutinize the voluminous computer-generated accusations.

Mentally rolling up her sleeves, Milan went over the detailed purchases. To her chagrin, there it was in black and white. Thousands and thousands of dollars spent on personal items. Jewelry, designer clothes, furniture, electronic equipment, perfume, a slew of expensive small kitchen appliances that looked good in her kitchen but had gone unused since Milan never, ever cooked. The list also included luxurious bed linens, beauty accessories, designer fragrances, and damn—she paused when she discovered she'd spent over three thousand dollars at Pier 1 Imports. She shook her head in amazement. *Did I really need so many candles?* Further down the list was a shocking nineteen hundred dollars' worth of items purchased at Toys "R" Us and seven hundred dollars spent at Gap Kids. She sucked her teeth, thinking about all she did for her ungrateful sister and her two bad-ass kids.

She scanned her online purchases. Her jaw dropped when she saw the company name, Freaky Pleasure Zone. Why, why, had she bought the gold-plated vibrator with the company credit card? Now, the conceited and self-righteous Kayla Pauley was privy to one of Milan's most intimate predilections.

After an hour or so of investigating, she had to concede that she'd gone buck wild with the company credit card and hadn't realized it. Beads of sweat began to pop out on her forehead, under her armpits, and on her neck.

She knew there was a little over nine thousand dollars in her piddly little personal checking account, but she picked up the phone to check her balance just to be sure of the exact amount. She stabbed the telephone buttons to input her account number but kept getting a ridiculous mechanical message that stated the account had been closed.

Frustrated, Milan turned to a different source of information and tried to log in to her checking account online. Instead of pulling up the page she was familiar with, an official-looking page appeared with a threatening red headline that boldly announced her account was unable to be accessed. She gasped in horror. The bank had frozen her checking account—put a hold on the only money she had to her name.

While she tried to make sense of the catastrophe, she noticed there was more information in small black letters. Leaning forward, Milan squinted at the screen. *To obtain more information on this account, please visit your local branch.* The small black-print letters had a more chilling effect than the glaring red print. There wasn't a chance in hell she'd visit *that* bank, which happened to be the same bank that she owed the money for the credit card purchases. For all she knew, she could walk right into a trap. The board could be trying to lure her out of her safe place so they could have her arrested for fraud.

Safe place? Milan looked around her apartment; she wasn't safe here. The board had her current address.

Oh God, what am I going to do? She felt queasy and, like the actresses of the golden era, Milan actually swooned. Her knees gave out and she collapsed into a bedroom chair—a hand-woven rattan armchair that she'd adored on sight and hadn't hesitated to purchase while browsing a few months ago in Pier 1 Imports.

In a burst of anger, Milan jumped up and kicked the accursed chair, toppling it. Working off more anger, she kicked it again harder, this time putting a hole the size of her foot in the back of the chair.

Breathing hard, Milan flopped down on her bed. The thought of making an emergency appointment at Tryst flitted across her mind. She needed to relieve the tension with an impromptu freaky sex rendezvous. Then disappointment caused her shoulders to slouch. Her critical financial situation had caused her to forget to make a payment and the monthly fee was now a couple of weeks late. Not too bad, she'd pay the fee and whatever penalty.

Feeling kicked in the gut, Milan suddenly remembered she no longer had access to her bank account or funds. Her membership, she sadly realized, was in poor standing and would soon be revoked.

But she had a back-up plan. Excitedly, she felt beneath the plump pillows, her hand seeking the object of tension release—the golden vibrator. *Oh damn!* It was inside the top bureau drawer on the other side of the room. Wound up with sexual tension and too badly in need of release to make the short jaunt across the room, she decided to pleasure herself the old-fashioned way—using her hand.

Milan quickly shed her clothing. She lay back and caressed her breasts, pinched her small nipples, applying pressure until they became sensitive to her touch. Aroused, she felt a rush of sensation between her thighs that was so intense, she moaned and drew up her knees, allowed them to part. Her right hand ventured down past the thatch of thick pubic hair, her longest finger leading the way. She massaged the bud of her clit until it throbbed and her finger became moist. Then, with two fingers of her left hand, she gently spread the dewy petals of her vagina, creating an opening that ached to be filled. Desiring instant gratification, she worked the longest finger inside, slid it in deeply, while simultaneously pressing her clit with a finger of the other hand.

One finger caressed gently, the other probed deeply. It never took very long to get what she needed; she knew exactly how to make her pussy purr. Solo sex was the only way she could achieve a really strong orgasm.

She had such an powerful pussy explosion, she cried out in ecstasy—a long, strident sound. When her heart rate slowed and her breathing returned to normal, she withdrew her sticky fingers.

Then, temporarily forgetting her troubles, she basked in the afterglow of self-administered satisfaction, slipped beneath the covers, and dozed off blissfully in the middle of the afternoon.

Printed in the United States
By Bookmasters